INDIGO DYING

Susan Wittig Albert

Thorndike Press • Waterville, Maine

Published in 2003 by arrangement with The Berkley Publishing Group, a member of Penguin Group (USA) Inc.

Thorndike Press® Large Print Mystery Series.

The tree indicium is a trademark of Thorndike Press.

The text of this Large Print edition is unabridged.
Other aspects of the book may vary from the original edition.

Set in 16 pt. Plantin by Minnie B. Raven.

Printed in the United States on permanent paper.

Library of Congress Cataloging-in-Publication Data

Albert, Susan Wittig.
    Indigo dying / Susan Wittig Albert.
        p. cm.
      ISBN 0-7862-5170-0 (lg. print : hc : alk. paper)
      1. Bayles, China (Fictitious character) — Fiction.
    2. Mines and mineral resources — Fiction.   3. Women
    detectives — Texas — Fiction.   4. Dyes and dyeing —
    Fiction.   5. Herbalists — Fiction.   6. Texas — Fiction.
    7. Large type books.   I. Title.
    PS3551.L2637I53 2003b
      813′.54—dc21   2002044724

To my sons,
Robert K. Wittig and Michael L. Wittig,
with love and admiration

Acknowledgments

This mystery grew out of a chance meeting on the Internet (if anything may be called chance in this synchronistic universe) with Lisa Shell, who lives on the edge of the Sandow Mine near Livingston, Texas. Lisa introduced me to her life as a shepherd, spinner, and weaver, and to the challenges of living on the outskirts of an ecological disaster area. I am grateful to her for acquainting me with the many fascinating aspects of a textile artist's life. I am also grateful to Carol Lee, whose generous description of her dye workshops shaped a scene in this book, and to the women whose emails gave me a whole new way of looking at the fascinating world of natural dyes. Mistakes that remain despite all their good advice are entirely my own errors.

I also want to offer special thanks to Billie Woods, for sharing her ballad, "An Ode to Alcoa"; Peggy Moody, whose patient and expert assistance makes so much possible; and to Catherine Cogburn, for her friendship over the past few years. I continue to owe thanks to Natalee Rosenstein at Berkley, whose support and encouragement have made this journey a more pleasant one. And ever and always to my husband and coauthor, Bill Albert, whose skill with plot is equaled only by his patient willingness to read what I've written. How can I be so lucky?

Note to the Reader

This novel is a work of fiction, and all names, characters, companies, places, and incidents are either the product of my imagination or are used fictitiously. However, even though Indigo, Texas, isn't real, it might be.

Times change, people change, and towns die: an unfortunate fact of rural life. However, a real town named Blue once thrived not far from the fictional Indigo (honest!), and the efforts to bring Indigo back to life recall the real-life revival of Gruene, Texas, a tiny community that died in the 1950s and was successfully resurrected some thirty years later. The Sandow Lignite Mine and the Rockdale Aluminum Smelter are also very real, and my descriptions of the mine's operation, its proposed expansion, and its terrible effects on the environment and the surrounding countryside are factually accurate. The herbs described here are real as well, and you should do your homework and use your common sense if you plan to experiment with them medicinally. China Bayles would certainly be upset if she lost any of her readers due to their uninformed or careless use of herbs. Do be careful, please.

— Susan Wittig Albert

How Plants Came to Have Color: A Legend of Liberia

Now Gala the Creator loved color. And he loved puzzles. When he made the plants he added color to each one. Sometimes it is hidden in the roots of a plant. Sometimes in the leaves. Sometimes in the bark. One day when he had finished adding colors, he ran his fingers over the ends of the twigs that made his brush. The many colors that had been used splattered over the big green leaves of a certain plant. Splatter. Splatter. We see that plant today. The *Kwi* people call it caladium. Gala planned to enjoy watching his children when they hungered for color and found at least some of it in the places he had hidden it.

Gala's favorite color was blue, every kind of blue . . .

You Cannot Unsneeze a Sneeze
— Esther Warner Dendel

Our lives are dyed the color of
our imaginations.

— Marcus Aurelius

One

Indigo, Texas, was founded in 1872 by Shelton Dobbs and named in honor of his daughter, Indigo Dobbs Crockett. The prairie around Indigo, about fifty miles east of Austin, was suited to the growing of cotton, and the town soon became a banking, ginning, and shipping center for area growers. But commerce began to decline when the boll weevil destroyed the cotton, and the stores started closing during the Depression. As highways bypassed the community, its death warrant was sealed. The most recent census shows that the population has dwindled to 27 hardy souls, all of whom swear that they would rather die in Indigo than live anywhere else.

"Notes on Some Notable Texas Towns,"
— *The Enterprise*, Pecan Springs, Texas

The man died fast and hard and in true Texas style, stepping into a shotgun blast that lifted his feet off the ground and slammed him backward through the door he'd just opened, into the powdery dust of the street. Nobody actually saw him die, but the report of his passing was loud enough to be heard by the amateur players in a makeshift theater across the alley, just at the end of the Friday night performance of *Indigo's Blue, or Hard Times on the Blackland Prairie.* The cast and most of the audience rushed out into the October night to see what had happened, followed by the San Antonio television crew that had come to shoot the performance.

That's why, on the following evening's TV newscast, you might have seen a dead man staring blankly up at the night sky, surrounded by a crowd of wide-eyed, open-mouthed women in the long skirts and puff-sleeved shirtwaists of the 1890s, a gaudy whore in red, white, and blue spangles, and a country doctor in a frock coat and top hat, groping inexpertly for a pulse. But from the gaping hole in the victim's chest and the amount of real blood that had soaked into the dust around the body, it was clear to the assembled crowd — which included Mike McQuaid, Ruby Wilcox, and me, China Bayles — that we might as well skip EMS and phone the sheriff.

But I'm getting ahead of the story, which

14

begins (for me, anyway) several days before the man opened that fatal door and ended up dead in Indigo. So I'll start when I first learned about the problem, on a sunny Monday afternoon in early October, as I was giving Allison Selby and Ruby Wilcox the two-bit tour of my backyard garden. That's when Allie told me about her uncle Casey and his plan to see the town of Indigo dead and buried.

I live in the Texas Hill Country, in a big Victorian house on Limekiln Road with my husband, McQuaid, and our thirteen-year-old son, Brian. To get to our place, you drive south on Brazos Street past the elementary school, where you turn right onto Limekiln Road and head west about twelve miles. Slow down when you see an old shed on the right, half-smothered under a mound of enthusiastic honeysuckle, a wilding planted by a passing bird. Just past the shed, you'll see a wooden sign that says MEADOW BROOK, decorated with faded bluebonnets. Turn left, and drive down the gravel lane about a quarter of a mile until it dead-ends at a two-story white Victorian with a green roof, a wrap-around porch, and a windowed turret. The house is surrounded by pecan and live oak trees and a couple of acres of grass that always needs either watering or mowing, depending on whether it's rained lately. September had been much wetter than usual and Brian (who is the chief lawn-mower in our family) had spent the last couple of weekends with his mother. The grass was ankle-high, lush, and generously decorated with seed-heads.

"Chiggers?" Ruby inquired dubiously, as we stood on the back porch, surveying the yard.

"You bet," I said. "Ferocious ones. I eat a lot of garlic, though, so they leave me alone." I reached for a small bottle of the herbal bug repellent that I sell at the shop. "Chiggers hate this stuff almost as much as they hate garlic." I handed it to her. "Want some, Allie?"

Allison shook her head. "Chiggers don't seem to like me," she said. "Guess I'm just not tasty enough." She leaned against the porch railing, gazing out across the yard. "Gosh, China, it's so green — and lush."

I grinned. *Lush* was a polite way of saying that the garden had gone back to the wilderness. "It's amazing what a little rain will do," I said.

While Ruby Wilcox is slathering on the repellent and Allison Selby is contemplating the overgrown landscape, I'll introduce the three of us. My name is China Bayles, and I'm the proprietor of Thyme and Seasons Herbs in Pecan Springs, a small town halfway between San Antonio and Austin, on the eastern edge of the Texas Hill Country. I came to Pecan Springs seven or eight years ago, single, approaching forty, and running from the law — from my career as a Houston criminal attorney, that is. I opened an herb shop, made friends, and settled into small-town life. Just about a year ago, I married Mike McQuaid and his son, Brian, who looks like his father, without McQuaid's broken nose. Brian came with a pessimistic basset hound named Howard Cosell and a varying assortment of footloose and fancy-free lizards, frogs, and spiders, which are supposed to live in his bedroom but have a habit of showing up elsewhere, especially where you wish they wouldn't. Howard Cosell has the good taste not to eat these items of biological bric-a-brac, but he's not above letting them think he might.

Ruby Wilcox is my best friend and business partner. She's slim and tall (six feet two in the open-toed blue slides she was wearing today), with frizzed henna-red hair, a liberal smattering of sandy freckles, and a generous mouth, lips firm and full. And if her height and coloring don't attract enough attention, she has her own unique — some might say outlandish — sense of style. Today, she was decked out in an empire-waisted, ankle-length, scooped-neck dress tie-dyed in various shades of indigo blue, with a matching indigo scarf twisted around her red curls, blue eyeshadow accenting her blue eyes (she likes to wear contacts that match her outfits), and blue polish on her finger- and toenails. A sight to make you sit up and take notice.

Ruby owns the Crystal Cave, the only New Age shop in Pecan Springs — not a surprise, for she's fascinated by things like astrology, tarot, divination, and channeling. Right now, for instance, she's teaching a six-week class on how to enhance your intuition — Tuning in to Your Right Brain, she calls it, because the right side of the brain is the switchboard where all the intuitive connections are spliced together. When she teaches a class, Ruby does all the exercises that she asks her students to do, which means that right now, she's working on sharpening her own intuitive skills.

But the left side of Ruby's brain works

just fine, too. She's a very sharp business-woman, and we're partners in a tearoom called Thyme for Tea, located in the same building as Thyme and Seasons and the Crystal Cave. This enterprise has been a challenge since we opened a little over a year ago, but we're finally beginning to settle into a more or less comfortable routine, with a light luncheon menu, afternoon tea, even the occasional catering job. Our shops and the tearoom are closed on Monday. That's why the two of us could stroll around the garden this afternoon and try to fool ourselves into thinking that we're ladies of leisure, which of course we're not. Being self-employed has a great many advantages, but leisure is definitely not on the list.

Allison Selby and I have been doing natural dye workshops together this summer. Nobody would ever call Allie pretty, for her face is too narrow, her nose too long, her chin tucked back too far into her neck. But her dark eyes flash with a vibrant electricity, her short, mahogany-colored hair is glossy, and her movements are energetic. Today, she was her usual casual self in worn jeans, scuffed leather sandals, and a T-shirt that announced the name of her business, Indigo Valley Farm.

Allie lives an hour's drive to the east and north of Pecan Springs, on beautiful Indigo Creek, near a tiny town that is also called Indigo, in Dalton County. Our workshops, which we call Colors to Dye For, take place on her farm, in her outdoor dye kitchen. I bring the dye plants and talk about them, and Allie teaches the students — some of whom come from as far away as Dallas and Houston — how to use them.

The four or five workshops we've given over the past several months have been fun for me, and I've certainly learned a great deal about using plants for dyeing. Even though I've studied herbs for years, natural dyes are a recent interest, and I'm continually amazed at the variety of plants that have been used throughout history to create color. Until the discovery of aniline dyes, fibers and fabrics were colored with plant and animal dyes. But in 1856, an eighteen-year-old British chemistry student named William Perkin stumbled over the first synthetic dye — the color mauve — when he was trying unsuccessfully to make quinine from coal tar. People were anxious to synthesize quinine, the herbal medicine that was the only successful treatment of malaria, because the bark of the cinchona tree, its natural source, was very difficult to obtain. (Quinine wasn't synthesized until World War II, when the Japanese seized the world's supply of cinchona trees.) Willy Perkin's mauve not only sparked a new color craze but became the first step in the development of modern organic chemistry.

In addition to helping me accumulate such fascinating oddments as the relationship between the cinchona tree and the color mauve, the workshops have also given me a chance to get to know Allison Selby better. She's a strong, intelligent woman with an ironic sense of humor, although she is often moody and private and . . . well, complicated. Our acquaintance goes back to our undergraduate years at the University of Texas (Allie was an art major while I was prelaw), but we lost track of one another over the intervening years, and I didn't even know where she lived until she got in touch with me last spring about collaborating on the workshops.

Ruby (who had agreed to help us with the next Colors to Dye For) finished fortifying herself against the chiggers and we waded through the grass, flicking off grasshoppers and pausing here and there to talk about the plants. My display gardens, which are designed to give people an idea of how various herbs look in a garden setting, are located on the grounds around Thyme and Seasons. Since they're open to the public, I am compulsive about keeping the beds trim and tidy. When you visit, you'll see squares and rectangles outlined with upright boxwood and principled brick paths, every weed (well, almost every weed) virtuously suppressed, as in a properly well-ordered English herb garden. If you are a gardener, you will appreciate that this takes time and dedication — a great deal of both, actually.

The gardens at the house get whatever time is left over. As a result, the herbs and flowers and veggies and weeds tumble together in a riotous anarchy that I fondly call my "cottage garden," but which might easily be mistaken for a stretch of impenetrable jungle. McQuaid refuses to go near it without a compass, a canteen, and a machete, and even I am careful about wandering through it, especially at twilight, when I can hear the plaintive cries of rain forest monkeys and the trumpeting of a distant elephant. At the far end of this tract of uninhibited chaos, I've planted some of the dye herbs we're using for the workshops — safflower, tansy, cosmos, marigolds, madder, woad — and I wanted to show them to Allie. I'd brought a basket, too, so we could gather some goldenrod.

We turned the corner. "And this," I announced, "is my dye garden."

I probably should have reconnoitered before I brought guests. Nobody said anything for a long time.

"Astounding," Allie remarked at last, in that half-ironic, half-amused tone of hers. "Would you look at that? I had no idea that sunflowers grew quite so tall."

Ruby craned her neck. "Somehow," she remarked, "they make me think of Jack and the Beanstalk. Maybe there's a pot of gold around here somewhere."

With all the rain we've been having, the Hopi dye sunflowers were taller and larger than usual, their orange-rimmed heads plump with purple-black seeds. The safflowers, too, were vigorous and woody, while the unruly madder (a distant cousin of that all-important cinchona tree) was thigh-high and sprawling. The goldenrod had catapulted across the path and leapt like a shameless hussy into the iris bed. And there was the woad, a garden gorilla that some fastidious states have unfeelingly designated as a Class-A noxious weed. My woad looked as fierce as the ancient Britons who terrorized the Romans when they painted themselves with it. The plants were obviously dead set on taking over Texas and were already eyeing the territory north of the Red River. It was going to take courage and determination, and maybe a legion of Roman soldiers, to bring them under control.

I sighed. "I think I'd better put in a call to the woad police. Before it goes to seed."

"I've got news for you," Ruby said, pulling off a dried seed pod and handing it to me. "What color do you get from woad?"

"Blue," Allie replied. "China's got enough woad here to body-paint a whole clan of Picts." She fingered a leaf. "In Europe, it was the major source of the color blue through the 1700s, but when the traders began importing indigo from the Far East, dyers sort of forgot about woad. If you want to know about blue, you need to ask Mayjean Carter. She's got quite a collection of blue-dyed textiles."

"Forget about woad?" Ruby asked nervously, gazing at my woad forest. "I don't see how they could. I'd be afraid to turn my back on this stuff, even for an instant."

As we paused to fill the basket with goldenrod blossoms, we talked about the dye plants Allie wanted me to bring to the workshop, which was scheduled for Friday.

"I've just finished shearing," Allie said as we started back toward the house, "so I've got some new fleece. And Miss Mayjean has promised to bring some of the pieces from her indigo collection."

"I'm looking forward to it," Ruby said. "How are your girls?" Ruby has never met Allie's family, but she's seen photos, of course. And she hears about them every time the three of us get together.

"They're having the time of their lives." Allie brushed a gnat off her arm. "Shangrilama is keeping an eye on things, and Buckeye and Bronco are fat and sassy. I'm getting rid of Rambo, though. He sneaked up behind me the other day and knocked me tail over teakettle. I told him it's time for him to hit the road." Her grin seemed tight. "I don't like to be knocked around."

I remember Allie saying something very similar during a painful divorce five years or so ago. She left her job as an art teacher in the Austin public schools and moved to a piece of land where her mother's family had lived for generations. Since then, she has painstakingly bred a small herd of

25

white and colored angora goats — the "girls," she calls them affectionately, although the herd includes a fiercely protective guard llama named Shangrilama, three conscientious angora bucks, and an assortment of rowdy kids. The angora is an ancient Turkish goat that is valued for its soft, luxuriant mohair. Colored angoras, however, have been bred only in the last few years. Their fleece is sold mostly to handspinners, who love the handsome dark colors of the fiber and the astonishing softness and strength of the spun yarn.

As a shepherd and fiber artist, Allie is one of the most talented and busiest women I know. She hand-shears her entire herd twice a year; washes, cards, spins, and dyes the fleeces; and weaves scarves and rugs and blankets that she sells, along with her fleeces and animals, at shows around the country. She also displays her hand-dyed items in various Hill Country shops, including Thyme and Seasons and the Crystal Cave, where she's developed a dedicated following. And she offers a variety of workshops and classes at her farm and in Austin and Pecan Springs. Most of the year, this woman has more work than she can possibly do and mostly she thrives on it. But like many artists, Allie chooses to live on the margin, investing her time and energy in return for the pleasure of her animals' company, the delight of her fiber creations, and not much money. Making ends meet must be a constant juggle, but, as I say, she seems to thrive.

Today, however, I had the unsettling notion that Allie was not thriving. She seemed taut, like a rubber band that's almost ready to snap, and there were blue shadows under her eyes. Her normal irony also seemed sharper than usual, less funny, more barbed. Her relationship, maybe? She'd been living with someone for the past couple of years — perhaps they'd split up. A failed love affair, coming after the divorce, would certainly be enough to turn her life sour.

Or maybe she really had taken on too much. She'd just gotten back from a fiber arts show in Colorado, and there was the Colors to Dye For workshop coming up on Friday and the Indigo Arts and Crafts Festival on Friday night and Saturday. Ruby and I had taken a booth, and we were planning to drive to Allie's place on Thursday afternoon to set things up for the workshop. Allie had invited us to stay at her farm on Thursday and Friday nights — a good thing for us, since Indigo has no motels. But maybe it wasn't a good thing for Allie. Maybe she ought to get some rest, instead of worrying about guests.

"Look," I said. "It's really kind of you to invite Ruby and me to stay with you and the girls at the farm this weekend. But maybe we should commute. It's only an hour's drive and having company just means extra work for you, on top of everything else."

Behind Allie's back, Ruby gave me a surreptitious thumbs-up, and I knew she shared my concerns. She and I have been friends for so long that we occasionally seem to read each other's minds — indicating, she claims, that I am finally beginning to develop my right brain. My biggest shortcoming, in Ruby's view, is that I am too rational, too logical. Linear, she calls it. I should learn to think in circles.

Allie lifted her head. "You can see right through me, huh?" She sounded irritable. "Allie's ready to snap?"

"Well," I said, "you do seem a little . . . edgy. Troubled, maybe."

Allie made a low sound in her throat. "You'd be troubled, too, if you knew what's going on in Indigo."

"So what's going on in Indigo?" I sat down on the old wooden swing that hangs from the live oak tree and patted the seat beside me. Allie sat down and stretched out her long legs. She didn't answer right away.

❦ Ruby pulled up a green-painted lawn chair, brushed leaves off the seat, and sat down. "There can't be much going on there," she remarked, "aside from the festival, that is. It's got to be the smallest living town in Texas. Why, it doesn't even have a post office anymore."

"You don't know the whole story," I said, pushing the swing with my toe so that we swayed back and forth. "People are really committed to bringing Indigo back to life." Allie had introduced me to several village leaders when we started giving our workshops early last spring. Shortly after that, the Historic Indigo Restoration Committee, HIRC for short, had invited me to meet with them as an informal advisor, since I had been involved with a similar group in Pecan Springs. I was impressed by the energy the group had brought to the task of enticing visitors to Indigo, scheduling events like the Festival for almost every weekend. This fall, they had already staged an antique car rally and a bicycle race and were planning a folk music fiesta, a farmers' market, and a holiday festival. If they kept coming up with good ideas like these, they were bound to succeed.

Five years before, nobody would have given a plugged nickel for Indigo's chances for surviving into the twenty-first century. It had been a lively little town once, with a busy cotton gin, a bank, a railroad depot, a two-story hotel, a grocery store, a feed store that also sold ranching supplies, a hardware store, a handful of saloons, and the Dalton County Jail, which provided overnight hospitality for the saloons' rowdier customers. It had been a pretty town, too, with pecan and willow trees along the streets and a large park that bloomed with colorful wildflowers in the spring and summer.

But times change and towns change. Indigo lost its vitality when the boll weevils chewed up the cotton, the Depression closed the stores, and the new highway swung ten miles in the opposite direction, taking the county seat with it. This sad business of dying towns, we've seen it happen all over Texas, from the oil-patch towns that dried up when the crude stopped flowing to agricultural towns killed off by drought and the loss of cheap farm labor. People with money in their jeans climb into their pickups and drive to the city, where they get cheaper prices and a greater variety of goods and services. People without money go elsewhere to look for work. When their customers and their labor force disappear, the town's businesses fold. Once they're gone, the schools go, too, and with them the sense of community. That's what happened to Indigo. In the end, there was nothing left but a few old folks, living on their Social Security checks while they watched Indigo die around them.

Until Allie, her friends, and HIRC began to bring Indigo back to life, that is. A dozen artists — spinners, weavers, dyers, potters, a wood-turner, even a blacksmith — formed the Indigo Arts and Crafts Co-op. They rented the dilapidated cotton gin from Allie's uncle, who owns most of what's left of the buildings on Main Street, and renovated it into studio space and a gallery where they could display and sell their work. Somebody opened a coffee shop across the alley, somebody else opened a gift shop, and everybody chipped in to buy planters for Main Street, which they filled with redbud trees, herbs, and native plants. In April, when the bluebonnets were blooming, they held a successful

Spring Arts and Crafts Festival, and now they were about to do it again. Indigo had died once, but Allie and her friends were investing their hearts and souls in the effort to resurrect it.

"The population is growing," Allie said, "but I'm afraid that's not going to make any difference." There was a bitter twist in her voice. "Looks like we've reached the end of the road."

"You can't mean that," I exclaimed. "Why, just think how hard you've worked to bring the town to life! And with all the events you've scheduled —"

"We'll get through the festival okay," Allie said, "and the events that are already on the calendar. But after that, there won't be any more town. The girls and I will have to move, too." She made a hopeless gesture with her hands. "No more Indigo Farm."

"Wait a minute," Ruby said, frowning. "I thought your farm belonged in your mother's family. I thought you were leasing the land from your uncle, or something like that."

"Right," Allie said sourly. "It does. I am."

"Then what's the problem?" I asked. "Why can't you —"

"The problem is called 'mining rights.' "
Allie leaned forward in the swing, her elbows on her knees, her head down. She looked angry and discouraged. "In another year or two, the town of Indigo will not only be dead, but buried, and so will the farm. Every building, every tree, every blade of grass, even Indigo Creek — it'll all be gone. Bulldozed, ripped away, dug up, diverted. What's left will look like a moonscape. The astronauts will be able to see the scars from space."

"Oh, no!" Ruby exclaimed. "That can't be! You can't mean it, Allie!"

"Oh, hell," I said, beginning to understand. "It's that strip mine, isn't it?"

"Right the first time," Allie said. She turned her head so we couldn't see if there were tears in her eyes. "And it's all Uncle Casey's fault, damn him!"

Two

Yellow and gold are related colors with conflicting symbolic meanings. Yellow can represent optimism, idealism, and joy on the one hand, while on the other it is the color of deceit, betrayal, and cowardice. Gold suggests abundance, but also the excesses of people who have too much.

"The Symbolic Meaning of Color"
— Ruby Wilcox

Goldenrod is a hardy, herbaceous perennial with plumes of tiny, yellow clustered flowers, which are excellent as cut flowers. All types can be used in the dye pot. Its just-opened flower blossoms yield clear, bright yellows, while later in the year, the flowering tops give greeny-yellow dyes.

Wild Color
— Jenny Dean

Ruby had to leave to go to the monthly meeting of her Breast Cancer Survivors group. Allie stayed a little while longer, while

I got as much of the bad news out of her as she seemed willing to tell me. After she left, I went into the kitchen to put on the teakettle, then got out my dye pot — an old stainless steel kettle I keep for this purpose. Working on the back porch, I weighed the goldenrod blossoms we'd gathered and made a note of the weight. The half-pound of plant material would give a good depth of color to a half-pound of fiber. The goldenrod went into the dye pot, and when the kettle boiled, I poured the water over the plant material and left it to sit overnight. The next morning, I'd strain out the plant material and bottle up the cooled dye bath to use at the workshop. If there was time after supper tonight, I'd make up a safflower dye bath as well.

That chore done, I wandered into the kitchen and began to pull leftovers out of the fridge, closely supervised by Howard Cosell, who likes to keep tabs on food preparation in his kitchen, in case a little something accidentally falls into his bowl. On Monday evening, we usually just have sandwiches, a salad, and whatever soup I am inspired to concoct. Today, I discovered the substantial remains of a roast chicken with some meat still on it; a small bunch of broccoli; some celery stalks with wilted leaves; a couple of over-the-hill carrots; an onion; and some naked cheddar that somebody (we will not mention names) had neglected to wrap. I gave Howard a few choice bits of chicken skin, then plopped the carcass into a large pot, covered it with water and tossed in the celery, carrots, and onion, all chopped. (Onion skins yield shades of orange, yellow, and rust, so they went into the paper bag with the others I've been saving.) Then I added four smashed garlic cloves, a couple of bay leaves, a dozen peppercorns, and a half-dozen sprigs of fresh parsley. After an hour's simmering, the broccoli would go in, too, and cook for a few minutes. Then a whirl in the blender and back into the pot to reheat, along with the grated cheese. Broccoli and cheese soup, to go with our sandwiches and salad. And in the process, I'd managed to clean out the fridge.

While the goldenrod steeped and the chicken stock simmered, I intended to do some simmering of my own. I poured a glass of rosemary lemonade and went out to the front porch, followed by Howard Cosell, who was worn out from his supervisory chores. With a weary sigh, he dropped down beside me as I sat in the rocking chair and began to reflect on what

Allie had said about the strip mine, Indigo, and her uncle Casey. Some of it wasn't news to me, of course, since the mine has been hitting the Texas headlines for several decades and a great many people have grown increasingly concerned about it. But some of it *was* news — ugly news, too.

If I asked you to name the natural resources buried beneath the surface of Texas, you'd probably think of oil, and maybe natural gas. But I'll bet you'd never think of coal. Most people associate coal with states like Pennsylvania, and Kentucky, and West Virginia, where miners sink underground shafts a mile deep and dig out veins of hard, black, glittery stuff — bituminous coal that burns hot and fast, with a minimum of residue.

Well, we have coal in Texas, too, but mostly it's soft, brown, and crumbly, a low-grade lignite coal that produces great amounts of sulfur dioxide and nitrogen dioxide when it's burned. If you're in the market for coal, the only thing good about this not-so-good coal is that it is buried just a couple of hundred feet below the surface, in a wide ribbon across the eastern quarter of the state. This shallow depth makes it easy and relatively cheap to strip mine.

And that's how the Sandow Mine came about. Located in Milam County, fifty miles east of Austin and a few miles north of Indigo, it is the largest strip mine in Texas, operated since the 1950s by Alcoa, the Aluminum Company of America. Draglines — twenty-story-tall behemoth shovels that scoop up 150 tons of dirt in one massive bite — strip away the earth and pile it off to one side in huge heaps, digging a pit big enough to bury a pair of *Titanic*s and exposing the lignite seam. The coal is chewed out by smaller electric shovels and trucked away in colossal 160-ton-capacity coal haulers. When the shovels and trucks have cleaned out the ten-foot-thick seam, the earth is pushed back into the pit and the dragline lumbers off to dig another huge hole. The whole process is something like the excavation of the Grand Canyon, except that it's not natural and it doesn't take millions of years. It takes only one year to strip the soil and rock from a 250-acre piece of Texas Blackland Prairie.

And yes, they do have to put it back again. Federal law requires that surface-mined property be restored — overburden replaced, fences and buildings rebuilt, trees and grasses replanted. But at

Sandow, the new grasses and trees don't grow very well. The draglines have brought large quantities of iron sulfide to the surface, where it decomposes into sulfuric acid and poisons the soil. The contours of the land may be repaired in a way that satisfies the letter of the law, but environmentalists believe that the prairie, with its amazingly rich diversity of plant and animal life, will be lost forever.

And something else is being lost. Over the fifty-some years of the mine's operation, huge quantities of precious groundwater have been pumped out to keep the pits from flooding. As a result of this pumping, the water level in the Carrizo-Wilcox Aquifer — the underground water source for a number of nonprofit water supply companies and thousands of private wells in a two-county area — has dropped alarmingly, up to 400 feet in places. With good reason, people fear that their wells will soon be dry, and if there's anything left, it will have such a high iron content that it will be undrinkable.

And where does all that coal go? In the case of the Sandow Mine, not far enough. Only a few miles, to Alcoa's aluminum smelter at Rockdale, one of the dirtiest plants in Texas, with a toxic plume that fans north to Oklahoma and west almost to New Mexico, annually emitting as much smog-forming pollutants as a million automobiles. Alcoa does not have to comply with the state's emissions requirements because it was grandfathered in under an earlier, more lenient code.

As you might guess, Texas environmentalists, ordinary citizens, and even a few lawmakers have been up in arms about this mess for years. They've filed lawsuits, masterminded letter-writing campaigns, and staged rallies on the steps of the capitol in Austin, where Billie Woods's ballad, "An Ode to Alcoa," is sung to the tune of "El Paso."

Out in the East Texas county of Milam,
Alcoa's smelter commanded the world,
With towering smokestacks and draglines
*   a hummin',*
Lignite did burn and pollution did swirl . . .

But everybody admits that it's hard to fight this powerful polluter, which has friends not only in Austin, but in Washington as well. In fact, Alcoa is now in the process of seeking permits to expand its lignite strip mine into an adjacent 16,000-acre area. The company already has access to much of the land through a coal-for-water deal it made last year with the San Antonio power company that owns the mining rights to the area of proposed expansion. Alcoa gets the lignite to power its smelter, while thirsty San Antonio gets the billions of gallons of water that will be pumped out of the new mine.

And that's where Indigo comes in, and Casey Ford, Allie's uncle. It seems that Casey has decided to —

With a low growl, Howard Cosell clambered to his feet, going into his I'm-a-ferocious-watchdog act. But when he saw McQuaid's blue truck coming around the curve in the lane, he wagged his tail energetically and put on the goofy doggie grin that says, *Ohboyohboy, here comes the rest of my pack. Now I know it's going to be a good day.* Howard is supposed to be Brian's dog, but he rarely smiles for anyone but McQuaid.

I guessed by the way McQuaid parked the car and slammed the door, however, that this had not been a good day for him. This suspicion was confirmed by the dark look on his face as he climbed the porch steps. He was limping, too. McQuaid ran into a bullet when he was on an undercover assignment for the Texas Rangers

41

about a year and a half ago. The wound was serious enough to keep him out of action for seven or eight months, but his recovery has been steady and he's almost his old self again — almost, but not quite. We probably won't be going on a three-day hike in the mountains this year.

He dropped heavily into the other rocking chair and leaned over to rub Howard's ears. "Hey, Howard, you good old dog," he said gruffly. "How ya been all day, pal?"

Howard said that he had been fine but was finer now that McQuaid was home and he could stop worrying that his best friend had walked out in front of a truck. Howard has a gloomy outlook.

"Hey." I held up my glass. "There's more where this came from. Want some?"

"Oh, hi." He gave me a sidelong look. "Yeah, thanks." McQuaid isn't handsome — his nose is crooked and there's a jagged scar across his forehead — but he's ruggedly good-looking, with dark hair that falls across his forehead and slate blue eyes that turn black and glittery when he's angry. Right now, they looked like pieces of hard coal.

I fetched the lemonade pitcher and another glass and poured. When I gave him his drink, he pulled my face down for a long, sweet kiss. "Sorry," he muttered, his lips against my cheek. "I shouldn't be taking this out on you, hon."

"Don't worry about it," I said, smoothing the dark hair back from his forehead. Like Howard Cosell, I was finer, too, now that McQuaid was home and I could see his face, finding something new in the familiar features, as I did almost every day. I know I had good reasons for putting our marriage off — wanting to hold on to my privacy, to keep myself independent and uninvolved, free of tangling commitments — but they don't seem all that compelling now. It's hard to think back to a time when we weren't a family, fitting together like pieces of a puzzle, sharing everything that comes along, good and bad.

I sat down and waited for him to tell me what was on his mind. Another run-in with the department chairman at Central Texas State University, where he teaches? McQuaid has a Ph.D. in Criminal Justice, but with more than a decade of real-world law-enforcement experience under his belt, he isn't your typical professor. He has zero tolerance for CTSU politics and less than that for his department chairman. Since he

43

went back to the university after the shooting, he hasn't enjoyed it very much. To tell the truth, I think he's been hankering after his old life, or pieces of it, anyway.

McQuaid rubbed his left leg, the one that usually gives him the most trouble. "Sally phoned today." His voice sounded gritty. "And I got a call from Brian's school counselor. He wants to see me this week."

I felt a twinge of uneasiness. "Ah, Sally. So that's the source of the heartburn."

Sally is McQuaid's ex-wife and Brian's mother. McQuaid takes the blame for their divorce, thinking that it was his work as a Houston homicide detective that unhinged Sally. I agree that being a policeman's wife is no picnic — I've seen plenty of law-enforcement marriages fall apart because of the uncertainty and danger. But I don't agree that McQuaid should take personal responsibility for Sally's retreat into alcohol and tranquilizers. We are all creatures of free will and moral choice, and Sally made her own decisions. But while McQuaid knows this in his mind — it's something all cops have to believe, or they can't be cops — it's a different story when it comes to Sally. He still feels heavily responsible for what happened to her and does what he can, whenever he can, to help her get her act together.

"Heartburn is right." McQuaid dropped his head back and drained his lemonade fast, as if he was pouring it on the fire. "Five alarm, at least." He gave me an unconvincing grin and refilled his glass from the pitcher. "Good stuff, China. A little more of this and I'll be just fine."

If he had Sally on his mind, I doubted that a few glasses of lemonade would help. When I first met Mike McQuaid — I was attorney for the defense in an ugly wife-abuse case, he was a prosecution witness — Sally had just gotten out of detox and was suing for divorce. McQuaid was doing his best to reassure Brian that the two of them could make it on their own. At the same time, he was trying to disconnect emotionally from his soon-to-be-ex-wife and encourage her to build a new life. Tough stuff.

The one ray of light in what must have been a dark, dismal episode was that Sally didn't demand custody. Perhaps she realized that she couldn't be a good mother at that point in her life. Or perhaps she knew that McQuaid would contest it and that the emotional battle would be terrible for

Brian, who is unusually sensitive and empathetic. He was only a little boy when his mother left, but even then he seemed compelled to please her and make her happy. (It's an impulse I understand, for my own mother was an alcoholic. When I was a kid I thought that if I could just relieve some of her worries, I could make her stop drinking. Not a very rational thought, of course, but a child trapped in codependency doesn't think like a brain surgeon.) Brian loves his mother and wants to help her, although, like his father, he can't seem to find a way.

Through the years I've known Sally, her life has been like a long-running soap opera, brightened by ecstatic highs, dimmed by abysmal lows. At one desperately low point a couple of years ago, she actually kidnapped Brian. When I caught up with them at the *Star Trek* conference where she'd taken him, she was so distraught that she tried to dive out of the window of the high-rise hotel. She would have succeeded, too, if it hadn't been for a six-foot Romulan with patent-leather hair and winged eyebrows, who restrained her.

Over the past few months, though, Sally has been on an upswing — happier, more stable, more optimistic about the future. Last spring, she moved back to San Antonio, where she took a high-paying job, got a high-rise apartment, started therapy, and fell in love with her stockbroker. I didn't think romance was a very smart move right away, given all the other changes in her life.

But when she told me about the affair a couple of months ago, it sounded as if she'd already thrown caution to the winds, so I kept my reservations to myself. And when Arthur began coming with her to pick Brian up, I understood the attraction. He was good-looking, charming, attentive, impressively dressed — and his Lexus smelled just like money. There was something about the man that troubled me, however. I couldn't put it into words exactly, but —

"Sally says that she and Henningson are getting married next month," McQuaid said woodenly. He turned to face me. "She wants Brian to go live with them for a while. She wants to get to know him before he grows up."

"But Brian's settled *here*," I protested in dismay. "He's involved in school and Science Club and a dozen other things. Anyway, he loves living in the country. He'd be bored to death in that apartment, and she'd always be after him to keep his feet off her white furniture. Where would he ride his bike? Where would he keep his lizards? And what would happen when his tarantula got loose? It would be worse than a snake in the plumbing."

"Sally's not thinking of Brian." McQuaid's tone was dour. "She's focusing on herself, as usual, and on this boyfriend of hers. According to her, Henningson likes the idea of being a dad. Instant family."

"I'm surprised to hear that. I had the impression that he was too engrossed in his work to have much time for parenting."

"Too self-engrossed, if you ask me," McQuaid growled. "Smug sonovabitch."

"I take it," I said delicately, "that you don't like him."

McQuaid looked at me, immediately defensive. "It's not that I don't like him. Who Sally shacks up with is her business. What I don't like is the idea of that macho creep being Brian's father."

"Stepfather." I didn't point out that McQuaid hadn't liked the term "shack up together" when we were doing it.

"Oh, yeah?" He gave me a skeptical look. "Do you consider yourself Brian's stepmother?"

That stopped me. To tell the truth, now

that I was beginning to get the hang of living with a teenaged son, I thought of myself as Brian's mom. I thought of Sally, when I thought of her at all, as Brian's irresponsible aunt, who appeared and disappeared on a whim, either bringing inappropriate presents or forgetting all about his birthday. A cold, hard knot twisted in my stomach, and I shivered in spite of the warm October sunshine. The thought of Brian going to live with his undependable, unpredictable mother was . . . well, it was unthinkable.

"I rest my case," McQuaid said, when I didn't answer. He wiggled his feet and Howard Cosell stood up and moved over to the edge of the porch, where he lay down with his chin on his paws, regarding McQuaid with watchful concern. McQuaid stretched his legs, slouching in the chair. "She's in for a battle. I'm willing to work out some sort of informal arrangement for weekends and holidays, but that's it." He rubbed his face. "Even if we had to go to court, I can't believe she'd win. Brian doesn't want to live with her. And he especially doesn't want to live with Henningson."

I lifted my head. "How do you know that? Has he said so?"

49

"Not in so many words." He gave a little shrug. "In fact, he shuts up every time I open the subject. My guess is that he can't say anything positive about this situation, so he won't talk about it at all. But I know how he feels, just the same."

I didn't doubt the truth of that. Brian and his father are extraordinarily close — after all, they were on their own together from the day Sally moved out until I came along. If the boy hadn't talked to McQuaid about his mother's relationship with Arthur Henningson, there was something seriously wrong.

"You said that you got a call from Brian's counselor." I asked. "What was that about?"

"She says that Brian seems to be depressed. She wanted to know if there was something going on at home that might be bothering him."

"I've noticed it, too," I said, "the last week or so. He's quieter, and he spends more time in his room, on his computer."

McQuaid's mouth tightened. "Well, I guess it's gotten to the point where it's obvious to his teachers. Anyway, I told the counselor I'd stop in and talk to her later in the week. And I'll try to get Brian to come clean with me about what's bothering him." He gave me a sideways look. "How do you feel about this relationship of Sally's, China?"

McQuaid and I had talked about Sally and her boyfriend several times before, in a casual, joking sort of way, but he was asking seriously and I answered carefully. "Henningson is certainly a charmer," I said. "And he's got an ego a mile wide and two miles long." I paused. "But the world is full of egotistical men. That's not what bothers me."

"What is it, then?"

I took my time before I replied. "This is all just my opinion, of course, and I've only seen him a few times. But Henningson seems like a controller. He tells Sally what to do. He even tells her what to think. And she's too quick to please him. She anticipates his demands, as if she's hyperattentive to what he wants. Almost as if she's afraid of him." I'd seen that look on the faces of battered women, but I didn't want to plant that idea in McQuaid's mind. Instead, I added, "A psychologist might say there's a power issue there somewhere."

"Oh, yeah?" McQuaid frowned. "How come I didn't spot all this?"

"Maybe because you're too close to the

situation. You know Sally very well." And maybe because he'd never been part of a relationship that involved a power struggle. McQuaid is a strong man who never needs to impose his authority on others. To make himself feel stronger at their expense. But as a child, I had witnessed my father exert his power over my mother and had watched it diminish her. Perhaps that's why I could see it now, in Sally.

⊕ "If what you say is true," McQuaid said, "marrying this guy is the worst possible thing Sally could do. Underneath all that bravado, she's breakable. If he's on a power trip, he'll destroy her. And if Brian's aware of the situation, no wonder he's troubled."

We sat for a moment in silence. I thought of Sally, just beginning to get her bearings after a decade of wandering in a wilderness of unhappiness, indecision, addiction. I thought of Brian, who felt his mother's pain and feared his mother's fears, as if the pain and fear were his own. And I thought of Arthur Henningson, who liked to have things his way. Or was I just imagining it? Somewhere in the trees a cicada began to buzz, vibrating shrilly in the quiet air. A hummingbird buzzed past, on its way to the feeder at the corner of the porch.

McQuaid was thinking, too. Finally, he said, "How much do we know about this man?"

"Only what Sally has told us. He works for a brokerage firm in San Antonio. He lives in the same apartment house she does, on the top floor. That's how she met him. They got stuck in the elevator together. She also mentioned that he's been married before."

"I don't want to get involved in Sally's stuff," McQuaid said in a low voice, "but I'm responsible for Brian. Maybe I'll check into Henningson's background." He gave me a questioning glance. "What do you think?"

"I think you should do whatever feels right to you," I replied, without hesitation. McQuaid always loved the part of his work as a cop that involved investigation — following clues, tracing evidence, searching people's backgrounds for hidden motives — and that's the part he misses most. Since he left Houston PD, he's occasionally taken investigative jobs, just to keep his skills sharp. But I knew he wouldn't go nosing around in somebody's past life just for practice. He's too principled for that.

There was another long, silent moment. "Sally is a grown-up," he said finally, "and her life is her business. But Brian is still a child and he's *my* business. I'm going to do some checking."

I grinned. "Just don't let Sally catch you. It would not make her happy."

"Oh, you bet," he said fervently. There was a brief silence. "Hey," he said, "what are you doing this weekend? Want to go camping with Brian and me?" Hearing the word *go,* Howard Cosell raised his head expectantly. "Sorry, Howard," McQuaid added. "I don't think you'd like roughing it. You can stay with the Carsons." At those words, Howard put his chin back on his paws. He likes the Carsons, who own a kennel up the road and treat him as if he were visiting royalty, which suits him just fine.

"I thought Sally was taking Brian to Dallas to see the Cowboys game," I objected. "He's been looking forward to it for weeks."

"That was something else she wanted to tell me. Some big client of Arthur's is coming to town, and Sally is supposed to entertain the man's wife. She says it's a command performance." A grin tugged at the corner of his mouth. "Her term, not mine. But I guess it supports your theory of the case, Counselor. His to command, hers to entertain. And Henningson's already given the tickets away, so Brian and I can't use them."

"I see," I said soberly. Brian was going to be terribly disappointed about missing the game. "But I'm afraid I can't go camping. It's the weekend of the Arts and Crafts Festival in Indigo. Allie and I are doing a dye workshop on Friday, and Ruby and I have rented a festival booth for Friday night and Saturday. We're staying in Allie's cabin Thursday and Friday night, then heading back to Pecan Springs after the festival closes Saturday afternoon." I paused. "Maybe you and Brian could camp at the tank on Allie's place." In Texas, for some reason that's never been clear to me, farm ponds are called tanks. "It's isolated and pretty, and she says the tank is full of bass. There's a picnic table and a place to put in the canoe. And Brian might enjoy the festival. They're staging an old-fashioned melodrama on Friday night."

"Sounds like a winner to me," McQuaid said. We sat silently for a moment, and then he said, "I guess I didn't ask about your day — just dumped on you about mine. How'd it go, China?"

"Fine," I said. "Until I learned that

55

Allie's uncle Casey has decided to sell the mining rights to the family land — including Indigo Farm, the place Allie's been leasing — and more than half of Indigo. Which means it'll all be chewed up and swallowed by the Sandow Mine."

McQuaid stared at me. "Indigo is going to be *strip mined?*"

I nodded grimly. "The festival won't be very festive, I'm afraid. More like a wake. When this deal is done, we can say *adiós* to Indigo. The town will be dead and buried, to the end of eternity."

Three

Orange can represent energy, warmth, and passion; it may also suggest a flamboyant demand for attention.

"The Symbolic Meaning of Color"
— Ruby Wilcox

The Osage orange, a cousin to the mulberry tree, takes its name from the Osage Indian tribe, which used the strong, resilient wood to make bows. It is native to the Red River Valley of Texas and Oklahoma but has spread across the plains because its thorny branches made ideal fences before the invention of barbed wire. The Osage orange is conspicuous in the autumn landscape, when its leaves have fallen and its yellow-green fruits, as large and fruity-smelling as grapefruits, hang on the bare limbs. (It used to be thought that the fruit would keep insects out of the house.) The wood itself is an orangy-coppery color. You can soak the chips or sawdust in water to produce a range of oranges, yellows, and golds.

"So what exactly are mining rights?" Ruby asked. "I don't think I understand." She finished filling the plastic tub with tarot decks and astrology books and straightened up, rubbing her back. "The next time we discuss whether to do a booth at a show," she muttered, "remind me just how much work it is. Then tie me to a chair and gag me, so I can't say yes."

Thyme and Seasons and the Crystal Cave are side by side in the same building, with a connecting door between and the tearoom in the back. Ruby and I were in her shop, packing for the festival. If you've ever undertaken anything like this, you know it's a major project. But we go to at least four shows a year — in Fort Worth, Houston, San Antonio, and Fredericksburg — so we've developed a system. I'd already gathered and packed in tubs (they hold up to hard knocks better than boxes) all the items I planned to sell on Friday night and Saturday: books, teas, potpourris, soaps and cosmetics, essential oils, culinary herbs. Then there are all the other necessities, such as bags, cash drawer and change, tables and table covers, display stands, and lawn chairs to sit in when we aren't standing up to wait on customers. Oh, and plants, too, of course, mostly four-inch pots in their own plastic trays. Not to mention the dye materials for the Colors to Dye For workshop on Friday. Ruby and I had been packing and loading for most of the day and we were nearly finished — only a few more tubs to go.

"Excuse me, but what are mining rights?" Ruby repeated, as I stacked another tub onto the dolly.

I straightened up, rubbing the crick in my back. I didn't need to be board-certified in property law to answer her question, because this is an issue that every lawyer in Texas knows something about. (I can still call myself a lawyer, because I've kept my state bar membership current. Not that I can imagine myself going back to the law. But it cost me a lot of effort to get it, so I might as well keep it. And anyway, you never know what might lie ahead.)

"Different states treat rights differently," I replied, "but under Texas law, owning the right to mine or drill on a property is separate from ownership of the property. You can sell your mining rights and keep the land, or vice versa."

Ruby put her calculator, a receipt book, and a bundle of Thyme for Tea advertising brochures into the tub she was packing.

"Which means?" she asked, reaching for a roll of Scotch tape and a stapler. She stuck them in the tub, then added a box of paper clips and several pens.

"Which means that if somebody's bought the mining rights to your property, they only have to give you six months' notice of their intention to mine before they begin knocking down your house and your garage."

That got her attention. "They can do *that?*"

I leaned on the dolly. "They sure can — if you sold them the mining rights. Or if a previous owner sold them the rights and you didn't happen to read the fine print in the reservations section of your title policy."

"But what happens to *me?*" Ruby demanded.

I shrugged. "You move someplace else, that's what happens. Of course, you can move back when they're finished digging up your property. They're supposed to return everything to its original condition, more or less." She looked so distressed that I took pity on her. "Relax, Ruby. This isn't going to happen to you. Not in town." I thought about what was about to happen to Indigo and added, "At least, not in a town the size of Pecan Springs, with newer, expensive houses."

"I think I'd better reread my title papers, just in case," she said. "Or you can read them and tell me what I'm supposed to know." She put the lid on the tub and fastened it down. "I left before Allie finished telling the whole story the other day, but I got the idea that her uncle has sold the mining rights to Indigo. Is that true?"

"I don't know if it's already happened," I said, "but Allie says that's what he's planning to do." I picked up another tub and swung it onto the dolly. "Of course, Alcoa doesn't yet have the permit it needs to expand the mine, but in the twenty years the Texas Railroad Commission has been issuing permits for lignite mining, they've only denied one. It looks like a done deal." I looked around. "Any more tubs?"

"No, that's it," Ruby said, dusting her hands on her overalls. These are overalls like you've never seen, hand-batiked in patches of exotic purples, reds, and oranges, and worn with a purple tee. "My suitcase is already in the van," she added, "and Janet and I have discussed the lunch menus. Looks like the tearoom is all set for the weekend." Janet cooks for us at Thyme for Tea, and Friday and Saturday are usually big days. "Is all your stuff loaded?"

"Just about," I said. "I still have to check with Laurel on a few things." A couple of years ago, Laurel Wiley came to work for me full-time, and when Ruby and I have something to do outside the shops — a catering job or a show — she takes over for both of us.

I glanced at my watch. It was four-thirty. I'd told Allie we'd be at Indigo Farm about six, since she and I were going to a HIRC meeting at 7:30, and I wanted time to get settled. "I also have to call McQuaid," I added. "And I need to speak to Ellen Holt. She hasn't told me how much longer she's going to be staying at Thyme Cottage, and I've got an herbal landscaping workshop scheduled for a week from Saturday." I frowned. "I hope I remembered to tell her that she had to be out by next Friday."

● Thyme Cottage is the stone building that's located on the alley behind the shop. The one-story structure was once a stable, but the previous owner of this place, an architect, turned it into a one-bedroom guest house with a skylight, a fieldstone fireplace, and a built-in kitchen. I like to hold workshops there, since the main room is large enough to accommodate tables and the kitchen is ideal for cooking demonstrations. And when there's no workshop scheduled, it's available as a guest house, which I advertise on the Internet and in the Pecan Springs Bed-and-Breakfast Guide. It's a good source of extra income, and not that much extra work. But I do have to juggle the schedule, and a guest who stays overtime can be a problem.

"Well, don't be too long," Ruby said. "We need to stop and get something to eat." As I reached for the telephone, she slung her bag over her shoulder and headed out the door.

My phone conversation with McQuaid was unsettling, and I was still thinking about it when Ellen, barefoot and wearing the briefest of denim cutoffs and a midriff top, answered my knock at the cottage door.

"Oh, hi, Ms. Bayles," she said. "I'm glad you stopped in. I wanted to ask you about your Colors to Dye For workshop tomorrow. I was in Indigo a couple of days ago, doing some research, and I saw a flyer in the café. Is there room for another person? If there is, I'd love to come. My grandmother used to dye fabric with plants from her farm in Ohio, and I've always wanted to know more about the process."

Ellen Holt — a young woman with long,

loose honey-colored hair, a flirty smile, and the figure of a Dallas Cowboys cheerleader — was my third or fourth paying guest and the first to book through the Internet. She said she was a writer on leave from her job with an Ohio newspaper to write a book on small towns, and wanted a place to stay while she did some local research.

"I'm sure there's room in the workshop," I said. "Dyeing is a lot of fun — I think you'll enjoy it. Laurel can give you a map, along with the other information. When we're starting, what to wear, stuff like that." I paused. "Did I tell you that the cottage is booked for a workshop a week from Saturday?"

"Yes, you mentioned it." She tossed her long hair back out of her eyes. "I may not be finished with my research by then, but if not, I'm sure I can find another place to stay." She glanced over her shoulder. I could see her laptop computer on the bar, along with some books and a stack of file folders. "It won't be as nice as this place, though. I really love it here."

"I'm glad," I said. "See you at the workshop tomorrow!"

An hour later, I was piloting Big Red

Mama, the van that Ruby and I recently bought, down a narrow, two-lane road that loops across the prairie to the east and north of Pecan Springs. We acquired the van because we couldn't squeeze all our stuff into our car, and we call her Big Red Mama because . . . well, because that's what she is, bless her capacious soul. She's become like a member of the family, and she proves her worth on trips like this, carrying us and our gear across the prairie.

❦ A great many people visit the Hill Country on vacation, and forever after, when they think of Texas, they remember the Edwards Plateau, a region about the size of Massachusetts with a landscape of rocky ravines, limestone ledges, and open meadows invaded by prickly pear, mesquite, and cedar. But the Hill Country isn't all there is to Texas, not by a long shot. The Edwards Plateau is cut off along its eastern rim by the Balcones Fault, an area of ancient uplift that you can see rising to the west as you drive down I-35 from Austin to San Antonio. To the east, you look out across an entirely different landscape: the Blackland Prairie, which stretches from the Red River on the north to San Antonio on the south, and east toward the Gulf of Mexico. This rolling country of moderate rainfall and rich black soil is the southern end of the tall-grass prairie that once extended into Canada. Before the area was settled by Europeans, there were over twelve million acres of open prairie here, home to an enormous variety of grasses, birds, and mammals, as well as the nomadic Indians who trekked through it.

But the Blackland clay soil (known as "cracking clay," because of the deep, wide cracks that crisscross it in dry weather) was easily turned by the plow, and by the 1930s most of that vast prairie had been planted to cotton. Now, it's all cropped and grazed, and the flood of urban development along the I-35 corridor from San Antonio to Dallas laps steadily eastward, submerging the once-rich grassland under an asphalt sea of subdivisions and shopping malls. Urban sprawl, runaway growth, the relentlessly rising tide of our civilization.

Once you're east of the suburbs, though, the prairie is still incredibly beautiful, especially on a clear evening in early autumn, when the setting sun slants low across the landscape. The sumac flushes crimson, the cedar elms are golden, and the roadside is glowing with color: Maximilian sunflowers, white-capped snow-on-the-mountain, green-eyed daisy, purple wands of gayfeather, mounds of yellow broomweed, stalks of blue boneset blooming with late-season butterflies, prickly pear cactus studded with purple-red fruit.

I did some research last year and discovered that many of these native plants can be used to make dyes. If you'd like yellow or gold, you can try snow-on-the-mountain, or sumac, or mistletoe. For shades of green, look for black-eyed Susans, or sunflowers, or willow. And if you want a special challenge, collect enough ripe prickly pear cactus fruit to make a magenta dye — although you might want to gather a few more and make jelly, too. (The challenge comes in collecting the fruit without getting bitten by its fierce thorns. The secret: Use a rake to knock the ripe fruit into a bucket of sand, then rub the fruit in the sand — use tongs and wear leather gloves — to remove the prickles.)

But I wasn't thinking about dye plants or dyeing right now. My mind was on Brian, and on what I'd heard from McQuaid when we talked on the phone. Brian's counselor had phoned again, more urgently this time, and McQuaid had made

67

an appointment to see her. When he arrived, Brian's P.E. teacher was there, too. When Brian was changing in the locker room the day before, the teacher had noticed two big bruises on his backside. Questioned, Brian had first been evasive, then stubbornly defiant. Finally, half-dressed, he'd run out of the locker room and cut his next class.

"On his *backside?*" I asked, startled. Kids get all kinds of cuts and bumps, but that seemed a strange place for bruising.

"Yeah. At first, I didn't quite understand what they were getting at. But then the counselor asked me point-blank how hard we spanked him. I got the message."

"You mean —" I was appalled. "But that's crazy! We'd never —"

"Probably not so crazy, given the kinds of stuff the school has to deal with. I told them that we'd never raised a hand to Brian. That he was an unusually co-operative kid and responded pretty well to a discussion of the issues, or time-out in his room. I think they believed me. But that leaves us with the sixty-four-dollar question. Who gave him those bruises?"

I frowned. It was October, and some of the school activities were just getting under way. "I hope there's no hazing going on." You'd think that thirteen-year-olds were too young for something like that, but in Austin, some middle-school band members were recently suspended from school for paddling a classmate during an initiation.

"I don't think it's hazing," McQuaid said, his voice steely. "I think Henningson did this."

"Henningson?" I was startled. I didn't like the man, but I wouldn't have thought that he would strike Brian. "Why do you say that? What have you found?" McQuaid doesn't teach on Thursday, and he'd gone down to San Antonio early that morning to begin a background check.

"*Nada* — yet. I've started checking the Bexar County criminal records, and Blackie is running a NCIC check for me." Blackie Blackwell is the sheriff of Adams County and McQuaid's fishing and poker buddy. A National Crime Information Center search should turn up any felony arrests and convictions. "And I made an inquiry through the National Association of Securities Dealers, to see if Henningson has ever been the subject of a disciplinary proceeding. It'll be a while before I hear back on that one." His voice became grim.

"Meanwhile, Brian and I are going to have a long talk, and he's going to strip butt-naked. I want to see those bruises for myself."

I felt a sharp wrench at the thought of how Brian must be feeling right now, mixed with a simmering anger at Arthur Henningson — if he was the one who had struck our son. If McQuaid's suspicions were correct, I would personally go to court to make sure that the man never again came within striking distance of the boy. But maybe McQuaid was wrong. Maybe Brian had gotten those bruises when he jumped off something and landed on his rear.

"I'm sorry I can't be there," I said.

"It's probably better that you're not," McQuaid replied. "This is going to be one of those old-fashioned father-son sessions. You've got your cell phone, right? I'll try to catch you a little after nine."

And that's how we'd left it. I agreed that this was something McQuaid could handle better than I could (Brian is a little old for me to ask him to take his pants down) but I couldn't help feeling left out. After all my hesitation about joining this family — my desire to protect my privacy, my fear of being hurt or of being responsible for someone else's hurt — after all that, this *was* my family now, and what affected one of us affected us all, which I suppose is the definition of family.

Ruby recalled me to the present. "It's like a painter's palette out there," she said happily, gazing out of the window. "And look! There's an Osage orange, loaded with fruit. Didn't you say you wanted some for the workshop tomorrow? Should we stop and pick up a few?"

"It's the wood that's used for dyeing, not the fruit," I said. "I found a tree on our property, and McQuaid turned a limb into a half-pound of chips. I made some dye bath from it, and I've brought it along."

We reached an intersection marked by a sign that said INDIGO, 3 MILES, and on an impulse, I swung Big Mama to the left. This wasn't the shortest way to Allie's Indigo Farm, but I hadn't been to Indigo for a couple of months and I wanted to have a look.

Indigo was no more than a cluster of three dozen or so small frame houses, most of them in poor repair, and what had once been a four-block business section, located on both sides of the intersection of Main and First. The Historic Indigo Restoration

Committee had done a nice job rejuvenating this small area. Ten or twelve commercial buildings were still standing, over half of them cleaned up and painted in bright, brave colors. A new restaurant called the Indigo Café had opened in an old saloon; Texas Antique Treasures occupied the former drugstore, kitty-corner across the street; Brown Brothers Hardware now hosted the Old Indigo Mercantile Emporium, with an impressive display of quilts and hand-woven rugs in the front window; and what had been the Garza Feed and Stock Supplies was now a candle and gift shop. The Dalton County Jail, a square stone building with a heavy plank door, had been cleaned up and bore a hand-lettered sign announcing that it was now the proud home of the Indigo Museum and Community Center. Planting tubs filled with Texas mountain laurels, salvias, and bright chrysanthemums were lined up along the cracked sidewalk, and wooden posts bore blue banners announcing the Indigo Arts and Crafts Festival. But the best part was what *wasn't* there, for no matter how hard you looked, you couldn't see a fast-food restaurant or a copy shop or a video store anywhere. If it weren't for a few late-model autos and pickup trucks parked along the curbs, this could be Indigo, Texas, 1925.

I slowed down so we could look around as we drove. Near the end of the first block, at the corner of Main and Second, stood the old cotton gin, where the Historic Indigo Restoration Committee and Allie's friends from the artists' co-op had focused their major renovation efforts. The doors were closed and we couldn't see inside, but I already knew that the main building had been converted into studio space and a gallery for the artists' work, with a stage at the back. The adjacent parking lot had been paved with old brick and transformed into an outdoor plaza, with picnic tables, a windmill covered with red, white, and blue morning glories, and rusty wagon wheels and tools hung on the corrugated-iron walls. As we drove slowly past, we saw a new sign on the front of the building. In old-fashioned blue letters it read,

COTTON GIN THEATER & GALLERY
Indigo, Texas

And beside the door, on a large poster, was the announcement of Friday night's melodrama:

Indigo's Blue, or
Hard Times on the Blackland Prairie
An Original Melodrama by Derek Cooper
Performed by the Boll Weevil Players

"Looks like Allie and her friends have been working hard," Ruby said. She shook her head sadly. "It's terrible to think that after all the effort they've invested, Indigo will be eaten by the strip mine."

"Some people seem to have made a pretty sizable financial investment, too," I said, pointing to my left. "Putting a restaurant into an old building can cost a bundle. The Indigo Café, in the old saloon, for instance. Can you imagine what it cost to meet the Health Department's kitchen and sanitary requirements?"

I could. Ruby and I had sunk what seemed like a small fortune into the kitchen for our tearoom, and our building had already been up to code for electrical and plumbing. I doubted whether the old saloon even had flush toilets.

"I wonder if the townspeople know about Casey Ford's plan to sell the mining rights," Ruby replied thoughtfully. "If they do, they can't be any happier than Allie."

Because of the paint-up, fix-up campaign, the small business section of the town looked clean and attractive. But we could see plenty of signs that the town's resurrection wasn't complete. Across the alley from the Cotton Gin Theater, the coffee shop I remembered — the Bluebonnet Coffee Shop — was closed and boarded up, and the store next to it, a shoe and saddle repair shop, had been razed, with nothing left but piles of bricks and boards. Farther down the street, the fine old limestone structure that used to house the *Indigo Weekly Chronicle* was coming down. Still farther, the old brick elementary school stood stern and silent, its windows covered with plywood. And on the outskirts of town there was the usual collection of trailers, with junky cars parked in front. From the look of it, the new Old Indigo was mostly a tourist attraction, and the people who had started the trendy businesses probably lived elsewhere.

Some moments later, heading east down the county road, we got our first glimpse of the strip mine, off to the north. The dragline was a mile or so away, on the other side of a clump of trees, but even so, it was huge and relentless, something out of a nightmare. I tried to imagine that enormous shovel lurching into town to gobble up the Cotton Gin Theater and

Gallery, but somehow I couldn't summon the image. All I could think of was the ironically prophetic title of the melodrama: *Indigo's Blue*. Without a doubt.

A few moments later, we were driving down Allie's gravel lane, which twists through a stand of oak, pecan, and elm along clear, spring-fed Indigo Creek, opening into wide meadows along the way. One fenced meadow was home to Allie's girls, and Ruby waved gaily out the window at them as we drove past.

"Oh, look!" she cried excitedly. "There's a big brown llama!"

I glanced toward the pasture. "That's Shangrilama," I said. "Allie's guard llama. His job is predator control. He —"

"Watch out for that Jeep!" Ruby shrieked.

I pulled the wheel sharply to the right and we bounced off the road and into the ditch, as a banged-up open-top Jeep, painted with bright orange stripes, hurtled past like a bat out of hell. The faded decal on the door read "Ford Enterprises." The driver wore a black cowboy hat and a blacker expression. In the back of the Jeep, barking savagely, was a junkyard dog.

Ruby was incensed. "The nerve of that jerk, taking his half out of the middle! If

76

you hadn't pulled over, he would have smashed right into us. Who *was* that idiot?"

"Uncle Casey, I think." Big Red Mama had stalled nose-down in the grassy ditch, her right front tire mired in mud. I started her again, shoved her into reverse, and jolted backward onto the road.

"If that's who it was, I'll bet Allie will be in no mood for company," Ruby replied grimly.

I didn't say anything. Given McQuaid's problem, Allie's dilemma, and the Indigo situation, this wasn't shaping up to be a very pleasant weekend. And we could all certainly do with a little less of Casey Ford.

Four

Created by the color opposites of hot red and cool blue, purple is associated with spirituality, royalty, and nobility — but also with creativity, unpredictability, and mood swings.

"The Symbolic Meaning of Color"
— Ruby Wilcox

Dark red- or deep pink-flowered hibiscus give attractive colors when used fresh or dried in the dye pot. The colors from these dark hibiscus flowers can range from lilac to maroon . . . Harvest the red and deep pink flowers every two to three days and use them fresh. Alternatively, dry the flowers until you have enough for a dye bath.

Wild Color
— Jenny Dean

A moment later we were pulling up in front of a two-story farmhouse that had been built sometime during Teddy Roosevelt's administration. The wooden porch sagged, the worn roof was an uneven patchwork of green and brown shingles, and the dingy siding was probably last painted about the time Harry Truman took office. But the old house had a certain ramshackle charm that was enhanced by the pink fall-blooming roses that tumbled across the porch roof and the cottage garden that filled the front yard. In the corner, behind a lush green screen of tall bamboo, was a chicken-wire dovecote, the resident pigeons spilling their plaintive songs into the evening air.

Allie was standing on the front porch, a black-and-white Border collie beside her. Her fists were clenched at her sides and her fierce look matched the scowl on the face of the driver who had run us off the road. But her mouth softened as we came up the flagstone walk and the set of her narrow shoulders relaxed.

"Hi, China," she said. "Hey, Ruby, I like those overalls. Very colorful."

"Thanks." Ruby glanced around. "Gosh, it's beautiful here, Allie. So peaceful."

It was the wrong thing to say. Allie's face tightened and her mouth turned down. "It's peaceful *now*. Five minutes ago, all hell was breaking loose."

"Your uncle?" I guessed. "He nearly ran us down."

Allie went to the screen door and held it

open so we could go in, the dog at our heels. "That's Casey, all right," she said thinly. "Puts pedal to the metal and never looks farther ahead than his front bumper. About as mean as that mangy old dog of his." She started down the hall toward the kitchen, tossing back over her shoulder, "Let's go to the kitchen and get some iced tea. I need to cool off."

Beyond the basics — electricity, running water, and propane — Allie's kitchen hadn't been modernized. The white-painted wood cabinets were still in place, scarred red linoleum covered both the counters and the floor, and the old hand pump, painted white, still sat beside the sink, a dishcloth draped over it, drying. The pump was no longer functional, but nobody had bothered to take it out.

But the kitchen wasn't just for cooking. Allie's favorite spinning wheel stood in one corner, surrounded by bags and boxes of carded fleece. A rack on one wall held a dozen hand spindles, and another wall was papered with photos of Allie's girls, all spiffed up for showing, and a couple of dozen prize ribbons, most of them blue. Through the door beside the fridge, I could see into the dining room that served as her studio, which was crowded with two large looms and more spinning wheels, a carding machine, and bins and boxes and bags of fleece and spun yarn in a rainbow of colors. Hand-loomed rugs and skeins of yarn hung on every wall, along with pieces of weaving equipment. A window looked out onto the garden, which was bordered by dark red hibiscus, yellow cosmos, and the tall yellow-green flowering stalks of weld — three plants that Allie often uses to demonstrate natural dyeing. Indoors and out, she had surrounded herself with the colorful chaos that often seems to energize creative people.

Ruby and I sat down at the old porcelain-topped kitchen table as Allie poured hibiscus tea out of a chipped pitcher into unmatched jelly glasses. The screen door was open and we could hear the velvety sounds of the birds in the dovecote.

"Have you eaten?" Allie asked.

"We stopped for a hamburger at the Sonic in Taylor," I replied. "But don't let us keep you from your meal."

"I'm too mad to eat," Allie said shortly. "It's going to take me a while to calm down. Anyway, Derek won't be here for another fifteen minutes, and he's cooking tonight." She dropped into the chair across from me and put her elbows on the table.

The Border collie, whose name was Lucky, sat on his haunches, his gaze fixed attentively on her face.

"Do you want to talk about it?" Ruby asked.

"Casey says he's signing over the mining rights on Monday," Allie said bitterly. "After that, it's just a matter of time until this house comes down." She glanced around with a hungry look, as if she were mentally recording her surroundings and storing the memory against the day when the farm would be gone.

"How awful!" Ruby breathed.

"How long?" I asked.

"I suppose I can stay until the dragline shows up on the doorstep, if that's what you're asking." Allie shifted in her chair, her mobile face even more restless than usual. "And I may have to. I don't have the funds to relocate — not after I put all that money into the girls' new barn last year. If Casey had let me know what he was planning, I wouldn't have built it." Her voice was corrosive. "But, of course, he wouldn't. He knows I'd do anything I could to stop him from doing this terrible thing. *Anything.*" Distractedly, she ran her fingers through her short hair.

"What about the people in town?" Ruby

asked. "Do they know what's happening?"

"Not yet," Allie replied. "He said he was going to come to the HIRC meeting tonight and give them the news. He's looking forward to it, if you ask me." She let out a shuddery sigh. "God, I dread the thought. Everybody's going to think I'm somehow involved with this scheme, even though I had nothing to do with it."

"How much of Indigo does your uncle actually own?" I asked. Not that it mattered. When a shovel seven or eight times taller and a hundred times hungrier than a brontosaurus moves into the neighborhood, sensible people have a tendency to pack their belongings and move somewhere safe.

"He owns all of the commercial buildings and about half of the houses," Allie replied, "although most of the houses aren't worth saving. He inherited the property when his father — my grandfather — died, four or five years ago. It was passed down from the original founder of the town, although I don't understand all the family connections." As if she couldn't sit still any longer, Allie got up, went to the counter, and brought a half-dozen old nylon pantyhose and a pair of scissors back to the table.

"What a sad thing," Ruby said. "China and I were commenting that people have money invested in those shops. Closing them is going to be traumatic, in more ways than one."

"You're right about that," Allie said, sitting down again, "Jerome and Carl just opened the Indigo Café last month and all their savings are in it." She began cutting the pantyhose into eight-inch lengths, tying a knot at one end to form a little bag. Tomorrow, the students would fill the nylon bag with dye plants, tie up the other end, and toss them into the dye pots to cook out the color. "Brenda spent plenty fixing up the inside of that old drugstore," she went on, "and the Masons — Maxine and Harry, who own the Emporium — sank a lot of money into their shop, too. Not to mention all the artists who've invested time and money in the Cotton Gin." She brushed the hair off her forehead. "We were all so happy, thinking that we finally had a place to show our work."

"But if people have leases," Ruby objected, "I don't see how he can throw them out." She reached out to stroke Lucky's smooth head, but he edged away, closer to his mistress. A one-woman dog.

Allie's laugh was short and harsh. "He

won't have to. When word gets around that Indigo is finished, they'll know there's no point in staying." She snipped another stocking. "Anyway, he put in a clause saying that if the building is scheduled for demolition, the lease is void." She snipped another stocking. "That's how he got Sandra out of her coffee shop. The building's still there, but it's coming down in another few weeks, or so he says. My guess is that it'll stay empty until they're ready to start mining this area."

"That's the Bluebonnet Coffee Shop?" I hazarded. Ruby and I picked up the snipped lengths of panty hose and began tying knots in one end.

"Right. The Bluebonnet belonged to Sandra Higgins. She was doing a fair amount of business, and she'd put a lot of effort into fixing the place up." Allie attacked another stocking with the scissors. "She wants to sue, but she doesn't have the money for a lawyer. So she closed down, and Casey nailed plywood over the front windows. Then he booby-trapped the building, to make sure people would stay out. It's not the only trap he's set, either — at least, so he claims."

"That is not smart," I said emphatically, thinking to myself that Casey Ford was a very bad actor. Booby traps are illegal in Texas, as they are everywhere else in the country. If somebody walked into one —

"Your uncle is booby-trapping empty buildings?" Ruby was indignant. "That's crazy! A child could be hurt. Killed, even."

I tied another knot. "Allie," I said seriously, "you'd better tell him to cool it. He can be charged with deadly conduct just for setting those traps. And if somebody's killed, it'll be manslaughter. For that, he could get life." He probably would, too. Texas law allows the use of deadly force to protect property, but it draws the line at booby traps.

"Nobody tells Casey Ford anything," Allie said, grim-faced. "He loves to walk on the outside edge of the law. My mother used to say that Casey would try to cheat the devil, just for the hell of it."

"Your mother is his sister?" Ruby asked.

"She was," Allie said quietly, putting down the scissors. "She died three years ago. Breast cancer." Her eyes went to Ruby, and she bit her lip. Ruby lost a breast just after Christmas last year. She opted against reconstructive surgery — "I prefer not to have a foreign object in my body," she says in a nippy tone, when anyone asks — and when her scar healed, she had a flower tattooed over it. She'll show it to you, if you ask her nicely.

"I'm sorry about your mom," Ruby said in a low voice. She put her hand over Allie's. "Cancer is terrible. I know it was difficult for you."

"It was," Allie replied. "It is, still. It never gets any easier. And now all this —" She pulled her hand away and reached for a wooden spindle that lay on the table. "Mom and Casey fought like cats and dogs," she said matter-of-factly, looping a yarn leader around the shaft and picking up a handful of carded mohair fiber, a soft gray color. "But Casey fights with everybody, so I don't suppose being brother and sister had much to do with it. He's brutal to poor Shirley, and God knows she's never done anything to cross him." She gave the spindle a hard turn, setting it spinning, and began drawing a thin, evenly twisted thread out of the fiber in her left hand. "She always acts like she's scared to death of him."

I finished knotting my pile of stocking lengths. "Shirley? Who's she?"

"Casey's younger sister — well, step-sister." She frowned as she turned the spindle again. "Come to think of it, I guess they aren't related by blood. Shirley's mother Janece was married to Grandpa Ford. Casey and my mother were his children by an earlier marriage — Grandpa was fifteen years older than Janece — and they both were grown up and gone by the time Janece and Grandpa got married. Shirley was in her teens then, and was pretty wild. After her mother died, she got into a whole lot of trouble, and after that, she went to live with Grandpa Ford."

Allie began twisting a figure-eight of spun thread around her fingers, and I thought that she seemed calmer and more relaxed with the spindle in her hand. Fiber therapy, spinners call it — a way of soothing and smoothing frayed nerves.

"Anyway," she went on, "after Grandpa Ford died, Casey moved back to the family place to keep an eye on Shirley. She cooks and keeps house and never goes anywhere. He doesn't like company coming to the house, either — even me." She cleared her throat. "Maybe especially me. Casey and I get along about as well as he and Mom did. Sometimes I just want to throttle him."

"That's too bad," I said. "Sounds as if Shirley could use a friend."

"I don't doubt it," Allie replied. "But Casey says he's afraid she might get violent

again and hurt somebody — although I
don't really believe it. Of course, I don't
see her very often, but she's never seemed
that way to me."

"Get violent *again?*" I asked curiously.

"She shot a man and spent three or four
years in prison." Allie spun another length,
then wound the yarn off her fingers onto
the spindle. "Les Osler wants to marry her,
but Casey won't allow it. Over his dead
body, he says."

"Won't allow it?" Ruby looked up from
her knotting. "How old *is* Shirley, anyway?"

"She's five or six years younger than I
am," Allie said, "which would make her
about forty." At Ruby's startled look, she
added: "Shirley's a little . . . well, slow,
mentally. Oh, she's definitely not crazy or
anything, although Casey likes to tell
people she is. She never learned to read, so
school was a total loss. She got pregnant
and dropped out when she was in her early
teens. And then she got into drugs, and
there was some serious trouble. After she
got out of prison, Grandpa Ford had himself appointed her legal guardian so he
could keep her under control. When he
died, Casey assumed her guardianship."

"But she wouldn't have to just stay

home," Ruby pointed out. "There must be some sort of social service in the county that would help her get out and make friends, or get some sort of job."

Allie's chuckle was dry. "You'd have to understand Grandpa Ford. He belonged to the old school, I guess you'd say. Wouldn't have any 'bleeding-heart social worker' interfering with his family. And Shirley has always seemed pretty content to just stay at home, so I don't think there was a problem, as far as she was concerned. But a few months ago Les Osler started hanging around — Casey hired him to tear down some buildings in Indigo — and the two of them apparently hit it off right away. Les asked Shirley to marry him. She said yes, but Casey said no." Her grin was crooked. "Actually, what he said was, 'Hell, no, I ain't allowin' no sister of mine to marry no scummy white trash.' " She gave the spindle another twist, setting it whirling.

"Poor Shirley," Ruby said softly. She knotted the last length of stocking. Allie put down her spindle and gathered them into a plastic bag.

"I don't know why I'm boring you guys with all this family stuff." She made a face. "I don't need to convince you that my

90

uncle is a sonovabitch. You already know. He wouldn't be doing what he's doing to Indigo — to this beautiful prairie — if he cared for anybody in the world except himself."

"Why *do* you think he's doing it?" I asked curiously. "What's his motive? Money?" I didn't have a clue to the current price of lignite mining rights, but I knew that the seller got an up-front fee plus a royalty, depending on the amount of coal that was extracted.

"Money?" Allie considered for a moment, pursing her lips. "I don't think so. I don't know the details, of course, but Grandpa Ford inherited quite a lot of property from Shirley's mother when she died twenty years ago. He must have left Casey plenty, although you wouldn't know it from looking at him. Drives that beat-up old Jeep, never fixes anything until he has to. He wouldn't put a nickel into the Indigo properties. Anything those people want done, they've had to do themselves."

"If his motive isn't money," Ruby asked, puzzled, "what is it?"

Allie shrugged. "He says he doesn't like what's happening in Indigo."

"But the town's going through a revival," I protested. "And the property is leased, so he's making money on it. In fact, if he leased more of those buildings, he could bring in even more money. What's not to like about that?"

"Well, let's see." Allie began counting on her fingers. "Casey doesn't like artists, he hates hippies, he can't stand gays — Jerome and his partner Carl, for instance — and he detests blacks." She picked up her spindle and gave it another whirl. "Brenda was probably the final straw. He leased the old drugstore to her through some real estate outfit in Taylor, sight unseen. When he got his first look, he was livid."

"A true-blue country boy," I murmured. City dwellers have learned to live with racial and ethnic differences, but rural Texas is full of people like Casey, which is why the state legislature finally passed hate crime legislation — over the governor's resistance.

"I guess you could say that," Allie said. She sighed heavily. "This is going to put a damper on the weekend, for sure. And the workshop, too. Most of the people who have signed up are from around Indigo. In fact, you already know them from HIRC — Carl and Brenda will be here, and Stella and Sandra as well. And Miss Mayjean, of course."

I was about to tell her that the young writer who was staying in my cottage would also be coming, but I was interrupted by the sound of a truck pulling up outside.

Allie lifted her head, her eyes narrowing just slightly. "That'll be Derek."

I'd met Derek Cooper when I came to Indigo Farm for the last workshop. He was Allie's live-in boyfriend, a thoughtful man in his early fifties, with a broad, full face, black hair that fell across his pockmarked forehead, a fan of wrinkles at the corners of his eyes, and a slow, quiet smile. He rarely spoke more than a few sentences, although when he did speak, it was with an almost surprising elegance.

Allie had met Derek at a Sheep to Shawl show in Colorado a couple of summers before — one of those shows where exhibitors sell everything from fleece on the hoof to knitted garments, wall tapestries, and finely woven shawls. He had hung around her booth, admiring the girls, watching her spin and weave, asking questions. When the show was over, he helped her load up the goats she hadn't sold for the long drive back to Texas. And when she got home, he was already there, leaning against the gate with that slow smile, waiting to help her unload.

"The girls were glad to see him," she'd said. "And so was I. I wasn't ready to jump into anything, of course. I'd been through too much pain for that. But Derek sort of eased me into it."

For a couple of weeks, Derek lived in his camper, which he had unloaded from his truck and set up twenty or so yards behind the cabin. He was writing, he told her, something he'd always wanted to try his hand at, although he wasn't sure the work was good enough to get published. But he took time away from his own work to lend a hand around the place — to cut wood, build fences, make repairs. In the country, there's always something that needs fixing or replacing, and it's a great relief to be able to turn to somebody for help.

Gratitude wasn't all Allie felt, though. It wasn't long before she invited Derek to move into the house, and a few days later, into her bed.

"It was November and the gas heater in his camper wasn't working very well," she'd said to me, as if her decision needed explaining. "Anyway, I was ready. The girls are my family now, but I need something more."

I looked through the screen door and saw Derek getting out of his red pickup. A mo-

94

ment later, he was coming into the kitchen, carrying groceries. He nodded at me.

"Hi, China," he said. "I thought that was your van. How are you? All ready for the workshop tomorrow?"

"Fine." I grinned. "I didn't know that you were a playwright, Derek. I saw your name on the poster announcing tomorrow night's performance."

He frowned as if he were displeased. "I didn't realize that they were going to give me credit. I wanted to be anonymous, in case it's a disaster." He swung a sack of groceries onto the counter. "But I suppose you don't have to be Tennessee Williams to write a melodrama for the Boll Weevil Players." He bent to brush his lips across the back of Allie's neck. "Hello, Allison," he murmured.

Allie stiffened, then pulled away. "Hi," she said, not looking up at him. I had seen them together before and felt that Derek had a positive effect on her — like spinning, he'd seemed to calm her, slow her down. I'd thought that they were a comfortable match, she with her restless energy, he with his quiet steadiness. But just now, there was something else going on here, something that wasn't quite so comfortable.

Allie stood up and moved away, out of

Derek's reach. "Ruby, this is Derek Cooper," she said shortly. "Derek, Ruby Wilcox. She and China are staying in the cabin tonight and tomorrow night." Ruby and Derek exchanged pleasantries.

"It's my turn to cook tonight," Derek said, beginning to take out the groceries. "Nothing creative — just hamburgers and coleslaw and applesauce. But there's plenty, and it'll be ready in a few minutes. You two are welcome to join us."

"Thanks, but we ate earlier," I said, pushing back my chair and standing up. "We'll take our stuff out to the cabin, and then I want to introduce Ruby to the girls. I've got stuff to put in the dye kitchen, too — dye plants and dye." I turned to Allie. "What time are we going to the HIRC meeting?"

Allie glanced at the clock. It was six-fifteen. "If we leave in an hour, we'll have plenty of time. I swept the cabin and put clean sheets on the beds," she added with a glint in her eye, "but you'll want to watch out for spiders. I've seen some big ones out there."

"Spiders!" Ruby spluttered as we got our bags out of the van and headed down the path toward the cabin. "You didn't tell me about spiders!"

Last year, Ruby and I accidentally got involved with several narcotics officers that we mistook for a gang of drug dealers, and Ruby handled herself in a way that led me to conclude that she is the coolest, bravest woman I know. If she wants to put up a fuss about a few spiders, I'll play along.

"I think Allie was teasing," I said in a consoling tone. But with Allie, you never know. There's a kind of enigmatic irony about her that sometimes makes it difficult to know how to take what she says. It was a characteristic I'd noticed when we were in college, and it seemed to have grown more pronounced over the years. "Anyway, we'll check the place out," I added. "Don't worry."

"Don't worry!" Ruby huffed. "I just don't understand how you can be so calm about *spiders*."

Five

According to Bobbi A. McRae, in *Colors from Nature*, the principle of mordanting fiber is fairly simple. Mordants bind the dyes to the fibers, brighten colors, and make the color more lightfast. When you dip the fiber into a mordant solution, the mordant molecules bind with the fiber. When you dip the mordanted fiber into the dye bath, the color molecules bind with the metal salt. In colonial America, dyers used whatever mordants they had handy: salt, vinegar, soda, iron filings, copper coins, even urine. They also used copper, aluminum, iron, or tin pots. If you're learning to dye with plants, you can manage with alum and cream of tartar, available from the grocery store.

The one-room wood-frame cabin was about fifty yards from the house, screened from view behind a clump of live oak trees. A honeysuckle vine grew over the screen door, and when we opened it and went inside, we found a small, square room with cheerful curtains at the open windows and a vase of yellow cosmos, zinnias, and yarrow on the table, with a bowl of apples beside it. In one corner of the room, twin beds covered with patchwork quilts were arranged at right angles to one other, the square space in the corner filled with a table that held a tall kerosene lamp with an old-fashioned red glass shade. In another corner stood a small woodstove, with a china pitcher of Maximilian sunflowers on it. Several handwoven rugs were laid across the painted wooden floor, and the walls were hung with Allie's woven hangings.

"This is cozy!" Ruby exclaimed. "I love it." She walked around, inspecting the walls and ceilings for signs of spiderwebs. Finally, she put her suitcase on a bed. "Okay if I take this one?"

"Whichever one you want." I put a bottle of herbal insect repellent and my cell phone on the table. I was already anxious about what was going on at home between Brian and his father. If McQuaid hadn't called me by nine-thirty, I'd phone him. I put my suitcase on the other bed. "There's only one wardrobe," I added, "and no closets. I hope you didn't bring much stuff."

"Oh, not much," Ruby said in a careless tone, beginning to pull items out of the suitcase. "Only a few things, really." Filling her arms with clothing, she went to the wardrobe and began hanging things up. "Just enough to see me through tomorrow and Saturday." She went back to her suitcase and took out another armload. When she was finished, there was about six inches of rod space left.

"It's a good thing I just brought jeans and tees," I remarked. "Otherwise, there wouldn't be as much room for you."

"I'm sure we'd have managed somehow." Ruby opened another bag and took out the wooden box that holds her tarot cards, a small leather bag filled with rune stones, and a red candle.

"I see you've brought your psychic tools," I observed, as she unfolded a black silk cloth and placed it on the table, then ceremoniously centered the candle, the cards, and the stones on it. "Planning to commune with your inner cowgirl?"

"I thought I might have some time to practice," she replied seriously, placing a quartz crystal and a cassette player beside the candle. "Getting quiet is important — that's what the candle and the music are for. The cards and the rune stones help you to focus. After that, you only have to be open and receptive to whatever comes." She opened a third bag and took out her cosmetic case. Holding it in one hand, she turned around in a slow circle. "Am I missing something? Where's the bathroom?"

I had to laugh. "Your intuition hasn't told you? It's in the house."

"In the house?" Ruby frowned. "But that's a long ways away!"

"Of course, you can always go pee behind the cabin. Just watch out for the poison ivy." I grinned. "It wouldn't do to get poison ivy on your you-know-what."

Ruby shuddered, as if poison ivy ranked right up there with spiders. She put down her case and groped for the switch on the lamp at the head of our beds. "Well, at least we have electricity." She frowned, fumbling around the lamp. "How do you turn this thing on?"

I went to the wardrobe, took a box of matches off the shelf, and handed them to her. She stared down at them for a minute, then up at me. "Does this mean that my curling iron won't work?"

"Yep," I said. "We're roughing it. No air-conditioning, no running water, no curling iron, no potty." I made enthusiastic motions with my arms. "Just antique quilts, handwoven rugs, gingham curtains, and fresh air scented with honeysuckle." I pulled in a deep breath as if I were savoring it, but something tickled my nose and I sneezed.

"Such a deal," Ruby said, sounding resigned. "But a potty would have been nice."

We spent the next few minutes arranging our stuff, then we dosed ourselves with bug repellent and walked down the lane to the pasture to get acquainted with the girls, several of whom came over to the fence to say hello and ask whether we had any special treats in our pockets. We'd neglected this important detail, so we just rubbed their soft ears and hoped they'd be satisfied with the attention.

Shangrilama hustled over, too, with that peculiar loud humming that llamas make when they are inconvenienced, irritated, or maybe just interested in what's going on. Shangrilama is six feet tall and brown-fleeced, an alert, aloof creature with large, thickly fringed brown eyes. He gave us a good looking-over and a chorus of inquisitive hums before he decided that we were tolerable humans with no ulterior motives — at least none that immediately threatened his goats. When he'd scoped us out, he trotted back to work, keeping one wary eye on us and the other on a trio of roughnecking youngsters.

"What a sweet llama," Ruby said fondly. "I wish I had eyelashes like that."

"He's not so sweet when there's a strange dog around," I replied. "He kicks butt." I'd seen Shangrilama in action just once, but it was enough to make a believer of me. A workshop attendee, unwisely, had brought her German shepherd puppy when she came to admire Allie's goats, not knowing that Shangrilama took a dim view of all dogs except Border collies. He hissed, bared yellow teeth, and charged with a shrill, high-pitched whistle that sent the puppy high-tailing. Guard llamas are definitely not pets, and the best ones, Allie told me after the incident, aren't terribly sociable where humans are concerned. Shangrilama's job is to protect his girls, and he takes his work seriously.

While the sun dropped low in the sky and the shadows slanted over the meadow, Ruby and I watched Shangrilama watching over the girls and their kids. Then we walked back to the van, got the dye materials, and carried everything to Allie's outdoor dye kitchen, a large shed with a porch across the partly open front, a wooden floor, two propane gas stoves and a couple of hot plates and Crock-Pots, a cast-off kitchen sink plumbed with a garden hose, and a couple of pieces of plywood laid across sawhorses to serve as worktables. Mordants such as aluminum, copper, tin, iron, and chrome (these serve as fixatives, permitting the fabric to soak up and hold the color) are highly toxic and require plenty of ventilation. What's more, it's never a good idea to work with dyes (even natural ones) around foodstuffs. All things considered, an outdoor arrangement works best, even if it's only a hot plate on a picnic table.

As Ruby and I put down our boxes, I could see that Allie had already done some of the prep for tomorrow's workshop. She'd mordanted some spun wool, cotton, and flax fibers and prepared ten yarn bundles, one bundle for each of the workshoppers to dye. Each bundle contained twelve-inch lengths of the fibers, the ends of which were knotted according to the universal dyers' code: one knot for alum, two for chrome, three for tin, four for copper, five for iron, none for no mordant.

If this had been a two-day workshop, the

students would have prepared and used the mordants themselves, but since we had only one day, Allie's preliminary work saved us some time. She had also set out two plastic gallon bottles, one filled with ready-to-use indigo dye bath made from plants that Mayjean Carter had raised. Miss Mayjean — the "Miss" comes from her days as a schoolteacher — was an expert on blue-dyed textiles and had assembled an impressive collection of items from many different cultures, some of which she'd be bringing to the workshop.

But it was seven-fifteen, and time to leave for the HIRC meeting. Ruby and I went back to the cabin, where she settled in happily with her music, candle, and cards. I stuck my cell phone in my purse and went back to the house to see if Allie was ready to leave for the meeting. I wasn't sure how she felt about it, but given the fact that her uncle was planning to make an appearance tonight, like an evil genie bearing bad tidings, I certainly wasn't looking forward to the evening.

My previous get-togethers with the Historic Indigo Restoration Committee had taken place in the Cotton Gin Theater, but this one was being held in the Dalton

County Jail *cum* museum. As a museum, the jail wasn't terribly impressive: a display of a dozen badly enlarged sepia photographs of the turn-of-the-century town; a few rusty guns and broken tools; a woman's ivory satin wedding dress with tiny buttons down the front and a waist that wasn't much larger than the diameter of my thigh; a shabby stuffed owl glaring accusingly from a branch in a glass case.

But the building itself was an interesting relic of the past and, like others in Indigo, worth saving. It was constructed of hand-hewn cypress logs, with a scuffed pine plank floor and a heavy plank door — complete with a couple of bullet holes. The doors to the lockups were constructed of hand-forged iron bars, the cells themselves weren't much longer than a bathtub, and the beds were nothing more than a wide board covered with a blanket. It wouldn't have been any fun to be locked up here, especially if you were claustrophobic — but maybe the jail's customers had been so drunk they didn't notice. I didn't see a stove or an opening for a stovepipe, so the winters wouldn't have been any picnic, either. Perhaps the chilly discomfort of the penal accommodations was meant to discourage people from breaking the law.

Three of the HIRC members were already there when Allie and I arrived. It was obvious from the casual tone of the conversation that Casey Ford had not yet stopped by to drop his bombshell.

The committee chairman was Jerome Buchanan, co-owner of the Indigo Café, a tall, stooped man in his forties, with thinning blond hair combed carefully forward to conceal a receding hairline, eyes the color of pale blue glass, and restless blond eyebrows that seemed to function independently of his other features. He was perched cross-legged on the wooden desk in the corner, moccasined feet drawn up under him, casually chic in khaki pants, an olive-green T-shirt, and a Zambezi travel vest that sported a generous collection of cargo pockets variously zipped, snapped, buttoned, and D-ringed. He held a clipboard full of papers, and he was going over a list with Maxine Mason, who was sitting stiffly in an old wooden office chair beside the desk. Jerome is the meticulous type, compulsively organized, covering all the bases. I suspected that he was single-handedly responsible for most of HIRC's past achievements, since he seemed to do most of the committee's work himself. Delegation wasn't Jerome's strong suit.

Maxine, on the other hand, liked to issue orders for others to follow. She was a bony, officious-looking woman in her late fifties, with gray hair pulled away from a severe face and a stern frown between small eyes. She was frowning now, as she listened critically to Jerome, pursing her narrow lips as if she were assessing his ideas and finding them seriously lacking in substance and style. Maxine and Harry, her husband of thirty years, owned the Old Indigo Mercantile Emporium. Although I'd never met Harry Mason, I pictured him as an exemplary order-taker and yea-sayer, who, if he had any ideas of his own, kept them to himself. If he hadn't, I somehow doubted that Maxine would have tolerated him for very long.

Maxine and Harry's daughter Stella was a different matter entirely. Stella was a renegade and nay-sayer who seemed to exist in a perpetual state of armed conflict with her mother. I hadn't managed to figure out why a woman in her late twenties was still living with her parents — unless, of course, she had tried to make it on her own and had given it up as a lost cause. Or unless she had some dependency issues that wouldn't allow her to survive unless she was battling with her mother — just another way of staying under her mother's firm control.

＊Tonight, Stella was sitting on the floor with her back to Maxine, a bored expression on her pinched, narrow face, eyes half-shut as if she could barely stay awake. Her mother was gaunt, but Stella was so dramatically thin that I had to believe that she suffered from an eating disorder. She wore her long black hair skinned back and fastened with a silver ring and was dressed in a black long-sleeved body shirt and skin-tight black jeans. A silver belt cinched her waist and a silver medallion the size of a saucer, inscribed with signs of the zodiac, hung around her neck. From something she had said at the last meeting I attended, I got the impression that she was studying to be a witch. Maybe she was planning to turn her mother into a frog. I had to smile at the thought of a froggy Maxine, *ribbiting* rapid-fire commands to an uncaring cadre of real frogs at the local watering hole.

Allie and I had just said our hellos, unfolded a pair of wooden chairs, and made ourselves comfortable when the door opened and we were joined by two other women. One of them was Betty Swallow, a pert, pretty young brunette with a wide smile who had recently opened a candle

109

and gift shop in the old Garza Feed Store. She took a seat on the splintery wooden bench in front of the owl's glass case.

The other woman was Sandra Higgins, a short, dumpling-shaped woman with stringy brown hair and a gloomy expression. Gloomy, probably, because she had less stake in the future of Indigo since Casey had closed down, boarded up, and booby-trapped her Bluebonnet Coffee Shop. Her reluctant greeting was sour, and I guessed that she was nursing a grudge. She sat down next to Betty.

Jerome glanced around, his smile showing stained teeth. "Carl sends his regrets," he said. "He can't be with us tonight. But now that the rest of us are here —"

"The rest of us aren't here," Sandra interjected grimly. "Brenda's late. As usual."

"Brenda's not coming," Stella said in a sleepy voice, examining her nails, which were painted a purple so dark it was nearly black. "She blew us off and went to Austin. Some friend is having a party."

"Okay," Jerome said mildly. "Let the minutes show that Brenda —" He frowned. "Since Brenda isn't here to take the minutes, would you like to be our secretary, Maxine?"

"I did it the last time Brenda skipped out," Maxine said, "and I'm not getting saddled with it again." She looked down her nose at Betty Swallow. "Betty, you do it."

Betty's smile was agreeable. "Sure, be glad to — as long as you don't take off points for spelling. It wasn't my best subject." She opened her bag and took out a notebook and pencil.

"Thank you, Betty," Jerome said. "Well, then, let's get started." He glanced at his notes. "Stella, I believe that you were going to look into possible dates for our Christmas at Indigo weekend. But before you give your report, maybe we'd better have a look at the list of vendors who have signed up for booths this weekend." He consulted his clipboard, counting silently. "As of five o'clock this afternoon, twenty-three vendors had signed up for the Arts and Crafts Festival, including —" he smiled at me "— our friends from Thyme and Seasons and the Crystal Cave, in Pecan Springs. At thirty dollars a booth, that comes to six hundred ninety dollars, which more than covers what we've paid out for advertising. In addition, I'm happy to tell you that the Boll Weevil Players have presold forty-two tickets to *Indigo's Blue*. Also, we were able to get a dozen folding chairs from the Methodist Church in Lexington, which will give us a total of sixty seats. We may not fill them all, but at five dollars a ticket, what we've already sold comes to —"

The door opened and Casey Ford stepped in, his thumbs hooked into his belt, the villain swaggering into the local jail to face down the town sheriff. In his mid-fifties, Ford was dark-haired and dark-mustached, big and brutish, with huge, ham-shaped hands and a square, dark-shadowed jaw. A beer gut sagged over his belt buckle and a second chin bagged down under his first. He was wearing a dirty suede vest over a blue work shirt that stank of beer and sweat, and a couple of cellophane-wrapped cigars stuck out of his pocket. His shirt sleeves were rolled to the elbows, showing forearms — the thick, muscular arms of a weight-lifter or black-smith — furred with curly black hair. He didn't take off his black cowboy hat.

Sandra half-rose from her seat, her frown darkening to a furious scowl. Maxine narrowed schoolteacherish eyes, as if to ask who had given this uncouth fellow permission to enter the room. Stella's eyebrows went up and she began to look half-awake.

Jerome smiled weakly. "Good evening,

Casey. This is a meeting of the Historic Indigo Restoration Committee. If you have a matter to discuss with us, we'd be glad to put you on the agenda. But as it is —"

"I got an announcement t' make," Casey growled. He looked at Allie. " 'Less you already told 'em, Allison."

Allie, grim-faced and silent, shook her head.

"Well, then." Casey's flinty glance went around the room, came to me without recognition, then back to Jerome, whose eyebrows were waving like flags. "I come to tell you folks that I'm sellin' the mining rights to all my propitty, includin' what I own in this town. Which means you got 'til the end of the year to get out." He pulled up the corners of his mouth in a smirk. "I know this ain't gonna please you none, but that's how it is."

Jerome sucked in his breath. "Get . . . out?" he whispered theatrically. "You can't be serious!"

"You're a fool, Casey Ford." Maxine was coldly contemptuous, her thin arms folded over her flat breasts. "Harry and I have a lease."

Casey laughed, a harsh, grating sound. "Read the fine print, lady." With his thumb, he tipped the brim of his hat and looked at her, dropping his gaze insolently to her breasts, then raising it to her face. "Lease gives me the right to evict you if the structure's scheduled to be d'molished, which it sure the hell will be, soon as the mine folks get their ass in gear and bring in their 'dozers." He scratched his nose with his forefinger. "Lease says I got to give you sixty days' notice. Hell, I'm givin' you ninety. Seems gen'rous to me. But you suit yerself. You wanna get out sooner, no skin off my nose." His eyes swept the group. "Any questions?"

Jerome was breathing fast and hard, as if he were about to hyperventilate, and his pale eyebrows were oscillating wildly. Betty's eyes were wide and disbelieving and her face had gone white, the freckles standing out across her nose like specks of cinnamon. She opened her mouth to speak, but nothing came out. The owl glared disdainfully over her shoulder, as if to suggest that we'd all gotten what was coming to us.

Sandra cast a pleading look at Allison. "This man is your uncle. Don't you have any control over him? Can't you stop him from doing this to Indigo?"

"I'm losing my place, too," Allie said thinly. Her hands were clenched on her knees. "I'm not responsible for anything this bastard does." The look she shot at Casey carried an almost savage hatred.

Casey chuckled. "Now, that's a fine fam'ly howdy, if I ever heard one." He seemed pleased at the reaction to his announcement. "Well, if nobody's got 'ny questions, I guess that's it. You folks'll be gettin' a notice in the mail soon as the papers're signed. You might want to spread the word around to the ones that ain't here."

"And when is the signing?" Stella asked.

"Monday mornin'. I figger there ain't no need to mess around, now that I made up my mind what I aim t'do. Hit that dogie while the iron's hot, y'know." Casey opened the door. "Y'all have a good evenin' now, y'hear?" The door closed behind him, and all hell broke loose.

"My God," Maxine shrieked. Her hand went to her heart. "My dear God! This is incredible! It's unspeakable! It's —"

"It's a load of crap, that's what it is," Stella said calmly. She was fully awake now. "Sit down, Mother, and don't be a goose. He's not going to get away with this."

"Oh, yeah?" Sandra asked, bitterly mocking. "And just who the hell is going to stop him? Are you going to cast some sort of spell?" She blew the hair out of her eyes. "I told you guys that he had something big and dirty up his sleeve when he closed the Bluebonnet, but you wouldn't pay any attention. Now you'll find out what it's like to lose your business, the way I lost mine. It's not fun, I'll tell you. Bills to pay, no money coming in —"

Betty stood up. "You people can sit around and wring your hands all you like," she said briskly, "but I intend to do something. I'm not going to stand idly by and see this town dug up by those monster machines. My brother is a lawyer in Dallas, with connections in Austin. He'll put a stop to this nonsense right away."

"Hang on, Betty." Jerome held up his hand. "We've got a lawyer on the committee. She can tell us what to do." He looked at me. "How about it, China? What's your advice?"

"I'm not a real-estate attorney," I replied, "but I know that you can't stop someone from selling the mining rights to his property, if that's what he's decided to do. And if it's true that each of you signed a lease containing a right-to-demolish clause, you probably don't have any recourse in the courts. I suggest that each of you read your lease carefully." Of course, they should have done that when they signed, but most people don't.

Betty threw up her hands, looking aghast. "But this building right here, this wonderful old jail — it must be over a hundred years old! He can't just tear it down! It's . . . it's *historic!* There's got to be a law against destroying historic buildings."

"I didn't see a state landmark plaque on the outside," I said mildly. "I haven't ever had occasion to look into the question, but I doubt that Dalton County requires an owner to obtain a demolition permit before he tears down a building. And anyway, Ford won't be doing the demolitions. The mine operators will take care of that, when they're ready to start digging in this area." I paused. I was letting them down, but they had to be realistic about their situation. "I'm sorry," I said sympathetically. "I know how awful you must feel about this. But that's —"

"Well, there's got to be a way to stop him," Maxine said determinedly. "And if it can't be done legally, we'll just have to find a different way." Her voice became fierce. "I move that we take whatever steps are necessary to prevent this . . . this desecration of our town."

117

"It isn't 'our' town," Sandra objected acidly. "It's his. He can do whatever the hell he wants with it."

"What do you mean, 'whatever steps are necessary'?" Allie asked.

Maxine didn't answer. She was staring at her daughter.

"Oh, all right, Mother," Stella muttered. "For God's sake. I second the motion."

"What was the motion, exactly?" Jerome asked.

"Discussion?" Maxine swept us with her glance. Without giving anyone time to speak, she said, "Call the question."

"What are we voting on?" Jerome asked weakly.

"We are voting to take whatever steps are necessary to prevent the desecration and destruction of Indigo," Maxine said. "All in favor say aye." She glanced at me. "Voting members only, please."

There was a straggly chorus of ayes. Maxine's was the loudest.

"All opposed, no," Jerome said, regaining control of the proceedings.

"Abstain," Sandra said.

"No," Allie said.

"You would," Maxine said, her tone acrid. "You're probably getting something out of this. He *is* your uncle, after all.

Don't tell me that the money won't stay in the family."

"Mother," Stella said, embarrassed, "you are acting like the village idiot." She glanced at Allie apologetically. "Forget it, Allison. My mother doesn't know what she's saying."

"Oh, I don't, do I?" Maxine said darkly. "Shut up, you wretched girl. I know a great deal more than you do."

"What do you intend by 'whatever steps are necessary'?" Allie repeated. "I can't vote for something as ambiguous as that. It could mean *anything*." She turned to Jerome. "So what are you planning to do?"

"I don't think we should get into the whys and wherefores tonight," Jerome said, trying to smooth things over. "Let the minutes show that the motion carried, three to one, with one abstention." To Allie, he added, "I think what the vote suggests, Allison, is that we realize that we can't just sit back and let Indigo die. We need to do *something*, if only to call attention to our dilemma."

"Sure, Jerome," Sandra said derisively. "Let's take off our clothes and chase one another down Main Street. That'll call attention to our dilemma — and it's just about as productive as anything else we could come up with."

119

"Harry and I will discuss options and let the rest of you know what we decide," Maxine said. "I move that we adjourn the meeting." She nodded at Stella, who shook her head.

"Second your own damn motion," she said.

"Second the motion," Sandra said wearily, standing up. "I'm sick of this. I'm going home — assuming I still have a home to go to."

"But the meeting's not over," Jerome objected. "We have to hear Stella's report. We need to set a date for the Christmas at Indigo weekend. We —"

"Haven't you got it yet, Jerome?" Sandra said harshly. "There's not going to be any Christmas at Indigo, or any of the other events we've planned, either. And you're not in charge here. Maxine is."

Betty stood up. "Are we finished? I'm going to call my brother." She gave me a frosty glance. "I want another legal opinion."

Bowing to the inevitable, Jerome said, "Meeting adjourned."

Over his shoulder, I saw a playbill taped to the wall. *Indigo's Blue*, it said. *Hard Times on the Blackland Prairie.*

You bet.

Six

If we go far back in time and space we find the colour blue associated with power, magic, and divinity . . . [The historian Pliny] describes the Roman legions' unusual encounter with blue-dyed Celts in A.D. 44 and 45: *"Omnes vero se Britanni vitro inficiunt, quod caeruleum efficit colorem, atque horribiliores sunt in pugna aspectu."* [All Britons dye themselves with woad, which makes them blue, in order that in battle their appearance may be the more terrible.]
Indigo Textiles: Technique and History
— Gösta Sandberg

We were silent as we drove back to Indigo Farm. Allie didn't speak at all until we turned the corner where the road to the mine branched off. It was full dark, but beyond the shadowy trees, we could see the lights of the dragline and hear its massive motors turning, the bucket chewing, the rock crumbling.

"It goes night and day," Allie said sadly. "Indigo Farm is almost two miles away, but when they're blasting, I can feel the ground shudder under my feet."

"It must be a dreadful thing to live with," I said, thinking how I would feel if a strip mine were set up on Limekiln Road.

Allie was silent for a moment, chewing her lip. "It's the wild things I fear for the most," she said, in a lower voice. "People can move if they have to, but where can the deer go, and the coyotes? More of their habitat is being destroyed every day, and when the mine is finished the soil will be poisoned and the springs and creeks will be gone. They won't have a home to come back to. I wish I could hold on to the farm, not just for me and the girls, but for *them*. As a refuge."

"I'm sorry," I said, not knowing what else to say.

"Yeah," she said bitterly. "So am I. There's no justice in a world where the wild things are destroyed and wicked men flourish." Her laugh grated. "Makes you wish for an old Western hero to put in an appearance, doesn't it? Somebody who'd come riding in on a white horse and set everything straight, make everything right again. It's a pity that life isn't more like those old movies where truth and justice always win out and there's a happy ending." She sighed. "Oh, how I long for a happy ending."

"What do you think they'll do?" I asked. "Those people in town, I mean." I hesitated, thinking of the threat implied in the motion Maxine had made. "I hope they won't come up with anything . . . radical."

All Indigo needed was a self-righteous, self-appointed vigilante committee convinced that it had carte blanche to do whatever it took to get rid of the problem. People have gotten hurt under similar circumstances. I hadn't met Harry, but Jerome didn't strike me as the kind of man who would last very long in a hostile confrontation with Casey Ford. One punch from that ham-shaped fist and Jerome would be flat on his back in the dusty street, or in a hospital bed. No happy ending there. Not much truth or justice, either.

"Radical?" Allie laced her fingers together. "Maybe they should. Who would blame them? Not me." She shook her head. "And this, on top of everything else." After a moment's silence, she added, "I don't mean to be obscure, China. You saw what happened this evening when Derek came home. I guess you won't be surprised to hear that I've decided to end the relationship."

"It's a difficult time," I replied cautiously. "You're under a lot of stress. Maybe you shouldn't make any major decisions about Derek just now." I smiled. "Remember what you told me once? Don't quit until you're ahead. Don't leave until you can do it with dignity. It was good advice then. It still is."

When Allie and I were both students, I'd gotten entangled in an unfortunate and sadly lopsided love affair with an older man. It took months to discover that I was a victim, not of him but of my own needs and desires and illusions. He had been as honest as he knew how to be about the way he felt; I just hadn't listened to what he was saying. Allie and I were close enough back then for me to share my misery with her. Over hamburgers at Dirty's and while we were lying on the grass beside Barton Springs pool, she'd given me several pieces of valuable advice.

"Stay in the relationship long enough to understand it," she'd said. "Stay until you can leave on your own terms and under your own power." Good suggestions. I'd never forgotten them.

"Advice is easier to give than to take," she said bleakly. "I just want to put my head down and sob. Or go to bed and sleep for a week or two." She knotted her fingers in her lap and stared down at them. "But crying won't help, and I can't sleep forever. I can't put a decision off much longer, either. First Marie, and now the woman Brenda saw him with." She stopped, as if she had lost her train of thought.

"The woman?" I prompted gently.

"I'm sorry. I shouldn't have brought it up. I haven't talked it over with Derek yet." She closed her eyes, fell silent for a moment, then opened them again. "However I feel about him now, I owe him a great deal for all he's done in the past couple of years — helping around the place, building the barn. I know I need to break it off, but I feel guilty." She laughed again, ironically. "Weird. He's been deceptive, and I'm the one who feels guilty. Go figure."

I reached out and squeezed her hand. We were driving past the pasture where the girls spent the night in the custody of Shangrilama. The moon had come out, and I could see their shadows under the trees, the lighter colored fleeces silvery in the half-light. It was a peaceful, pastoral scene. No wonder Allie loved it here.

"I'm sorry we've got the workshop scheduled for tomorrow," I said. "It's just one more thing for you to worry about."

She raised her head and I could see a streak of bright tears glinting on her cheek. "To tell the truth, I'm glad we're doing it, China." She pulled in a ragged breath. "Work is my salvation just now. It's a lot better than sitting around feeling sorry for myself, or wishing that Derek weren't —"

She broke off again as we pulled into the graveled area in front of her house, where Derek's red pickup was parked. There was a light in the upstairs bedroom.

"Damn," she said fiercely. "I was wishing he'd gone out."

I parked the van beside the truck. "Good night," I said, when we'd gotten out. "I hope things look better in the morning."

"They won't," Allie said. "But thanks anyway." She put her hand on my arm and then, impulsively, gave me a hard, wordless hug — unusual, for her. Then she went off toward the house and I started down the path to the cabin, glad for the moon that gave just enough light to see.

The night was full of late-summer music: the high-pitched chirping of crickets, the occasional *ga-rrumph* of a bullfrog, the complaining call of the poor-will. As I walked, I thought that while Allie might be saddened and distressed by the changes in her life, she still seemed to be in control. However unhappy she was in her relationship with Derek, I had the feeling that she knew how she felt, understood why, and was prepared to do what she had to do. Casey Ford was probably a much larger threat to her long-term happiness than Derek Cooper.

I hadn't gone far when my cell phone rang, its tinny sound an artificial and imperious summons interrupting the night music of the prairie. I fished it out of my purse and flipped it open. It was McQuaid, with a report on his talk with Brian.

"How'd it go?" I asked, suddenly anxious. I'd managed to put Brian's situation aside for the last couple of hours, but now my worry came flooding back. "What did you find out?"

"I got him to come clean. But he's one troubled kid. He may be just a thirteen-year-old, but he's hauling around a pretty big load of adult-size problems."

I had come to the edge of the grassy area behind Allie's house, where the dark woods embraced the garden. A white-painted wooden swing hung from a live oak tree, luminous in the moonlight. As I sat down, a great horned owl sailed past, a huge black shape against the sky. Instinctively, I shivered. The owl was as innocent as the trees and the frogs and the musical crickets, its flight as graceful as a benediction. But I could understand why it has been feared as an omen of death.

I shook off the thought. "What did he tell you?" I asked, sitting in the swing.

"The whole story. Henningson spanked him for getting mud on the backseat of that fancy new Lexus. Whacked him hard, too, judging from the size of those bruises. It happened last Sunday, and they're just beginning to fade."

"Mud on the backseat?" I asked incredulously. I brushed a mosquito off my arm before it could settle down to dinner. "It might be a good idea to take a photo of the evidence."

"Spoken like a lawyer," McQuaid said dryly.

"Or a cop," I retorted. "You know as well as I do that you can't allege abuse without something to show for it."

"Actually, Brian suggested the photo. He says that when it happened, he didn't want to tell his mom. But now that he's thought about it, he's changed his mind. He thinks she ought to know, although he doesn't want to be the one to tell her." He chuckled. "Guess I can't blame him for that."

"So where was Sally while her son was getting knocked around?" The more I thought about this, the angrier I felt. If Henningson had caught Brian tormenting an animal or threatening a younger child, it might have been a different matter. But mud on an auto seat? "Why didn't she intervene?"

"It happened in a corner of the parking lot, after she'd gone up to the apartment. Henningson told Brian it would be just between the two of them — that he wouldn't tell Sally about the damage that Brian did to the car."

"What Brian did to the *car?*" I exclaimed angrily. "This jerk has his priorities upside down. We could be talking injury to a child here, McQuaid." I stood up and began pacing back and forth in the grass. "Just wait until we haul Henningson up in front of a judge. He's going to be sorry he ever —"

"Hang on, China." I could hear the familiar creak of McQuaid's recliner as he sat down. "Brian's really upset about what happened, but he's more concerned about his mother — afraid for her, even. You were right about the power trip. Brian says he hasn't witnessed any physical abuse, but he's heard the way Henningson talks to

129

Sally. He's worried that the guy will hit her. Which is why he's willing for her to know about the bruises. He thinks maybe it will make her change her mind about marrying the guy."

"Then we'll put Sally on the stand, too," I said between my teeth. "When I'm through asking questions —"

"We're not putting anybody on the stand," McQuaid replied wearily. I could picture him rubbing the back of his neck, trying to knead the weariness out of his muscles. "I can't drag Brian through an ordeal like that — and neither can you, if you'll calm down and think about it."

I stopped pacing and sat back down in the swing, grateful for McQuaid's calm. I was overreacting and I knew it. "You're right, of course," I said more quietly. "So when are you going to talk to her?"

"I agree that Sally has to know. But if I go down there and raise Cain about Henningson spanking Brian, I'm afraid she'll get defensive, then try to make light of it. I want to see if I can turn up anything else on the guy. In the meantime, we'll have to find a way to keep Brian away from Henningson."

We were silent for a few seconds, each of us digesting all this. "You guys are still

130

coming out here for the weekend?" I asked. Allie had been happy to let McQuaid and Brian camp at her tank, so I'd drawn a map and left it on the refrigerator.

"We sure are, and looking forward to it. Brian's out of school about three, so we'll drive over tomorrow, put up the tent, then meet you in Indigo for supper and the show. Okay?"

"Sounds good to me," I said. "I hope Brian's not too unhappy about missing the Cowboys game."

"He didn't make a big deal about it," McQuaid said. "I think he's got more important things on his mind. This business with Henningson and his mom really has him down."

"More important than the Cowboys? This *is* serious!" I said it lightly, but I knew it wasn't anything to joke about.

"Right." McQuaid's voice softened. "Hey, China, I love you. I'd hate to be trying to handle this on my own."

"Me, too," I said simply. "And I'm sure Brian feels better, knowing he's not in this alone."

We said good night and I walked slowly along the path to the cabin, thinking of McQuaid and of the comfort of what we

131

had together, thinking, too, about Allie, and her longing for a happy ending. I didn't picture my life with McQuaid as an ending, though — it was more like a different beginning every day, a work-in-progress, with no way to calculate how it would turn out. I smiled to myself. Emphasis on work. I don't know what I'd expected, but in the year since our wedding I'd found that a good marriage is something you *make*, both of you working together, not something you just luck into.

Ruby had managed to light the kerosene lamp, and it cast a golden glow around the cabin. She'd already taken a shower and was sitting cross-legged on her bed, a henna-haired buddha in a floral-print caftan. There was a book on her lap, the latest *Cat Who* adventure; a bottle of blue nail polish and shiny nail implements on one side of her; and a box of chocolates on the other. Delicately, so as not to mar her freshly painted blue nails, she screwed the cap back on the polish bottle.

"You know," she said, "I could get to like this pioneer life."

"Some pioneer," I replied with a laugh. "I'll bet you wouldn't be wearing that caftan if you had to spin every inch of thread that went into it."

"Oh, absolutely," Ruby said. "I'd go naked." She reached for a chocolate. "Spinning must be very hard on the nails," she added thoughtfully, popping the candy into her mouth. "To tell the truth, I'm just as glad to let the machines do it." She picked up another chocolate. "Chocolate-candy making, too. I might not like chocolates so much if I had to stand and stir for hours and hours." She glanced at me. "How was the meeting? Did Casey Ford show up? How did people respond to the news about Indigo?"

"If you'd stepped outside, you might have seen the fireworks from here," I said, and told her all about it.

"Sounds like a very bad situation," Ruby said worriedly, when she'd heard the story. "Is there anything that can be done?"

"Maybe Betty's legal-eagle brother can come up with some kind of delaying tactics," I said. "But whatever they do, Casey will probably end up by having his way. The law favors property owners." I stretched. "Think I'll read for a while before I take a shower."

I'd brought a book, too, one that Miss Mayjean had recommended to me. It was Gösta Sandberg's fascinating study of the cultural and economic history of indigo —

for which, it turns out, men have been willing to sacrifice their lives. Especially in India during the eighteenth century, where the production of indigo dye was under the control of the empire-building and fortune-hunting Brits, the plant was as notorious an instrument of human oppression as cotton in the American South, coffee in the plantations of South America, or sugar in Cuba. "Not a chest of indigo reached England without being stained with human blood," I'd read. It had probably been a very good thing when indigo blue was finally synthesized in the 1890s and the plant was abruptly devalued.

After an hour, I decided it was time for my shower. I picked up my flashlight and dropped my toothbrush, soap, and towel into a tote. "I'm off to the bathroom," I announced, slipping my feet into flip-flops. "Don't let the boogeyman bite while I'm gone."

"Shangrilama will run him off," Ruby said absently, still intent on her book. Ruby thinks of Quilleran and Kinsey Millhone and V. I. Warshawski as her alter egos, and when she reflects on her childhood, she pictures herself as Nancy Drew, solving the mystery at Lilac Inn or finding the heirloom necklace at the bottom of the old trunk in the attic. There's something quintessentially Ruby about this small obsession, and I enjoy watching her indulge herself.

It was already dark, so I turned on the flashlight for the trek to the bathroom in Allie's old farmhouse, which had been fitted into what used to be a kitchen pantry, beside the stairs. The space was cramped, but the water was hot and plentiful, the soothing lavender scent of the soap filled the small room, and in a few minutes, I felt like a new woman.

I had just stepped out of the shower and grabbed for the towel when I heard Allie and Derek come into the house and start up the stairs. They must have been out for a walk. Now, however, they seemed to be arguing. Loudly.

Unfortunately, I am the kind of person who has never been above listening to other people's arguments. In fact, in my previous incarnation as a defense attorney, this habit frequently stood me in good stead, providing bits and pieces of information that I might not otherwise have picked up. But this situation was a little different, for Allie and I were working together and I had no desire to learn intimate details of her personal life that she did not intend to share with me.

The voices were getting louder. Not wanting to eavesdrop, I made sure I had closed the bathroom door, but that didn't help. I looked up. The footsteps had arrived in the room over my head, and the wooden boards that made up the bathroom ceiling seemed to be the floor of Allie's bedroom. There was no way to keep the words from sifting through the cracks. I was a captive audience.

"I'm sorry you're upset, Allison," Derek was saying in an exaggeratedly patient tone, "but I promise you, there's nothing to it." Something thudded on the floor, probably a shoe.

"You're saying it wasn't you in your truck, or that it wasn't your truck?" Allie's voice was heavily sarcastic. "You're telling me that Brenda made a mistake — or that she's lying?"

There was a pause. I was hastily pulling my underwear on, but I hadn't quite finished toweling. It was like trying to skinny, wet, into a dry bathing suit. I pulled off my bra, turned it right-side out, and tried again. This time I couldn't get it fastened.

"No," Derek said warily, "that was my truck. But the woman's a writer. All she wanted was an interview. There's nothing

136

between us. I swear it." His words were clipped and an odd tension vibrated in his voice. I couldn't see his face, but I knew I was hearing a lie. And if I heard it, I could bet that Allie did, too.

"An interview?" Allie snapped. "If that's what it was, you could have talked here, in the kitchen. Or at the Indigo Café. You didn't need to take her out to the old quarry — unless there was more to it than just talk, of course." There were quick footsteps, and the floor creaked. Allie was pacing.

I made a couple of fast swipes with my deodorant and reached for my toothbrush and toothpaste. I had to hurry up and brush my teeth and get out of here, before I learned something I'd rather not know. When people are angry, they say all sorts of things they don't mean. Allie and Derek might patch things up and forget all about what they'd said to one another. But I'd remember, and the recollection would color my reactions to both of them for a long time.

"And why would she want to talk to you, anyway?" Allie went on. "She's writing about Texas, and you're not even a native Texan. You're just —"

"Just passing through?" Now it was

Derek's turn to be sarcastic. "By that, I suppose, you mean that my usefulness here has come to an end. I've built your goat barn and fixed the house roof and done all the other odd jobs you'd been saving up. And I've given you enough good sex to hold you for a while. It's time for me to pack up and hit the road. Is that it?"

"Of course not!" Allie cried. "But after you slept with Marie, I made up my mind that I wouldn't put up with —"

"I've apologized for my mistake," Derek said flatly. "I was wrong, and I'm sorry." His laugh was short and harsh. "I am *very* sorry, believe me, Allison. It only happened once, when I had too much to drink. It wouldn't have happened at all if she hadn't made the first move. I —"

"Oh, now you're saying that Marie seduced you?" Allie's voice was corrosive. "That it was all her fault?"

"No, it wasn't all her fault. But some of it was, that's for damn sure. She threw herself at —"

"Marie was my *best* friend! And now you're messing around with some cute little thing young enough to be your daughter. You're —"

"I am *not* messing around!" Derek said

138

sharply. "Knock it off, Allison. You don't have a clue to what's going on in my life, or who I am, or who I was before I met you. You don't trust me. You don't know how to trust."

"If I knew who you were," Allie said, very low, "I might be able to trust you."

There was a long silence, and when Derek spoke, his voice was sad. "Trust is *trust*, Allison. It's not a commodity that you trade for information."

Hey! I wanted to say. *That sounds good, but it's wrong. You can't trust somebody you don't know.* The bed creaked and I could picture Derek standing up, going to Allie, putting his arms around her, holding her tight against him.

"I love you, Allie, and I'm very sorry about what happened with Marie. But that's past, and it will never be repeated. I'm committed to you, with my whole heart. I want us to stay together for the rest of our lives, if that's possible."

"But not get married." Allie's words were etched with pain. "You're committed, but your commitment doesn't include marriage. You tell me what's going on in your life today, but not in the past. You're like an iceberg, Derek — only a tiny part of you is visible, and it's not the most important part."

"I'm trying. I'm giving as much as I'm able to give. I say I love you. Isn't that enough?"

"But we're never completely *together*, Derek. A part of you is somewhere else, someplace I can't reach. And now this writer comes along and —"

She broke off. There was a long silence, while the pain and pity twisted inside me. I knew exactly how Allie must be feeling, for I'd been there once myself, when McQuaid had been involved with another, much younger woman. Jealousy isn't an emotion that you can pack up and put away and forget about. It settles in your flesh, it aches in your bones, as if you've been poisoned by some toxic heavy metal. Even when jealousy is overshadowed by another powerful emotion — as it was for me, when McQuaid was shot and I feared that he was going to die — you don't forget how it feels.

Derek cleared his throat. "There are things I can't explain, Allison. All I can do is ask you to trust me. Can't you just settle for what we have? Can't we —"

"Stop it!" I imagined Allie putting her hands over her ears. "I don't want to hear it! Stop." After a moment she went on. "I can't talk about this any longer, Derek. I've got too much else on my mind. I'm losing this farm and I'll be lucky to keep the girls together. The town I've fought so hard to save is being destroyed." Her voice became muffled. "I think you'd better sleep in the camper tonight. Or maybe you'd rather go over to Pecan Springs and see if Ellen is free."

Ellen? A writer, staying in Pecan Springs, working on a Texas book? Toothbrush frozen in one hand, toothpaste frothy in my mouth, I stared at my reflection in the mirror, realizing what I should have realized several moments before. The woman Derek was seeing must be the Ellen Holt who'd rented my guest house. The sexy, petite blonde with the Barbie-doll dimples, who was planning to come to the workshop tomorrow!

I heard feet scraping. Derek was putting his shoes back on. "All right," he said, "I'll sleep in the camper tonight, if that's what you want."

Steps across the floor. The sound of the door opening and Derek clattering angrily down the stairs. I pulled the shower curtain open and ducked inside, thinking that he might make a pit stop on his way out. But to my enormous relief, the back door

141

slammed. He'd gone out into the night, and upstairs in the bedroom, Allie was weeping despairingly.

I stepped out of the shower, feeling Allie's anguish, an echo of my own remembered pain. I wanted to go upstairs and comfort her, the way she had comforted me so many years ago. But what could I say? That I'd been hiding in her bathroom, eavesdropping on her private conversation? That I'd met Ellen Holt, who was young and pretty and sexy, and that her jealousy was perfectly understandable? That I thought Derek was a unconscionable rat who —

But maybe Derek wasn't a rat. Maybe, like McQuaid, he was simply a man who found himself caught in a situation he didn't know how to handle. Maybe, if Allie gave him some time, the relationship could be repaired. But it wasn't up to me to offer advice, especially when I knew how embarrassed Allie would be at the idea that I had invaded her privacy, inadvertently or not.

I gave it up, gathered my things, and crept quietly out of the house, like a burglar weighed down by a bag of guilt. There wasn't anything I could say to make Allie feel better. She needed to get some sleep, and maybe tomorrow morning, she would wake up and her world would look brighter.

In the distance, thunder rumbled and a jagged flash of lightning split the sky to the east.

And then again, maybe it wouldn't.

When I finally fell asleep, I dreamed of bloodstained casks of indigo dye stacked in the old Dalton County Jail, while Allie and I and members of the Historic Indigo Restoration Committee, barricaded in the building, held off Casey Ford with shotguns. Derek and Ellen Holt, as stiff and beautiful as Ken and Barbie, stood across the street, watching. They were holding hands.

Seven

HOW THE SNAILS CHEWED BLUE: A LEGEND OF LIBERIA

Gala, the Creator, loved blue. That is why he made the sky blue. He hoped that blue would be the first dye color found in a plant. He had called the snails to chew in order to give a little hint. The plant they chewed was indigo. When they had finished chewing, each little hole had a rim of blue around it.

The woman who did not fear the forest saw the blue edges of the little holes. She picked a handful of the chewed leaves and ran to ask Gala the meaning of the round holes. When she opened her clenched fist, her palms and her fingers were stained blue. Blue. Blue. Blue dye had been discovered.

Gala was overjoyed . . .

You Cannot Unsneeze a Sneeze
— Esther Warner Dendel

If you've never experimented with natural dyes, I hope it's something you'll try. It's

144

hard to imagine the many subtle shades and hues that are hiding in such ordinary-looking herbs as bronze fennel, purple basil, and Saint-John's-wort, as well as the brighter reds and blues of the classic dye plants: madder, indigo, woad. It's also interesting to think about the fact that, with dye plants (as with people who are concealing their own true colors) what you see is definitely *not* what you get.

But until you have a chance to do some experiments of your own, you might be interested in hearing what went on at our Colors to Dye For workshop — and not just because it was a good day for dyeing, either. As things turned out, it was also a good day for meeting a number of people who might have had a strong interest in dying of a different sort.

The previous night's thunder and lightning had been a false alarm, and the sun was shining brightly as Ruby and I climbed out of bed and put on old T-shirts and jeans. (Dye has a tendency to splash and splatter, and if you've made it right, it won't wash out.) The nine workshop participants — seven women and two men — began to arrive shortly after breakfast. Two women drove down from Waco, and one of the men, a member of a historical reenactment group that stages the Battle of the Alamo, came up from San Antonio. Reenactors have a great interest in re-creating the past as accurately as possible, down to the natural dyes that they use for their homespun costumes.

And Ellen was there, too. At breakfast that morning, trying not to reveal that I had any special knowledge about Derek and Ellen, I mentioned casually that the woman writer staying in my guest house had said she wanted to come to the work-shop and that I'd told her yes. From the startled look on Allie's face and the imme-diate frown that followed, I guessed that she'd made the connection and wasn't pleased at the news. When Ellen arrived and I introduced her, I could read Allie's feelings on her face, a mix of jealousy, anger, and frustration. I was sure that Allie was feeling every year of her age, while Ellen was fresh as an April breeze and pic-ture-pretty in shorts and a T-shirt, her honey-colored hair piled carelessly on top of her head. She was probably in her late twenties, but she might have passed for eighteen, with a year or two to spare.

The five other workshop participants, as Allie had said, were from Indigo, and four were members of HIRC. Sandra Higgins and Stella Mason, who'd been at the meeting the night before. Carl Holland, Jerome's partner in the Indigo Café, and Brenda Davis, the ebony-skinned black woman who owned Texas Antique Treasures, both of whom had missed it.

And Miss Mayjean Carter was there, too, of course. She was a spectacled, white-haired lady scarcely five feet tall — but Lord help you if Miss Mayjean suspected that you were looking down on her because of her age or her size. I'd met her at our first workshop and had been impressed by the range of her knowledge — and even more impressed by the textile collection she showed me when I stopped at her house, a half-mile up the road. She'd been dyeing with blue for decades, so she had provided the indigo and woad dye baths for the workshop and also brought a few pieces from her impressive textile collection of adire cloth, lengths of indigo resist-dyed cotton that are made and worn by the Yoruba women of Nigeria as wraparound dresses. Miss Mayjean might be close to eighty, but she had the spirit and energy of somebody half her age, and she'd never once thought of retirement. Last year, she spent several months in Nigeria, apprenticing to an old woman indigo dyer in Oshogbo.

The group was just the right size for a workshop, but most of the local people didn't have their minds on dyeing. They were, as we say in Texas, madder than a boiled squirrel. Madder than a mama wasp. And the target of their collective wrath, quite naturally, was the man who planned to take Indigo off the map.

"Casey's not going to get by with this," Carl muttered furiously, as the group gathered around the tables in the dye kitchen and Ruby and I began handing out instructions and worksheets. Carl was a good-looking man with one gold earring, slender, of medium height and build, his light brown hair worn in a buzz cut. His idea of old clothing (we'd told everybody to wear things they wouldn't mind getting splattered) was a light blue Izod shirt and khaki shorts, with penny loafers and no socks.

He turned to the slender, attractive black woman on his right, whose graying hair was cut in a crisp, curly Afro. "You're smart about stuff like this, Brenda," he said. "How can we stop that crazy man from turning Indigo over to the mine?"

"Legally, you mean?" Brenda's voice was razor-sharp. "There's not a damn thing we can do. When Sandra called early this

148

morning and told me what was coming down, I dug up my lease and read it. There was the right-to-demolish clause, big as life. I just hadn't noticed, that's all. My own damn fault."

I noticed that Ellen was listening closely. Well, if she was interested in small-town Texas, this conversation ought to give her some new insights. Towns like Indigo might look cute and cozy from a distance, a writer's ideal subject, but they are vulnerable in the face of change. Scratch that placid exterior, and you'll find plenty of anxiety and fear for the future.

Miss Mayjean was scowling. "You don't want to fool around with those Fords," she said. Her face was age-splotched and as wrinkled and leathery as a dried apple, but her mouth was firm and uncompromising, and her dark eyes were birds' eyes, quick and bright and alert. "They're mean folks. Frank Ford, Casey's daddy — when he was alive, he'd as soon shoot you as look at you. And Casey's not much more civilized." She shook her head sadly. "The one I feel sorry for is Shirley. She must have had a hard time of it, living with those Fords all these years. Her poor mother would feel so bad about the way things've turned out. She never intended it to be like this."

149

I wanted to ask how Miss Mayjean knew about Shirley's mother, but Sandra had spoken up, her voice rising passionately. "There's got to be a law against what he's doing!" she cried, her round chin quivering. "Breaking leases on a technicality, selling the town out from under us — it's *wrong!*"

"It's not as if he needs the money, either," Stella put in. She was looking witchy in skinny black pants and an old red T-shirt painted with cabalistic signs, her black hair twisted into a straggly knot on top of her head. "He's just doing it because he doesn't like us." She gave Carl a meaningful glance. "Because he's *prejudiced.*" Her eyes went to Brenda. "This could be a civil rights matter."

Ellen cleared her throat. "Maybe you ought to hire a lawyer," she suggested tentatively. "I don't know anything except what I've heard this morning, but it does seem that this man ought to be stopped before he does something that can't be undone."

Sandra fastened on the suggestion. "My idea exactly. Everybody in town — all the merchants, anyway — should chip in and hire a lawyer. Betty's brother, maybe. She was going to talk to him today."

"A lawyer? Give me a break." Brenda was scornful. "After we've forked over a couple of hundred dollars for an hour of his precious time, he'll tell us that a property owner can do whatever the hell he likes with his property. Period. Paragraph. End of story."

"What about an environmental suit?" the woman from Waco asked.

"A half-dozen suits have already been filed against this mine, and they're all stalled," Carl said quietly. "Anyway, it would be hard to find somebody we could afford who isn't on the company payroll already, or wants to be."

Carl was probably right. It's hard to find a local lawyer who doesn't have some ties to the local political power structure, which includes not just the elected county commissioners but big property owners and employers. Money walks and talks. It doesn't always buy justice, but it can put a heavy thumb on the scales.

"But surely somebody can stop this awful thing!" Tears had squeezed out of Sandra's eyes, already red from crying, and were running down her pudgy cheeks. "Allison, he's your uncle. *You* make him stop."

I looked at Allie, who was handing out

151

the bundles of premordanted fiber. Her movements were stiff and jerky and her mouth was set in a hard, bitter line, as if she were holding back feelings so fierce that they threatened to explode out of her. Derek had been nowhere in sight when Ruby and I joined Allie at breakfast this morning, and I felt a sharp twist of sympathy. If I'd known that Derek and Ellen had something going — or that Allie thought so, at least — I'd never have encouraged Ellen to come.

At first Allie pretended that she hadn't heard Sandra's plea, but when Carl repeated it, louder, she turned to him. "I've known Casey Ford a lot longer than the rest of you," she said, snapping off the words. "When he decides to do something, he does it. Nobody stops him. Not me, not you, not anybody."

Miss Mayjean nodded, agreeing. "Just like his daddy," she said in a low, sad voice. "I was friends with Shirley's mother Janece, and I told her she shouldn't ought to marry him. 'Those Fords, they're bad news,' I told her. I was right, too. Frank came between Janece and me, and even when she got sick, he wouldn't let me go to see her."

"I might try a few protection spells,"

152

Stella offered diffidently. At Brenda's scornful look, she muttered, "Well, it can't hurt, can it? It's not black witchcraft."

"You try all the spells you want, Stella," Miss Mayjean said in an encouraging tone. "It's not much different from making a prayer."

"Of course it can't hurt," Ruby said. "I'll be glad to show you some charms I know."

"Oh, would you?" Stella asked eagerly. "I'm just getting started in the craft, and I've got a lot to learn."

"Sure," Ruby said. "And I can tell you which herbs have been used traditionally to protect property. Allie is growing some of them in her garden. We could gather them at lunch and make up bundles that people could take home to hang on their doors and fences."

"Wonderful!" Stella exclaimed, looking truly awake for the first time since I had met her. "Thank you, Ruby."

"Witches' spells." Brenda gave a contemptuous snort. "They'll do about as much good as lawyers getting into a circle and chanting whereases. In my opinion, the only way to deal with this bastard is to get rid of him."

"That's what Maxine told Harry after the meeting last night," Sandra replied seriously. "She said somebody ought to take a gun to Casey Ford."

I frowned. I certainly hoped that Maxine wasn't giving Harry his marching orders. Casey might be armed, and I was willing to bet that he could draw faster and shoot straighter than Maxine's husband.

"Please don't repeat that, Sandra," Stella said uneasily. "Mother was only joking."

"Oh, she was? Well, it's not such a bad idea." Brenda's laugh had a sharp edge. "Remember what happened to that town bully in Missouri a few years back? He'd been terrorizing some little village for over a decade — Skidmore, I think it was — until somebody shot him."

"Oh, sure, I remember," Sandra said excitedly. "Everybody in town knew who did it, but they wouldn't tell, not even after the FBI came into the case. Maybe we ought to —" She broke off, casting a swift look at Ellen, as if she had just remembered that outsiders were present. "But of course that's silly." She turned up the corners of her mouth in what might have passed for a smile. "Nobody in Indigo would do a thing like that. We're peace-loving people."

"I think we ought to let the sheriff know about those booby traps Casey claims to have set," Carl put in. "You've got to be crazy to do something like that. Maybe we could get him locked up as a menace to the community."

"He's definitely crazy," Brenda said firmly. "That sister of his, she's a fruitcake, too."

"I doubt that," Miss Mayjean replied in a snippy tone.

"How do you know?" Brenda looked at Allie. "Didn't she kill a guy once, Allison?"

This was getting out of control. I was about to say something, but Allie clapped her hands. "I understand that some of you are very angry," she said. "But there's nothing we can do this morning about the situation, so let's get started, shall we?"

The purpose of a dye workshop is to give the group a chance to go through the entire process, while each person gets acquainted with as many colors as possible. Allie began by reviewing what we'd be doing, while the students filled the panty hose bags we'd made the previous afternoon with the dye stuffs: madder root, annatto seeds, and brazilwood chips for red; calendula, Osage orange, and coreopsis for yellows and oranges; and willow and comfrey for greeny-browns, tans, and browns. We'd also be using the indigo that Miss Mayjean had brought, already prepared, and woad from my garden.

When the bags were all filled, they were dropped into the simmering dye pots. While the plant material released its color into the hot water, Allie talked about the bundles of fiber we were about to dye, describing how she had treated each bundle with a different mordant and briefly demonstrating how to make the five different mordant solutions. After a short break, the students fished out the bags of dyestuffs, wetted their fiber bundles (wet fiber absorbs color more evenly), and plopped them gently into the hot dye baths to simmer for another hour. Allie added some wool fleece to each pot, as well, for comparison.

It's fascinating to watch the pale wool gradually absorb the dye in the dye pot, changing color and taking on an entirely new look. While we waited, I handed out samples of the herbs we were using and talked about their traditional uses as dyestuffs. Then Miss Mayjean took over, showing the unusual indigo-dyed textiles she'd brought: resist-dyed Yoruban adire cloth, a piece of Chinese blue print, a wax batik from Java, and a dark blue kimono from Japan, handwoven in the early 1900s. Looking at the cloth and reflecting that it came from different times and different places gave us a new perspective on the age-old art of dyeing.

When Miss Mayjean was finished, it was almost time for lunch. The students took their bundles of dyed fibers out of the dye pots and washed and rinsed and hung them up to dry in the shade of a large pecan tree, while Ruby and I went into the farmhouse and made ham sandwiches to go with the macaroni salad Allie had already fixed.

While everyone was eating, I looked for Ellen, thinking that it might be a good time to get to know her a little better. But she seemed to have taken her lunch and slipped off somewhere. So I sat with Allie, Miss Mayjean, and the out-of-town people, noticing that the Indigo folks were all gathered off to one side, their heads together and their voices low. They might have been discussing the melodrama they were going to perform that night, or they might have been plotting a way to thwart Casey Ford.

After Ruby and Stella finished lunch, they went through the garden, gathering rosemary, rue, dill, basil, and Saint-John's-wort to hang on the doors for protection. I supposed that Ruby was sharing spells with Stella, as well. I wished them luck, but if you asked me, it would take more than a few herbs and incantations to keep that dragon-shovel from gobbling up Indigo.

After lunch, we filled out worksheets, recording what and how much dyestuff had been used, how long it had simmered and at what heat, and where the dyestuff had come from. By that time, the dyed fibers were about as dry as they were going to get, and we could get a good look at the colors and discuss and compare them. Everyone tied their dyed yarn samples through the holes punched in the margins of the worksheets, next to descriptions of each of the dyes, mordants, and fibers, so they could take their worksheets home and use them for reference when they repeated the experiment. And when that was finished, Ruby and Stella handed out the bunches of herbs they'd gathered, with instructions for tying them up with red thread and hanging them beside a doorway to keep evil spirits from invading our homes.

By three o'clock, we'd tidied the dye kitchen, put things away, and said goodbye to everyone. I breathed a sigh of relief as Ellen, the last to leave, drove away. Given the mix of emotions that had been simmering in the group all day, I could only be grateful that things had gone as smoothly as they had.

The workshop might be over, but the weekend had barely begun. Ruby and I changed out of our old clothes and into something more suitable for an arts and crafts festival — khaki twill pants and a green Thyme and Seasons T-shirt for me and a long, loose gold challis dress for Ruby, the bodice quilted with patches of brown velvet and gold embroidery.

As we started to climb into the van, Allie came out of the house and locked the door behind her. She walked down the path toward her green Dodge truck, a shotgun in one hand and her costume for the show, on a hanger, slung over her shoulder. She was absorbed in her thoughts, and when she looked up and saw us, she was startled.

She held up the shotgun. "A prop for the show." Her grin looked forced. "I don't want you to think I'm gunning for Casey."

"Why not?" Ruby asked, opening the door of the van. "Everybody else is. Judging from today's group, the whole town has turned into a gang of vigilante wanna-bes."

"Yeah, sure," Allie said wryly. The corners of her mouth tipped up. "The problem is, everybody's chicken, including me. All boots and no cowboy, as Grandpa Ford used to say." She leaned the shotgun against her truck, opened the door, and hung her costume — a black skirt and white Gibson Girl blouse — on a hook. I noticed that there was a bale of hay in the truck bed — for the goats, maybe? "Are you guys coming to the play tonight?" she added, putting the shotgun into the rack across the back window. That's how you tote rifles and shotguns in Texas, out in the open, for everybody to see. If you want to carry concealed, you have to get a permit.

"China and I drew straws," Ruby replied. "She gets to go to the play. I'm staying with the booth."

I'd felt guilty about winning, but it was fair and square. "McQuaid and Brian will also be there tonight," I said.

"I'm sorry you'll miss it, Ruby," Allie remarked. "This might be the last performance, under the circumstances. There's no point in raising money to support a town that will be six feet under by this time next year."

She turned to get into her truck, but at that moment, a big red Harley motorcycle came roaring down the lane. It skidded to a stop and a man and a woman, neither wearing a helmet, climbed off.

The man, in his late forties, was powerfully built. He wore a sweat-soaked black tank top that showed his biceps, grease-stained jeans, and grimy workboots. His full mustache was as black as his shaggy hair, and he seemed twice the size, in weight and girth, of the woman. Thin and fragile, she was almost lost in a red shirt that hung down to the knees of her jeans. Dark hair, streaked with gray, tumbled around a face that wore a look of desperately fearful anxiety. The skin around her left eye was purplish-green, and she had a bruise on her temple.

The man gestured to a small orange duffle bag secured to the back of the Harley. "We've brought Shirley's stuff, Allison. She's got to stay in your cabin for a couple of days. She's havin' problems with Casey." He gave Allie a pointed look. "Real serious problems."

I looked at the woman again. Shirley. Casey Ford's crazy sister, who kept house for her stepbrother and wanted to get married, against his wishes. And the shaggy-haired, mustached biker must be Les Osler. What was it Allie had said about him? That he was as stubborn as Casey? I didn't doubt it. He had the look of a desperado.

"I'm sorry, Les." Regret was heavy in Allie's voice. "I told you before, it isn't a good idea for Shirley to come here. You know how mad Casey gets when I interfere. This is the first place he'll look when he misses her, and he'll just take her back home." She put the shotgun into the truck, then nodded toward Ruby and me. "Anyway, the cabin's not available. My friends are staying there this weekend."

The man flicked a dismissive glance in our direction. "Then how 'bout lettin' her sleep in the camper out back? That'd probably be better than the cabin, anyway. Casey ain't likely to bother around Derek's stuff."

"The camper isn't available either," Allie said flatly. "I've told you before, Les. If Shirley wants to leave Casey, the two of you have got to handle it yourselves and leave me out of it. Why don't you take her to Austin and check her into a motel? Use a different name, so he can't trace her."

At the suggestion, Shirley seemed to curl up like a leaf in a hot wind, turning her face into Les's shoulder. As he put a protective arm around her and drew her close, I saw that she was trembling. I guessed that she was terrified to stay by herself in a strange place. Les probably couldn't stay with her, and he couldn't leave her alone.

"Don't reckon that'll work," Les replied, tightening his arm. "Got any other bright ideas?" He smiled mirthlessly. "How about us takin' out a contract on Casey? If that sonovabitch was out of the picture, everybody'd sleep better nights."

Shirley shuddered convulsively and raised her head. "Casey Ford is a bad man," she said. Her voice was low, her words vibrating, awkwardly pronounced, as if she weren't used to speaking out loud. "He's very, very mean to me. He hurts me." Tears were gathering in her eyes, and she lifted a trembling hand to her temple. "He *hurts* me," she whispered.

I spoke gently. "If your stepbrother gave you that bruise, Shirley, you need to tell the sheriff." If she could provide evidence of Casey's abuse, his control over her could be terminated very quickly. "The law can protect you, find you a safe place to stay, away from —"

"No!" Shirley stiffened, her whole face twisting in a spasm of sudden fear. "If I tell, Casey says he'll get Les thrown in jail." She thrust out her fist as if she were pummeling Casey. "I won't let him do it.

163

I won't, I won't!"

Casey's threat sounded like blackmail to me, and pretty effective blackmail, at that. If Casey had a court-authorized guardianship over his sister, all he had to do was get an injunction forbidding Les Osler to see her. Defy that, and Casey could get the law on Les faster than a duck on a June bug. The whole business would be ugly and traumatic for both Shirley and Les — especially if the sheriff or the county attorney happened to be one of Casey's cronies. Things like that shouldn't happen, but they do, all the time. And looking at Shirley, I guessed that she didn't have the courage or the stamina necessary to bring charges of abuse against her stepbrother.

Les put his big, grease-stained hand over Shirley's small fist and held it against his chest, restraining her violence. "Don't fret, Shirl," he murmured into her hair. "I can take care of myself. And I won't let you go back to that bastard. We'll find someplace where you can be safe."

"I'm really sorry, Shirley," Allie said sadly. "I feel so damn helpless. There's just no way to deal with Casey. When he gets like this, he's irrational. He's sick."

"I can think of a way to deal with him," Les growled, his mouth set and angry under his mustache. He turned Shirley around and guided her toward the Harley. The back of his shirt said "Avenging Angels."

Eight

A simple method of making an herbal protective was used extensively not more than one hundred years ago in the British Isles and on the Continent. Pick several protective herbs [such as basil, mistletoe, dill, horehound, rosemary, mugwort, rue, Saint-John's-wort.] and bind the stems together with red thread, then hang beside the door.

Magical Herbalism
— Scott Cunningham

In Germany, braids of onion and garlic, woven with red yarn, were hung on the doorpost to repel evil spirits.

Oxford Dictionary of Plant-Lore
— Roy Vickery

In many cultures, the color red was believed to protect against evil influence. The fleshy, reddish-orange roots of madder (*Rubia tinctorum*) produced a clear red dye, and the cloth dyed with it was used for many ritual purposes.

"The Symbolism of Color"
— Ruby Wilcox

Ruby and I got into Big Red Mama and followed the dust cloud raised by the green truck ahead of us. Ruby was silent for a few moments. Then she said, "How about calling the Whiz and asking her opinion about all this? I'll bet she'd love to jump right into Shirley's case."

"I was just thinking of Justine myself," I said approvingly. I picked up my cell phone and handed it to Ruby. "Her number's in memory. Why don't you call and invite her to the festival tomorrow? We can introduce her and Shirley and she can take it from there, if she thinks she can help."

While Ruby punched in the numbers, I thought about Justine — Justine Wyzinski, familiarly known as the Whiz, because she could untie legal knots faster than anybody else in our class at the University of Texas School of Law. When I left the law, Justine expressed the opinion that I was certifiably *non compos* and ought to be filed in the loony bin. But we've remained friends, and every now and then, we manage to be useful to one another. The Whiz now practices family law in San Antonio and is passionate about women's issues. This case of Shirley's, complicated by claims of abuse and threats of jail, raised exactly the kind of legal questions she loves to unravel.

She'd probably share my opinion about Shirley's relationship with Les, too. While I had no reason to question his feelings for Shirley, I didn't think it was a good idea for her to flee from the clutches of one man straight into the arms of another. Les might look to her like a knight in shining armor, but rescuers can have self-serving motives, just like the rest of us. He could turn out, in the long run, to be every bit as exploitative as Shirley's stepbrother.

Having left a call-back message on the Whiz's answering machine, Ruby turned toward me with a probing look. "I noticed that Allie wasn't very cordial when Derek came home yesterday evening. And just now, she said he was sleeping in the camper. I don't suppose it's any of my business, but are they having problems?"

I hadn't planned to tell Ruby what I'd overheard, especially since I hadn't yet told Allie that I'd been trapped in her bathroom while she and Derek were quarreling. But sharing something with Ruby often helps me to sort it out, so I sketched what I'd heard.

"What a jerk," Ruby said indignantly. "No wonder Allie was so uptight today." She made a wry face. "Funny how Ellen manages to look young and beautiful even when she's wearing old clothes."

"I guess it's because she *is* young and beautiful," I said with a little laugh. "But maybe Brenda didn't actually see what she thought she saw," I added. "Derek could be telling the truth."

"Well, maybe." Ruby's eyebrows went up and her tone was skeptical. "It seems pretty fishy to me, though. If you were an extremely attractive young writer, would you drive out to a deserted quarry with some guy you didn't know, just to interview him? That's asking for trouble."

I had to agree with that. If Ellen had only wanted an interview, why all the secrecy? "A comment of Derek's keeps coming back to me," I said. " 'You don't have a clue to who I am.' And Allie retorted with something like, 'If I knew who you were, I might be able to trust you.' " I paused. "It seems like a sad commentary on a two-year relationship. You'd think they'd know one another better, after all that time."

"Really?" Ruby's expression was serious. "How many people do you know, China? Really *know*, I mean."

"Well, there's McQuaid," I replied. "And Brian, and you, and my mother." I stopped. "No, we'd better take my mother off the list."

A few months before, I'd gone to the Mississippi plantation where my mother Leatha grew up, to help her with the care of Aunt Tullie, who is dying of a degenerative neurological disease. In the few days we spent together, I'd unriddled a few of my mother's mysteries and we'd grown much closer. But there are complexities there I still don't understand.

"And sometimes I'm not sure about you, either," I added with a smile. I'd been amazed at the way Ruby handled her breast cancer. It showed me a side of her I'd never seen before.

"See?" Ruby gave me a wise look. "The problem is that it's hard to stay with somebody long enough to really understand what they're like. And just about the time you finally get them figured out, they change." She sighed. "Or they don't, which might be even worse."

This cryptic comment actually makes sense, in Ruby's case, anyway. She's dated quite a few men since her divorce ten or eleven years ago, but none of them for more than a few months. I have the feeling that once she feels she knows someone intimately, she loses interest in him.

On that philosophical note, we drove into Indigo, parked, and walked around, looking for our booth location. We finally ran into a harried-looking Jerome, wearing a yellow badge that identified him as the festival director. He consulted the list of vendors on the clipboard he was carrying and directed us to the brick-paved plaza next to the Cotton Gin Theater and Gallery — a good location, not far from the public potty. You might not guess it, but a spot near the bathroom is one of the very best vendor locations at a festival, second only to a spot near the hot dog stand.

We put up our tables in the shade of a mesquite tree and hauled our displays, merchandise, signs, and sales equipment from the van. Then all we had to do was unpack all our tubs, put up our signs, and arrange our tables, displays, plant racks, and sales area. This is something that Ruby and I do three or four times a year, so we know pretty much how we want everything to look. We usually finish setting up the booth in something like thirty minutes, then sit down in our lawn chairs and take a breather while we admire our handiwork and wait for the first customer to arrive on the scene.

We didn't have long to wait. We'd barely unfolded our lawn chairs and sat down when two sweet little ladies came along, oohed and ahhed over our displays, and bought a half-dozen herb plants, some herbal soap, and two of Ruby's astrology books. One of them wanted to buy a small fresh wreath made of rosemary, mistletoe, rue, fennel, and mugwort that Ruby had just hung on the tree, tied up with a piece of red yarn.

"I'm sorry," Ruby said, "but that's not for sale. It's a protection wreath."

The lady arched her eyebrows. "You're expecting trouble?"

"Not as long as we have the wreath," Ruby said blithely. When they had gone, we put their money into our plastic cash box and gave each other a congratulatory hug. We were open for business!

After that, the trickle of traffic turned into a steady stream, and it was a while before I got to sit down again. When I did, I'd just gotten comfortable when somebody came up behind me and began to massage my shoulders.

"How's business, hon?"

"McQuaid!" I pushed myself out of the chair and greeted my husband and my son. "Hi, Brian. Got your camp all set up? I thought you guys weren't coming until later."

Brian, with a typical thirteen-year-old's

slouch, hung out a few cautious yards away, as if he wasn't sure that he wanted to be identified with this particular group of adults. "It *is* later," he pointed out, in that tone of condescending indifference that teenagers use to address the older generation. "Quarter to seven." He dodged away, boy-fashion, from my hug, then grabbed me around the waist, just to show that there were no hard feelings. That's how it is with thirteen-year-olds. Pseudo-sophisticates one minute, great little kids the next.

I looked at my watch, pretending astonishment. "No kidding. I wouldn't have guessed."

McQuaid surveyed our booth with a critical look. "Wouldn't that plant rack look better over here, China? You could put it at right angles to —"

"Forget it, friend," I said pleasantly. "Unless you want to take everything down and move it yourself, that is."

"Aren't we going to get something to eat before the show?" Brian demanded. "I'm starving." He doubled over, grabbing his stomach to demonstrate that death from malnutrition was imminent.

"Are you guys going to the Indigo Café?" Ruby asked. "Would you mind bringing something back for me?"

"I'm afraid you'll have to settle for a hot dog or a fajita," McQuaid replied. "I don't think there's time to get anything from the café. It was pretty crowded when we walked past."

Julia Child would no doubt be dismayed, but a hot dog slathered with yellow mustard (mustard is an herb, too) and loaded with pickle and onion tastes just great, especially when it's eaten while you're doing something interesting in the company of people you care about. McQuaid, Brian, and I sauntered up one side of Main Street and down the other, munching our hot dogs and slurping our sodas as we made a quick survey of the booths and I filled McQuaid in on the HIRC meeting of the night before and some of what had been said at the workshop. The stores were open, of course — the Mercantile Emporium, Texas Antique Treasures, Betty's Candle and Gift Shop, the Indigo Café — but the festival had also attracted a large vendor turnout, with displays of fascinating handcrafted wares: pottery, jewelry, clothing, art. Fascinating to me, at least, although Brian wasn't greatly impressed, since he couldn't locate any vendors selling lizards or spiders, and there weren't any out-of-print book stalls for McQuaid to browse. We sent Brian to deliver Ruby's hot dog and a large cup of iced tea, while McQuaid and I got in line for tickets to the melodrama.

⚘ As we stood there, I looked around and spotted several people I knew. Stella, wearing an exotic gold turban and an all-black dress painted with gold signs of the zodiac, had set up a fortune-telling booth near the front of the plaza. Sandra, with a look of forced cheerfulness, was selling theater tickets and handing out programs. Jerome was standing in the doorway of the Indigo Café across the street, his arms folded across his chest, a nervous traffic cop surveying the action, his eyebrows fluttering like pennants in the breeze. I smiled when I saw the clump of rosemary, rue, and mugwort, tied with red yarn, hanging beside the café's front door.

None of these three seemed to be having the time of their lives, and as McQuaid and I waited for Brian to catch up with us, I thought to myself that this must be a very difficult evening for all those who knew that Indigo was doomed to die — and that there wasn't a thing they could do about it. Unless Stella and Ruby came up with a pretty powerful protection spell, that is, or unless someone could persuade Casey to change his mind about signing the town's death warrant.

At that moment I turned and caught a glimpse of Les Osler ducking around the building, and wondered where he had stashed Shirley. After the play, I needed to track him down and learn her whereabouts. If the Whiz decided to weigh in on her behalf, I wanted to know where to find her.

Brian joined us and we went inside, where we could see just how hard everyone had worked to convert the old cotton gin into an art gallery and theater. The renovation was only partially completed, of course, and the building might not be habitable on a cold day in the middle of January. But on this balmy October evening, the corrugated iron walls, rusty metal trusses, and unfinished plywood floor faded into the background. What caught everyone's attention was the brightly illuminated display of large paintings, weavings, rugs, hangings, metal sculptures, turned wood vases, and even a few large pieces of blown glass, all artfully arranged in the large, open gallery space. Most of the work was displayed with a photograph of the artist and brochures about his or her work. Whoever had installed this show had done a masterful job, and I thought how sad it was that the gallery, with all the artistic potential it represented, was destined to be razed to make way for a strip mine.

A shallow wooden stage had been constructed near the back of the large building, with a black curtain rigged in front of it. McQuaid and I found seats on the wooden chairs in front of the stage. Brian had already latched onto a girl, and he brought her over to sit with us. He's a friendly kid who strikes up acquaintances as easily as striking a match, so I wasn't entirely surprised. She was slender and cute, with a pert grin, each ear studded with at least a half dozen earrings. When I asked her name, I learned that she was Diana Higgins, Sandra's daughter.

McQuaid gave Brian some money and he and Diana went back outside to get some buttered popcorn. (What's a melodrama without popcorn to munch and throw at the villain?) As they left, I happened to glance around and noticed Ellen Holt, standing up at the back of the seating area. She had changed since the workshop, into red slacks and a silky, cream-colored sleeveless top that was a perfect match to a flawless complexion. With her honey-colored hair tumbling down her back, she reminded me of a young Farah Fawcett.

Ellen caught me staring and gave me a friendly hi-there wave and a smile that showed dazzling white teeth and winsome dimples. I returned the wave with a smile, but I couldn't help feeling curious — and critical. Why had she come? Was she collecting more background for her book? Or was she meeting Derek?

But that was none of my business, and I turned resolutely around. If I hadn't been trapped in Allie's bathroom, I wouldn't know anything about Ellen and Derek. Anyway, I had something more pressing on my mind. While the kids were fetching the popcorn, I asked McQuaid how Brian seemed to be feeling since their discussion the night before.

"I think our talk helped," McQuaid replied. "And he's enjoying tonight — especially now that he's found a girl. He was acting a little bored before she came along." He grinned. "Why is it that teenagers have to pretend that they've been everywhere and done everything?"

"Don't ask me. I think I skipped being a teenager." I paused. "Did you find out any more about Henningson?" McQuaid had mentioned that he'd made a couple of phone calls that morning. As an ex-cop, he seems to have friends everywhere, and all of them owe him favors.

"My contact in San Antonio located a divorce record from four years ago, but that's it so far." McQuaid frowned. "The property settlement was handled out of court, and Henningson and his wife got a no-fault decree. Which covers a multitude of sins, from boredom, to one or both parties engaging in hanky-panky, to spouse abuse." McQuaid was right. In the old days, husbands and wives filed all kinds of interesting allegations against one another, while today's divorce court records don't begin to tell the real story behind the breakup. "I'll check the newspapers around that date, though," he added. "Henningson seems to be the social type, and his name may crop up in one of the society columns. And I'll try tracking down the ex-wife. Raissa Lennartz. She took back her maiden name."

Brian and Diana came back just then with an armload of popcorn and sodas, and we settled in comfortably as the curtain opened and the performance began. Scanning the program, I was reminded that the play had been written by Derek Cooper. Was that why Ellen was here? To witness his debut as a dramatist?

Whatever, *Indigo's Blue* was surprisingly well written, with plenty of fast, smart repartee, sly double entendre, and downright slapstick humor. Getting into the spirit of things, the audience gleefully hissed the villain, sighed with the heroine, and cheered the hero. The action took place in Old Indigo, in 1896. The town seamstress, Mrs. Violet Stitch (played by Miss Mayjean), and her widowed daughter, the beautiful, buxom Azure Knits (played by Sandra Higgins), are about to lose their modest home and business to the local bank. Just as the foreclosure papers are being served, in strides wealthy, ruthless Randy T. Lechalot (Carl), who magnanimously offers to pay Mrs. Stitch's debt and set her up in a posh retirement home in return for kisses on demand from the alluring Azure. Azure, however, is in love with The Lonely Stranger (Jerome), a tall, taciturn masked man who has Azure's best interests at heart.

The cast was rounded out by the severe librarian (Allie), the bumbling doctor, and the uninhibited madam, plus a few bit players. Madam Mamie, who is in league with Lechalot and eager to include Azure among her bevy of besmirched beauties, was costumed briefly and memorably in red, white, and blue spangles. Mamie was a special hit with the TV crew from San Antonio, who had brought their cameras to shoot some footage of the performance. I didn't see Derek anywhere — he was no doubt backstage, making sure that everything went smoothly — but I did catch another glimpse of Ellen. This time, she was slipping out the side door that opened onto the alley, the light glinting on the silvery clip that caught her tawny hair.

The play was a great hit, and the audience brought the cast back for several curtain calls. Afterward, everyone strolled through the gallery, admiring the artwork and actually buying some of it. Brian and Diana had gone off on an adventure of their own, and McQuaid and I were looking at one of Allie's handwoven rugs and wondering whether it was the right color for our living room, when a dull, hollow boom rattled the glass in the window beside us. The crowd stopped chattering and exchanged apprehensive looks.

Jolted, I stared at McQuaid. "That was a —"

"Truck bomb?" a man said beside me.

"A gas explosion?" his wife guessed.

"Shotgun," McQuaid snapped, and headed for the side door, with me on his heels.

The rest of the audience and some of the cast followed. Which was why, if you saw the film footage on the television newscast the next night, you might have seen Carl Holland holding back the crowd of spectators in front of what had once been Sandra Higgins's Bluebonnet Coffee Shop. You might have seen me there, too, standing open-mouthed next to Ruby, with Brian and Diana beside us, and Ellen, white and trembling, next to Diana. Loud country music was coming from the plaza — Willie Nelson and Waylon Jennings singing "Mama, Don't Let Your Babies Grow Up to Be Cowboys" — but the crowd itself was eerily silent.

It might have been a scene from the play, illuminated by the TV crew's lights. McQuaid knelt to take a brief look at the dead man, who had a gaping and bloody hole in his chest, and then disappeared into the boarded-up building from which the shot must have been fired. The man who was playing the town doctor took McQuaid's place beside the body and clumsily picked up a limp wrist. Then, looking as if he were about to throw up, he stood and said, "I can't feel any pulse."

Mrs. Violet Stitch looked grim. Madam Mamie stuffed her fists into her mouth to stifle a shriek, while beside her, Derek stood shocked and silent. The Lonely Stranger, still masked and wearing his white cowboy hat, put a protective arm around the shaking shoulders of the librarian, who stood stunned, her face under her stage makeup as white as her Gibson Girl blouse.

The man lying flat on his back, bleeding into the dust, was the librarian's uncle. Casey Ford was dead.

The music stopped suddenly and the silent crowd began to shuffle and mutter. In front of me, Carl leaned over to whisper into Brenda's ear, with cruel satisfaction, "Sonovabitch walked right into his own booby trap, did he? How obliging."

And Brenda, her voice grimly elated, replied, "Serves the bastard right, and saves the rest of us the trouble. Let's make him Citizen of the Year."

"Yeah, right." Carl grinned ironically. "Nothing's too good for the man who shot Liberty Valance."

I looked around and saw the same sentiment on the faces of a half-dozen other spectators. The town tyrant was out of the picture, and the townspeople were celebrating. Casey Ford's death had given Indigo a whole new lease on life.

Nine

One drop of indigo is enough to spoil a
whole bowl of milk.

— Javanese proverb

In rural counties, things don't happen as fast
as they do in cities. It was nearly thirty minutes before the sheriff's car drove up and
screeched to a stop in the street, sirens
howling and bubble lights searing the dark
night, followed fifteen minutes later by the
EMS ambulance, whose crew seemed to
have gotten the word that there was no point
in hurrying. By that time, McQuaid, who
had identified himself as a former homicide
detective and taken charge of things, had
moved everyone back to the other side of the
street, closed the Bluebonnet's open front
door, and found a sheet to cover up the
body.

After McQuaid had secured the building, Jerome, who seemed to want to be
useful, took off his mask and cowboy hat
and announced that he would take the
name of anyone who had seen anything
that might help the police with their inves-

185

tigation. That request, of course, was the crowd's clue to melt away. Crime scenes hold a morbid fascination for most people, but the same folks who crowd curiously around a dead body are usually not very anxious to be connected with it, especially when they're asked to leave their names. This was probably especially true here, since the victim's demise was being secretly celebrated by every citizen of Indigo.

Ruby and I collected Brian — and Diana, who seemed to have attached herself to him — and went back to our booth in the plaza, where we packed the merchandise into our tubs and stashed everything in Big Red Mama for overnight safekeeping. Taking the booth down always goes faster than putting it up, especially after we've sold out of a few items. Tonight, I noticed that I was low on herbal soap, potpourri, and four-inch pots of rosemary and Saint-John's-wort, and Ruby said that she had sold out of a couple of favorites. We also had a pair of helpers, who made the work go faster. Brian, of course, was nonchalantly indifferent, but Diana was willing and interested. She even offered to help us out the next day.

"I think it would be really beast," she said enthusiastically. "I've worked for my mom lots of times when she ran the Bluebonnet, and I'm really good at handling loot."

"Beast?" I asked.

"Awesome," she said. "Choice. Cool. I'm stellar when it comes to making change."

"Sure, you can help," Ruby said, smiling. "There's always room for a stellar helper." Her smile included Brian. "Even two stellar helpers."

"I could help," Brian said, his eyes going to Diana, "if Dad and I weren't fishing." We all looked up at the sound of the police siren. "Hey!" he said excitedly. "It's the sheriff. Cool! Come on, Diana. Let's beagle on over and see what my dad is doing. He used to be a cop, you know. He's probably got this case solved already."

Beagle on over?

"Well, he ought to have it solved," Diana retorted tartly. "Weren't you listening to what people were saying? Everybody in Indigo knows that Mr. Ford blew himself up with his own booby trap. I bet my mom thinks it's bitchin'," she added knowingly. "It was shiznits when that hairball wouldn't renew her lease. She definitely zoned out. Had a real melt-down. Now he's cashed it in, maybe she can open up again."

I couldn't have translated word for word, but I managed to get the general gist. Now that Casey was dead, Sandra Higgins would have a shot at reopening her coffee shop — although she probably wouldn't appreciate her daughter telling a stranger how glad she was that the owner had been shot.

"Don't you have to go home, Diana?" I asked. "It's after ten. Your mother will be worried about you."

"Oh, she's cool," Diana said with careless assurance. "Anyway, we live right behind the Bluebonnet, so I'm practically home already. If it was daylight, you could see the back of our house from here. My rabbit hutch, too," she added, with a glance at Brian. "That's where Ethel and her babies live."

"You've got baby rabbits?" Brian asked enviously, forgetting for a moment about the arrival of the sheriff. "Cool. Can I see?"

"Sure," Diana agreed, and the kids raced off.

"Better baby bunnies than dead bodies," I said to Ruby. Especially a dead body with an indecently large hole in the chest.

"Diana's found the way to that boy's heart already," Ruby agreed. She closed

Mama's door and took her keys out of her purse. "Would you like me to drive? We've been up since six this morning. I really hate to miss all the excitement" — she nodded toward the Bluebonnet — "but I need to get some sleep."

I stood still. Casey Ford's death might have been an accident, but on the other hand, maybe it wasn't. And if it was murder, there was no shortage of suspects. While I didn't want to interfere with the investigation, I should probably tell the sheriff what I knew. The way the towns-people felt about Casey, it was very un-likely that they would volunteer any information. Anyway, I needed to talk to Allie.

"If you're tired, why don't you go on to the cabin without me?" I suggested. "I can ride back with Allie, or with McQuaid. He probably won't be staying much longer — there's nothing for him to do, now that the sheriff is here." Law enforcement officers take a strongly proprietary attitude toward crimes committed in their jurisdiction. This sheriff wouldn't want McQuaid hang-ing around.

Ruby frowned indecisively, torn between her curiosity about Casey's death and her very real weariness. Then she sighed and climbed into Mama.

"See you later," she said, closing the door and turning the key in the ignition. Then, as an afterthought, she rolled down the window. "I forgot to tell you that the Whiz returned our call while you were watching the play. She'd like to talk to us about Shirley, and maybe meet her. She'll be here tomorrow around noon."

Shirley. I paused. Casey Ford's death was going to have a great many interesting consequences. I could guess what it might mean to the town. I wondered what it would mean for his sister.

The front door of the Cotton Gin Theater was locked and the gallery area was dark, but when I went around the building and walked down the alley, I found the side door propped open with a brick. Inside, only a couple of bare bulbs were lit, and the backstage area looked like a setting in a grainy black-and-white film. I found Allie, alone, in a screened-off area that bore the crayoned sign WOMEN'S DRESSING room. She had changed and scrubbed off her makeup. She turned and saw me. She was very white. Her eyes were large and dark, and her chest was rising and falling as if she had been running.

"What a terrible thing, Allie," I said, going to her and putting my arms around her with instinctive compassion — not for Casey, who was past sympathy, but for her, for all she was going through. "I know this must be very painful for you."

She stepped back, turning away. "He brought it on himself," she said, her voice thick. "He made people hate him. Everybody in Indigo hated him. His sister hated him. I hated him." She swallowed audibly. "Isn't that awful, China? My mother's only brother, the only connection I had left to her in the whole world — and I despised him! All I feel inside when I think that he's dead is a terrible kind of rejoicing, for me, for Shirley, for Indigo, for all the land that he planned to destroy." She clenched her fists, her face twisting with raw pain. "Casey's dead, and I'm glad. God, I'm so glad it hurts. And I keep thinking how terrible Mom would feel if she heard me say it. I'm glad *she's* dead, too, and doesn't have to witness this."

"You don't sound glad," I said in a practical tone. "You sound like you're in shock. Anyway, regardless of how you feel — glad, sad, whatever — your uncle's death isn't your fault. You had nothing to do with it. What you need is a stiff drink and a hot

191

shower and a good night's sleep." I paused and added, "But the sheriff showed up a few minutes ago. It might be a good idea if you postponed the drink and the shower long enough to introduce yourself to him."

Her head snapped around. "The sheriff? Why would I want to do that? I don't know anything about —" She stopped and swallowed again, and her gaze slid away. With her next words, something in her voice changed, and her face had taken on a sullen, closed look. "I don't have anything to tell him."

I acknowledged the uneasiness that prickled at the back of my neck and pigeon-holed it for now. "Well, for starters, you could tell him that you're Casey Ford's niece and give him your phone number and address. And you could offer to help him with his investigation in any way you can." I put on a wry grin and lightened my tone. "Hey, I wouldn't tell you to do this if it wasn't important, Allie. This cops-and-robbers stuff used to be my business, remember? I'm an expert at what to tell the police, and when. Trust me."

She stared at me for a moment, her eyes giving nothing away. "I don't need an attorney, China. *Nobody* in Indigo needs an attorney. This was Casey's own doing.

After he closed Sandra's coffee shop down, he told everybody he was booby-trapping the building, and that anybody messing around would be sorry. He bragged about it."

"Did he say what kind of trap he'd rigged?"

"What kind? A shotgun." She frowned. "That's what killed him, wasn't it?"

"Well, do you think he rigged the trap and then forgot about it?" That didn't seem likely. Somebody who was determined enough to set up a trap would surely be smart enough to stay away from it.

"Maybe he thought he'd disarmed it, and he hadn't." Allie's voice was stronger, with an edge. "Anyway, that's what happened. He was killed by his own booby trap. And that's what I'm going to tell the sheriff." She picked up her purse and slung it over her shoulder. "Let's go, for God's sake. Let's get this over with."

Sheriff Montgomery was a tall, thin young man with an unlined face and eyes that hadn't yet seen a great many shotgun deaths. He was also, as I found out when Allie and I were introduced to him in the street in front of the Bluebonnet, one of

McQuaid's former Criminal Justice students at CTSU. I managed not to frown when I heard this, although I could see that it might lead to complications.

"The best and the brightest," McQuaid added, with pride. "I didn't realize that you'd gone and gotten yourself elected Dalton County Sheriff, Charlie. When did that happen?"

"I wasn't elected," the sheriff said, in a slow, self-conscious drawl. "Sheriff McFarland, he had a heart attack six weeks ago and had to resign. I'd just signed on as his chief deputy, so the county commissioners appointed me to fill out the few months he had left in his term." He looked down at his shoes and added, in a lower voice, "Hate t'say it, sir, but this is my first murder case. We get the usual stuff — traffic accidents, cows on the road, dogs after the neighbor's goats. But we don't have many shotgun killings here in Dalton County."

I looked at McQuaid, knowing exactly what I was going to hear. I could have mouthed the words as he said them.

"I'd be glad to help if I can, Charlie. A job like this, a man could use a pair of extra hands."

Charlie looked up quickly and I could

read the relief on his face. "That 'ud be fine, sir. 'Preciate any help I can get, 'specially from you."

"Speaking of help," I said, and nudged Allie. In a quick, terse sentence, she recited her name, her relationship to Casey Ford, her address, and her phone number. The sheriff took a notebook out of his shirt pocket and jotted it down.

"I guess you'll want to talk to me," she went on, "but I hope it won't be tonight. I'm really tired, and I don't feel very good. This —" Her eyes went to the EMS ambulance, where the justice of the peace, a bearded, heavyset man, was peering at the motionless figure that had been loaded onto the gurney. In Texas, the JP is required to certify every death, from gory roadkills to the quiet deaths in the local nursing home with the family gathered around. "This is quite a shock."

"I understand, ma'am," the sheriff said quietly. "But there's one thing I need to ask tonight, if you don't mind. One of the owners of the Indigo Café — Jerome, his name is — says that your uncle rigged a booby trap in that building. Do you know if that's true?"

Allie nodded. "When I saw what had happened, that was the first thing I thought of. I guess everybody here thought of it, too." She licked dry lips. "That he'd set off his own trap, I mean. And it killed him."

"I see." The sheriff wrote something down, then looked up. "You're his next of kin?"

"Not really. He has a stepsister, Shirley. But I don't think you should . . ." She hesitated, as if she were trying to decide how much to say. "That is, it probably wouldn't be a good idea for you to go over there tonight, if that's what you're planning to do. Shirley isn't . . . well, she's not legally competent. My uncle is . . . was her guardian. They lived together. This is going to be a shock to her, too."

"I see," the sheriff said gravely. He closed his notebook and put it back in his shirt pocket. "Well, Miz Selby, what d'ya reckon is the best way to handle this? This stepsister oughtta be notified, and it sounds like she might need some help."

I looked at Allie. "Maybe we could drive over there," I suggested. "I know you're tired, but —"

"That might be the best idea, at least for tonight," the sheriff said gently. "If you don't mind."

Allie's mouth tightened. "Well, it's com-

196

plicated. Shirley and Casey have been having some trouble and —" She frowned and added, reluctantly, ". . . she might not be there."

"Trouble?" the sheriff asked without inflection.

✿ "Oh, not really." Allie looked away. "Just a sort of . . . well, family thing. But you're right. Shirley might need some help." She sighed and turned to me, resigned. "I guess you're right, China. Let's go over there and see what we can do."

I thought of lingering to speak to the sheriff, but since it looked as if McQuaid was going to be involved in this investigation I could tell him what I'd heard from the townspeople — but not now, not in Allie's hearing.

McQuaid walked with us to Allie's truck, which was parked on the street near the Cotton Gin Theater. Allie got in and turned the key in the ignition, but before I could slide into the passenger seat, he took me by the arm.

"I'm going to hang out here for a while," he said in a low voice. "I'd like to do what I can to help Charlie. The kid could be in over his head."

"Yeah, right," I said dryly. "What about the other kid? Won't Brian be bored while

197

his dad's playing detective?"

McQuaid motioned with his head, and I turned to see Brian and Diana sitting on a bench in front of the Indigo Café across the street, the light spilling from the window onto their shoulders. They were taking turns drinking out of a soda can, and she was laughing at something Brian had said. Their hands were touching.

"Love at first sight," McQuaid said with a smile. "I can recognize the symptoms from here."

"But he's too young," I protested. "He's not even fourteen, for pity's sake!"

"I had a girl when I was his age. And he's forgotten all about Sally and Henningson — a good thing, in my book." McQuaid bent and kissed me swiftly, still speaking low enough so that Allie couldn't hear him. "Charlie and I can't do much here tonight, so I'll take Brian back to the camp as soon as we wind up a few things. I've got eggs and bacon and stuff in the cooler. How about you and Ruby joining us for breakfast tomorrow morning, say around seven? I'd like to pick your brain about these Indigo folks."

"Allie, too?"

"No, I —" He paused. "No, not Allie." He gave me a quick kiss and raised his voice. "Oh, and bring your bug stuff. It looks like a great fishing tank, but there's some heavy-duty mosquitoes in the neighborhood. Strong enough to haul off a horse."

He sauntered off, hands in his pockets, whistling tunelessly. I shook my head as I climbed into Allie's truck. There's nothing like first love to bring out the man in a boy, and nothing like a murder to bring out the boy in an ex-cop.

Ten

FALSE INDIGO

Don't be deceived by the beautiful blue flowers of *Baptisia australis,* a showy wildflower that's very popular in perennial gardens, nor by the Latin name of *B. tinctoria* ("tinctoria" means "used by dyers," a misnomer in this case). Both are called wild indigo or false indigo, but I've never gotten appreciable color from any part of them, and I've never met anyone else who did, either. Grow them for their beauty, not for dyeing.

> *A Dyer's Garden*
> — Rita Buchanan

The nautical term "sailing under true colors" comes from a time when the only way to identify a ship was by the flag it flew (its colors). A ship might carry the flags of many nations; it would fly false colors to lure another ship within striking distance, then raise its true colors, showing its real intentions, and attack.

> "The Symbolic Meaning of Color"
> — Ruby Wilcox

200

The house where Shirley and Casey lived was less than a mile from Allie's place, down a narrow, winding gravel road densely overhung with trees. The road dead-ended in front of an old frame farmhouse, where a mercury-vapor yard light illuminated a sagging clothesline, the towels and pillowcases stirring like pale ghosts among the restless shadows. I surmised that Shirley preferred to hang out the laundry, or her stepbrother hadn't bothered to invest in labor-saving appliances; knowing something about Casey, I could guess which. There was one light in the two-story house, on the lower floor, at the back. There was no sign of Les Osler's red Harley.

"The light's on in the kitchen," Allie said. "Shirley must still be up." She put her hand on the horn and held it there, then tapped it twice. A long and two shorts. It might have been a signal.

A light went on somewhere else in the house, followed by the porch light. The lace curtain on the door was pushed aside, then Shirley opened the door and came out onto the porch. She was wearing the same shirt and shorts that she'd worn earlier, only now she was barefoot.

We got out of the truck and went up on the porch. Shirley stared at us, her hair a dark tangle, the purple smudge under her eye standing out against the pallor of her face.

"He's dead," she said in a high-pitched, childlike voice. "Casey's dead." It was an announcement, not a question, and she didn't bother to hide her jubilation. Under the circumstances, I couldn't quite bring myself to blame her.

"So much for breaking it to her gently," Allie said to me in a low voice.

"News travels fast," I said. Then more loudly, "How'd you find out so quick, Shirley?"

"Me 'n Les was in town." She pulled her shoulders back, straightening up as though she had shed a burden, and stretched her arms above her head, all quite unself-consciously.

Allie seemed wary. "Where's Les now?"

"Went home to feed his dogs and get some clothes. He said to put on some coffee and he'd be back." She lowered her arms and pushed her hair out of her face. "You want some coffee?"

Coffee was the last thing I needed at this hour of the night, but after we'd sat down at the yellow formica-and-chrome kitchen table, I let her pour me half a cup, then filled it the rest of the way with milk she took from the fridge. A quick glance told me that in spite of the peeling wallpaper, the bare lightbulb over the sink, and the heavy odor of cigars that fouled the air, the room was clean and tidy — a few dishes stacked in the drainer on the counter, the linoleum floor swept, the table cleared except for a plastic caddy shaped like a rooster that held salt, pepper, sugar, and two squeeze bottles, red for catsup, yellow for mustard. A tempting pie with a deliciously browned crust sat under a clear cake cover. If Casey Ford had valued clean clothes and pies, I could see why he might want to keep his stepsister around.

Shirley poured herself a cup of coffee, black, then took a fresh package of filter cigarettes out of a drawer and opened it. She put one in her mouth, turned on a burner on the gas range and bent over, holding her hair back, to light the cigarette — inexpertly, as if she were just learning how. I wondered if Casey had forbidden her to smoke, and now that he was dead, she intended to do it. She sucked in a lungful of smoke, proudly, then came back to the table.

"Yep, he's dead," she said with gleeful satisfaction, sitting down and putting a black glass Coors Beer ashtray on the table in front of her. "Wouldn't of b'lieved it if I didn't see it myself." She touched her cheek gingerly. "Now he cain't hit me no more."

"So you were in Indigo when he got killed?" I asked in a conversational tone. "Near where it happened?"

"Near 'nough." She took a swallow of coffee. "Jes' down the street, across from the old schoolhouse. I was sittin' on the curb next to the Harley, waitin' for Les."

Allie took a deep breath. "You actually saw it happen? You saw Casey walk into his booby trap?" Her voice was strained.

"Booby trap?" Frowning, Shirley pulled on her cigarette and blew a stream of smoke out of both nostrils. She coughed, then broke into a fit of coughing. When she'd managed to get her breath, she said, "I don't know nothin' 'bout no booby trap."

Allie didn't look at me. "Casey bragged to *everybody* about setting booby traps in the buildings he'd boarded up. He didn't tell you?"

Still holding her cigarette, Shirley picked up her cup and held it in both hands, the smoke curling around her face. She took a swallow of coffee. "Casey didn't talk much," she said. "Lots of times three, four days 'ud go by with him never sayin' a word. I got so lonesome I'd sing to myself, just for comp'ny." She smiled, anticipating. "Les says I can have me a tee-vee, now Casey's gone. A radio, too."

"So you didn't actually *see* your stepbrother get shot," I said gently.

"I heard it." Shirley put her cup down. "I had my head turned the other way, lookin' for Les." Her eyes glittered. "Shitfire, did I hear it. Scared me. Great big *blam!*" Another long pull on the cigarette, and ragged blue curls of smoke escaping from the nostrils. "Then I turned around and saw somebody layin' in the street, and people come runnin' from ever'where. Didn't figger it was Casey, though. Not then."

"When did you find out?"

"When Les come back. He told me."

Allie leaned forward. "And where was Les when it happened?"

A soft smile played around Shirley's mouth, and for a moment she looked almost pretty. "Findin' me a place to stay. When he heard 'bout Casey whoppin' me, he said I couldn't stay here no more. I couldn't stay at your place neither, so we rode into town so's he could see if one of his friends could hide me." She lifted her head at the sound of a vehicle. "Somebody's comin'."

"I'll see who it is." Allie got up and went down the hall to the front door.

"What do you think happened to your stepbrother?" I asked, when she had gone.

Shirley shrugged. "Reckon somebody shot him. Weren't many liked him, 'specially after he began to figger on sellin' out to the coal mine."

"He told you about that?"

"He said he had to get my name on the papers."

I frowned. If Casey owned the property, he could do as he wished. If she had an interest in it and he was her legal guardian, he could act for her. Either way, he wouldn't need her signature. What was going on here?

My question was forestalled by the sound of voices at the front door and steps in the hallway. Allie and Miss Mayjean came into the kitchen.

Shirley hurriedly stubbed out her cigarette, her face breaking into a wide smile. "Miss Mayjean!" she exclaimed, jumping up. Her face was suffused with a childish pleasure. "I cain't believe it's you!"

"I figured you might need some company, Shirley," Miss Mayjean said. She put the dish down on the counter and held out her arms. "It's been too long, child. Come here and give your old teacher a big hug."

"Teacher?" I whispered to Allie, as the two women put their arms around each other.

"Miss Mayjean taught first grade in Indigo," Allie said. "She had every kid in town."

After an emotional embrace, Miss Mayjean poured herself a cup of coffee, sat down at the table, and blew her nose loudly on a hanky she took from her pocket. "It's been years since I was in this kitchen," she said, looking around. "Janece and I used to sit at this very table — it was new then, and belonged to *her* mother — and talk about who we were going to marry when we grew up. That was when we were just girls, hardly big enough to bake a pan of biscuits." She sighed. "Life has got a way of sendin' you stuff you wouldn't've ordered for yourself."

"Janece?" I asked.

"My momma," Shirley said. I noticed that she had scooped the cigarette package and ashtray off the table, as if she didn't want Miss Mayjean to see that she had been smoking.

"Shirley's mother and I were real close,

once," Miss Mayjean said. "Shirley's daddy didn't mind us bein' friends, but Frank Ford, he was a different story. When Janece married him, he told me to stop comin' around. Said I was a bad influence." She waved a hand, grinning crookedly. "Hell, he was prob'bly right. The older I get, the badder my influence is. You weren't around then, were you, Shirley? How old were you when Janece and Frank got married?"

"Seventeen," Shirley replied. She blushed. "That was when I got myself in trouble."

"Well, that's water under the bridge," Miss Mayjean said briskly. "We won't talk about it now. I brought my suitcase, Shirley. I thought you might like me to stay a few days. Till you get straightened out and know what you're going to do."

Shirley pulled her eyebrows together, giving this some thought. "Well," she said finally, "I'd like that, Miss Mayjean, I really would. But Les, he said he'd stay, and —"

"I thought so," Miss Mayjean said. "I've been seein' that big motorcycle of his buzzin' up and down the road past my place. I figured he was comin' here to see you when Casey wasn't around."

Shirley sighed. "Yeah. That's why Casey

hit me. 'Cuz he came home and found Les sittin' here at the table. Les talked back to him, and after he left, Casey whopped me." She brushed a hand to her cheek.

Miss Mayjean leaned forward, her eyes warm, her wrinkled face grave. "You're a grown woman, Shirley, and I don't aim to tell you what to do. But I will tell you straight out, as your momma's nearest and dearest friend, that she would not like Les Osler sleepin' in this house with you. Not till you get married — if you do. Marriage is something you need to give some serious thought to, 'fore you go jumpin' into it."

She lifted a hand, tenderly, and touched Shirley's bruised cheek. "Now that Casey's gone, things'll be different, Shirley. You don't need Les to rescue you and take you away, like some fairy-tale knight rescuing a princess out of a tower. You're on your own now, which means you've got to learn to be independent and take care of yourself. That doesn't mean you have to stop seein' Les, if that's what you really want to do. But you don't have to marry him to get away, or to have some company."

It was a long speech. Shirley listened intently, looking down at her fingers twisted together, mulling it over. At last she said, "I reckon you're right, Miss Mayjean.

About Les stayin' here, I mean. It ain't gonna please him none, but —"

She was interrupted by the deep, full-throated roar of Les's Harley. We heard a spray of gravel, hurrying steps on the porch, and the front door opening.

"Shirley?" Les yelled. "Shirley, you okay? Who's in there with you, Shirley?"

Shirley got up, fetched a mug, and poured it full of coffee. As Les strode into the room, a ring of keys jingling from his wide leather belt, she put it on the table. "Want some pie to go with your coffee, Les?" she asked.

Les stopped inside the kitchen, his eyes going from one of us to the other. He was still wearing the same tank top and dirty jeans that he'd had on earlier, and the scent of motorcycle oil, cigarette smoke, and cheap whiskey hung around him like a fog.

"Good evenin', Miss Mayjean," he said, with a curt nod. He dropped his head and looked bullishly at Allie, then at me. "What're you two doin' here?"

"Why, they come to see me, Les," Shirley said, surprised. "Why else would they be here?"

"The sheriff asked China and me to tell Shirley about Casey," Allie replied. She pushed back her coffee mug and stood up. "But she already knew, so I guess we'll go on home."

"The sheriff?" Les's tone was sharp. He pulled out a chair and turned it around, straddling it, leaning his elbows on the back. His right bicep carried the tattoo *Born to Raise Hell.*

"The sheriff is investigating Casey's death," I said.

Les made a noise in his throat. "Stupid waste of time," he said scornfully. "Any damn fool can see that Casey set off his own booby trap. It was an accident."

"Maybe so. But that's for Sheriff Montgomery to decide." I stood and put a hand on Shirley's shoulder, smiling down at her. "When he comes to talk to you tomorrow, Shirley, be sure you tell him exactly what you told us a few minutes ago."

Les had picked up his coffee. He put it down and scowled at Shirley. "What did you tell them, Shirl?"

"Only what happened." Shirley's eyes were wide, and she sounded anxious. "That I was sittin' beside the Harley when it happened, and then you come along an' told me it was Casey got killed." She swallowed nervously. "Did I say something wrong?"

211

"Wrong?" Les didn't look pleased to be stuck with Shirley's version of the evening's events, but he forced a tight grin and his tone softened. "No, I don't reckon you did, babe. Best to stay out of this as much as you can, though. You don't know nothin' 'bout it." He picked up his mug and said it again, more emphatically. "You don't know *nothin'* 'bout it, y'hear? Now, how 'bout rustlin' me up some of that pie?"

I turned to Les, remembering that I had seen him when McQuaid and I were standing out in front of the Cotton Gin Theater. "Did you have any luck locating a place for Shirley to stay in town?" I asked amiably.

"No," he growled. "As a matter of fact, I didn't. Nobody I asked had any room. Then Casey got blown away and I figured Shirley might as well come back here." He took a swallow of coffee, his eyes flinty over the rim of his mug. "How come you're askin'?"

"Oh, no reason," I said. It would be up to the sheriff to get a list of the people Les claimed to have talked to, which might or might not establish an alibi. "Thanks for the coffee, Shirley."

"Come any time," Shirley said. She gave

212

us a ghost of a smile. "Now that Casey's not around to run you off."

Les looked at Miss Mayjean. "Miss Mayjean," he said, "ain't it a little late for you to be out? Maybe you better go on home, too. I told Shirley I'd stay over."

"These may be old eyes but they still see in the dark," Miss Mayjean retorted tartly. "Anyway, I'm stayin' the night, so you don't have to." She smiled, a school-teacher's smile, showing pink-gummed dentures. "It was neighborly of you to offer, though, Les. I'm sure Shirley 'preciates it."

Les blinked. "Shirley? I thought we was gonna —"

"It wouldn't be right, Les," Shirley said. "People might talk. Anyway, with Casey gone, I got to do some thinkin'." She stood up and took a knife out of a drawer. "But I'll get you that pie before you go. It's apple." She looked at Miss Mayjean. "Miss Mayjean, you want some, too?"

"I surely do," Miss Mayjean said pleasantly, folding her hands on the table. "There's nothin' I like better in this world than a big piece of apple pie before I go to bed."

Les hunched his shoulders and growled something I couldn't quite hear. When

Allie and I left, Shirley was cutting the pie.

"WHOZZIT?" Ruby muttered sleepily as I came in.

"Just me," I said, stripping off my clothes. I didn't have to light the kerosene lamp, because the moonlight was streaming through the open screened windows, tracing shadowy bars across the floor. The light made the room seem mysterious, as if it held hidden secrets.

Ruby rubbed her eyes and sat up. "Did you talk to Shirley? How did she take the news?"

"It wasn't news to her," I said, setting my travel alarm and putting it on the corner table between our beds. "She was close enough to see the action." As I pulled on the old pink T-shirt I sleep in, I sketched the events of the last hour, concluding with Miss Mayjean's neat ouster of Les.

"I'm glad Miss Mayjean came over," Ruby said sleepily, rearranging her pillow and lying back down. "It was sweet of her to step in and help." I could hear the smile in her voice. "I hope she doesn't just take over, though. Shirley doesn't need somebody else to take charge of her life. She has to learn to be independent."

214

I smiled into the darkness, thinking of the way the old lady had handled the situation. "I think independence is high on Miss Mayjean's priority list."

Ruby turned over, face to the wall. "But the way you describe the situation, China, it doesn't sound like there's a thing wrong with Shirley." Drowsy, she was slurring her words. "With her thought processes, I mean."

"I agree," I said, sliding between cool sheets that smelled faintly of lavender from Allie's garden. "And if that's true, it raises another interesting question. What kind of power did Casey — and his father before him — wield over Shirley? How did they manage to keep her under their control for so long?" I thought for a moment. "Maybe she was being blackmailed. Maybe the Fords, father and son, knew something, something she did in the past. Maybe they were holding it over her head." I frowned, not liking the scenario I was spinning. It provided Shirley with plenty of motive for getting rid of her stepbrother. She wouldn't have had to do it herself, either, as long as she could persuade Les to do it for her.

I raised up. "What do you think, Ruby? Does it sound like blackmail to you?"

But the only answer I got was a soft, buzzy snore. Ruby had conked out.

I lay awake for a while, watching the silvery moon-bars slide across the shadows, listening to the serenade of cicadas and frogs in the woods behind the cabin. Then I fell asleep and didn't wake up until the alarm went off at six-thirty in the morning.

Eleven

CINNAMON BASIL HONEY

1 cup honey
2-inch cinnamon stick,
    broken into several pieces
$1/8$ teaspoon cloves
1 tablespoon brandy
3 sprigs cinnamon basil

In a saucepan, gently heat together honey, spices, and brandy. Put the basil sprigs into a sterilized jar and pour the hot honey mixture over it. Cover and allow the flavor to mellow for about a week. Tasty on French toast, pancakes, and waffles.

"What time is it?" Ruby asked groggily, when the alarm went off. She propped herself up on her elbow to peer at the clock, then slid back down and pulled the sheet over her face. "It's only six-thirty," she said in a muffled voice. "The festival doesn't open for hours and hours. Why are we getting up so early?"

"Because McQuaid is fixing breakfast at the camp down at the lake," I said cheerfully, zipping my jeans. "He'll have coffee. Juice, too, and eggs."

"Coffee," Ruby mumbled, under the sheet. "Coffee."

"And be sure to put on plenty of bug stuff," I added, pulling on a sweatshirt. "He says the mosquitoes have teeth."

"Coffee before dawn," Ruby said blurrily. "Mosquitoes with teeth." She groaned. "I'll be a good sport if it kills me. How do I get to the camp?"

I combed my short hair with my fingers. As I glanced through the window, I saw that the morning sky was heavy with ominous clouds — not the sort of weather you like to wake up to when you're planning a day at an outdoor craft festival.

"Go past the dye kitchen and take the path along the creek." I pushed my feet into my sneakers. "Or you can walk around by the road. It's a little longer, but there probably won't be as many chiggers."

"Chiggers," Ruby muttered. "Mosquitoes. Spiders. Nature with tooth and claw, in the raw." She jerked the sheet off her face and raised her head, eyes wide. "What was that noise I just heard, China? It can't be —"

"Thunder, I'm afraid," I said regretfully. "But it's still pretty far away. I don't think it will rain on breakfast, but the sky isn't getting any lighter."

"Oh, no," she groaned. "Don't tell me the festival's going to get rained out!"

"One rumble doesn't make a thunderstorm," I replied optimistically. "Anyway, we've got several hours before we have to leave for Indigo. Maybe it's just a passing shower." I slathered on some repellant, gave Ruby a wave, and left.

Outside, where I could see the sky, I didn't feel quite so optimistic. The clouds to the north were building, and the wind stirred the leaves. I took the path along the creek, braving the chiggers. If you prefer a sanitized country life — closely clipped lawns, brick paths, electronic bug zappers — the Texas Blackland Prairie is not the place to linger, especially in October, when the brambles and greenbriar are at the peak of their glory and the bugs have heeded the divine directive to be fruitful and multiply. But if you prefer nature uncivilized, there's nothing better than a narrow green path along a clear creek, on a cool, cloudy morning when you can smell the rain in the air, liberally laced with the heady scent of wild honeysuckle.

219

And bacon. I could smell the bacon long before I saw the blue tent that McQuaid and Brian had set up in a clearing next to the lake. Brian, wearing a cap with the bill turned backward, was fishing along the shore about thirty yards away, under a huge weeping willow. McQuaid, dressed in jeans and a blue plaid shirt, was stirring pancakes under a yellow plastic tarp slung over the picnic table, while bacon strips sizzled in a cast-iron skillet propped on large rocks over a small, neat campfire — a Boy Scout's campfire.

"Morning, China," he said cheerfully. "Nice that you could drop in."

I came up close, put my arms around his waist, and snuggled against his broad back. "Good morning," I said. "Sleep well?"

He set down the pancake bowl and turned to hold me, tipping my face for a kiss. "Would've slept better if you'd been in my sleeping bag." He pushed his hands up under my sweatshirt, touching my breasts, and I shivered.

"Hey, look what I found," he said, his lips against mine. "I've got a great idea. Let's you and me duck into the tent for a quickie before my wife comes along and catches us. She's the jealous type."

I laughed, kissed him again, and pushed

him away. "I thought you invited me here to feed me, and now I find out that you've got sex on your mind."

"Always." He turned and cupped his hands to his mouth. "Hey, Brian, come on back. I'm about to cook up a mess of pancakes."

"But the fish are biting!" Brian yelled, pulling up on his rod. As we watched, he reeled in a wriggling fish so small I could scarcely see it. He held it up proudly. "See? I'm going to have it for breakfast. But it's not big enough, so I'll have to catch another one."

"I hope he remembers how to clean that fish," I said. Thunder rumbled again. "Drat this weather. If we get some serious rain, we can scratch the festival."

McQuaid went back to the pancakes. "Can't the vendors set up their booths in the Cotton Gin Theater?"

"Probably. But people don't come to an outdoor festival in the rain. No customers, no sales." I was being realistic. Ruby and I have been rained out before. When it happens, you can hang around and discuss the weather with the other vendors, or you can pack your stuff and head for home.

McQuaid poured two large pancakes onto a hot griddle on the camp stove.

"Coffee's ready," he said, motioning with his head to the blue enamel pot beside the fire.

McQuaid learned how to make camp coffee in the Boy Scouts, where they dump ground coffee and an egg, shell and all, into a pot of water and bring it to a boil. The egg is supposed to settle the grounds, or at least that's the theory. In practice, you pour carefully and strain the liquid through your teeth. I sampled, shuddered, and opted for the bottle of cranberry juice that was sitting on the table.

McQuaid flipped the pancakes. "The coffee'll be better tomorrow." He was deadpan.

"It can't help but be better," I said, taking a couple of eggs out of the cooler. "It couldn't be worse." I bent over, peering into the pot. "You don't suppose one of Brian's sneakers jumped in here by accident, do you?"

"Ha-ha. Old Boy Scout joke. Old as the hills and twice as dusty."

Smiling, I forked the bacon out of the skillet onto a plate covered with a paper towel. We don't often eat bacon at home, but I operate on the hypothesis that when you're dining under an open sky, fat grams don't count. I poured out most of the grease, cracked a couple of eggs into the little that was left, let them cook for a minute, then slopped a glug of water into the hot skillet and clapped on the lid. Eggs cooked this way are steamed, sort of. If I'd been at home, I would have added fresh parsley and garlic chives, but McQuaid's camping pantry doesn't include such niceties.

McQuaid slid the pancakes onto a plate and poured two more puddles of batter onto the griddle. A few minutes later, we were sitting across from one another at the picnic table, our paper plates filled with bacon and eggs and pancakes covered with cinnamon basil honey.

"Ah," McQuaid said happily, swallowing coffee. "Strong enough to raise blood blisters on a boot." He looked at me over the rim of his cup, laugh lines crinkling the corners of his eyes. "Sure you don't want a cup, China?"

"Thanks, I'll pass." Enjoying the fresh air and the food, enjoying the sight of my husband across the picnic table, I lifted my plastic cup of cranberry juice in a toast. "Here's to investigations. What time did you and Brian get back to the camp last night?"

"Just before eleven. Charlie and I taped

off the crime scene and left a deputy parked out front to keep an eye on things." McQuaid picked up the honey jar. "I looked for Allison's truck in front of the house as we drove past, but I didn't see it."

"I guess we hadn't got back from Casey's house yet," I said. "Shirley's house, I suppose it is now. Want to hear?"

"I'm all ears." McQuaid dribbled honey on his pancakes. "How did she react when you told her that her brother was dead?"

"She already knew," I replied, and reported as much of the conversation as I could remember, prefacing it with a quick outline of the visit that Les and Shirley had paid to Allie the previous afternoon.

"One of the things that interests me," I went on, "is that Shirley is supposed to be in such dire mental straits that the court assigned her a keeper. But while she may be uneducated and doesn't seem to have much experience of the world, I saw no evidence of mental disability — certainly not enough to cause her to be declared incompetent. And she mentioned something about having to sign the documents for the sale of the mining rights. I'm wondering whether she really was Casey's legal ward, or whether he — and his father before him

— managed to pull the wool over her eyes."

"Is that really likely?" McQuaid was skeptical. "In Queen Victoria's day, maybe, but not now." He grinned. "Not after women got the vote — and the Pill."

"What's the vote and the Pill got to do with it?" I licked honey off my fork. "Allie said that Shirley was involved with drugs at one time. Maybe she was in a lot worse shape fifteen years ago than she is now, and her stepfather thought it was the only way to keep her out of an institution." That was putting it into a charitable light. "Or maybe they knew she had done something pretty terrible and they were using the knowledge to control her. Allie says she went to prison for three or four years for shooting a man. Maybe she got into more trouble, and —"

"Let me see if I have this straight," McQuaid said, frowning. "This woman is being knocked around by her stepbrother, who refuses to let her marry her boyfriend. The boyfriend takes her into town and parks her on the curb beside his Harley while he's supposedly out finding a place for her to stay. Immediately after the stepbrother is gunned down, the woman goes back home, with the intention of letting the boyfriend move in. Is that it?"

"In a nutshell," I said. "Boiled down, it sounds pretty suspicious, I guess."

"Boiled down, it sounds like a motive for murder." McQuaid dredged a forkful of pancake in egg yolk. "Hers, his, or both. Who inherits the deceased's property?"

"Shirley?" I guessed, averting my eyes from the yolky mess on McQuaid's plate. "Allie, maybe? I wonder if he left a will." I picked up a slice of bacon in my fingers. "Murder, huh? So you and the sheriff aren't buying the theory that Casey Ford stumbled into his own booby trap?"

With his finger, McQuaid fished a chip of floating eggshell out of his coffee. "Oh, he stumbled into a booby trap all right. No doubt about that. Somebody took the butt stock off of a twelve-gauge shotgun and —"

"Coffee," Ruby gasped weakly, emerging from the woods. She was wearing a loose blue cotton shirt and blue leggings, and she hadn't bothered to run a comb through her frizzed hair. She staggered to the table, one hand at her throat, the other held out in a dramatic plea. "Coffee! I need coffee!"

"Uh-oh," I said. "Will you settle for cranberry juice?"

"Cranberry juice!" Ruby cried theatrically. "I didn't trek all this way through the jungle, fighting off lions and tigers and chiggers every step of the way, for cranberry juice!"

I held out a coffee mug. "Fill 'er up," I instructed McQuaid, and passed it, filled, to Ruby. "You asked for it, sweetie."

"Ah, coffee." Ruby hiked her leg over the bench, sat down, and took a large swallow while I watched, waiting for her reaction with a suppressed smile. When she got a taste of that awful coffee —

"Oh, heaven," she breathed, rolling her eyes. She took another swallow, cradling both hands around the mug. "Oh, McQuaid, this is absolutely the best coffee I have ever drunk in my whole, entire life! I'd ask you to marry me if you weren't already married to my best friend."

McQuaid beamed while I shook my head in amazement. There is no accounting for tastes. I picked up a plate. "Pancakes and honey? Bacon? An egg? Something to cut the taste of that coffee?"

"Not to worry," Ruby said, holding her mug up and inhaling the steam that rose from it. "I'll just have more coffee." She turned to McQuaid. "You were saying something about a booby trap?"

"Right." He gestured with his fork. "See,

you take the butt stock off a single-action twelve-gauge shotgun and set it into a wooden footlocker, which has a hole cut in one end for the barrel and a cradle, sort of, to keep the gun from shifting. Then you run a length of fishing line from the door handle about thirty feet to the rear of the room, where you set up the footlocker. You thread the line through a hook screwed into the rear end of the footlocker, then loop it around the trigger. The range will give you a decent pattern."

"A decent pattern?" Ruby asked.

"So you won't miss," McQuaid said, holding up his hands as if he were holding a basketball. "At a range of thirty feet, the spread of the shot is about like that. The trap was set so the gun was aimed chest-high."

Ruby shivered. "It sounds lethal."

"It was." McQuaid went back to his bacon. "But maybe it wasn't originally set up to be lethal."

I frowned. "Originally set up? What do you mean?"

"It was too dark to give the place a good going-over last night. But I did notice that the business end of the footlocker was propped up on a couple of bricks, elevating it just enough to catch the victim in the chest, instead of the knees. Making it lethal."

"But if Casey was going to set a trap to scare off intruders," I said thoughtfully, "he'd have aimed it lower and loaded it with rock salt, not the real thing."

"Rock salt?" Ruby asked. "The stuff you use to make ice cream, and put on the sidewalk to keep it from freezing?"

"Right," McQuaid replied, forking another pancake onto his plate. "Sometimes people load it into shotgun shells, instead of birdshot or buckshot — metal shot."

"But that chest wound wasn't inflicted with rock salt," I pointed out. "What killed Casey Ford was the real thing."

"Right again," McQuaid said. "Double-aught buckshot. That's my guess, anyway. We'll know for sure when Charlie gets the medical examiner's report. And of course, we'll probably turn up some other evidence at the crime scene when we go over it this morning. Fibers, hairs, prints — no matter how careful a killer is, he's bound to leave something behind and never even know it. The big problem is in making a match." He looked from Ruby to me. "You two have met some of these folks. Is there anybody who'd want this man dead?"

"Anybody?" Ruby laughed. "How about *everybody?*"

I nodded. "Casey was the town bully, to hear folks talk. If this was murder, you won't have any shortage of suspects. The whole town was gunning for him. You and Charlie Montgomery are going to have your hands full."

A shadow of a smile crossed McQuaid's face, and I thought again that he was enjoying this investigation. Once a cop, always a cop. He took a pencil and notebook out of his shirt pocket.

"Okay," he said, "how about naming the people who were gunning for him?"

Ruby gave me a quick look, and I knew what she was thinking. She didn't feel comfortable naming people who'd been angry and might have spoken on impulse, saying far more than they meant. On the other hand, a man had been murdered — or at least the police would have to proceed under that assumption until they concluded otherwise. I'd already decided, the night before, that I would share what I knew — even if it amounted to a suspect list.

"Well, there's Jerome Buchanan and his partner, Carl Holland," I said. "They run the Indigo Café. They're gay, and Casey

230

didn't much care for them. He didn't like Brenda Davis, either — she owns the antique shop — because she's black. Allie thought maybe he decided to close Indigo down because he didn't like the kind of people who were attracted to it — hippies, blacks, artists, gays."

McQuaid was scribbling. "Anybody else?"

"I've barely gotten started. You should talk to Maxine Mason. She and her husband Harry and their daughter Stella — she's a witch — run the Mercantile Emporium. Maxine got HIRC to pass a motion that they would take any steps necessary to stop Casey from turning the town over to the mine. Oh, and Betty Swallow, and Sandra Higgins, Diana's mother. Sandra used to run the Bluebonnet Coffee Shop before Casey closed it down."

"A witch, huh?" McQuaid grunted. "What kind of witch?"

"An apprentice witch," Ruby replied helpfully. "I don't think Stella knows enough to do much good, though — and, of course, she's already taken the witch's oath. To do no harm," she added, in an explanatory tone, when McQuaid looked puzzled.

"So Casey Ford was cast as the town

231

bully, huh?" McQuaid finished writing the names and put down his pencil. "Is it possible that these people put their heads together and decided to kill him as a group project? Vigilante justice?"

"I suppose it's possible," I said, not liking the sound of the words. "It's also possible that one person did it, feeling confident that the others would never give him — or her — away." I paused. "But before you stop writing, you'd better add Les Osler's name."

"The boyfriend," McQuaid muttered, scribbling. He looked up. "And Allie?" he asked.

I sighed, remembering what Allie had said about being willing to do anything she could to keep Casey from selling the mining rights. "I suppose she had a motive," I said reluctantly. "Like everybody else, she hated the idea of losing the town to the mine."

"And she was going to lose this place, wasn't she?" McQuaid asked. He looked up and glanced around the tank, his gaze lingering on the willows along the edge, where Brian was contentedly fishing. "It's beautiful here. Now that he's dead, she won't have to leave."

"Right. But I don't think Allie would be capable —"

"I know," McQuaid said. He gave me a crooked grin. "Where have I heard that before? Nobody likes to believe that their friends are capable of murder." He glanced down his list. "Nobody's mentioned Allie's boyfriend. Don't I remember you telling me that she has a live-in?"

"Derek Cooper," Ruby put in.

"But as of Thursday night, he stopped being Allie's boyfriend," I said. "He doesn't have much of a stake in the community, so he probably doesn't have much of a motive."

"That's good," McQuaid said, putting his notebook back in his pocket. "The suspect list is already as long as your arm. Not exactly a slam dunk."

"I'm glad this isn't my investigation," I said. Thunder rumbled again, a little nearer now, and the cool breeze that had sprung up was blowing steadily toward the clouds — usually a sure sign that rain is on the way.

McQuaid got up and went toward the shore. "Pack it in, Brian," he called. "Come on and get your breakfast before it rains."

"Aw, Dad!" Brian protested. "They're bitin' real good. Just one more fish, puleeze?"

McQuaid shook his head. "Nope. The lightning's getting closer."

Ruby frowned up at the yellow plastic tarp overhead. "That wasn't a raindrop I just heard, was it?"

"That's rain," I said, as the lake's surface began to dimple. "Let's go back to the cabin before it gets serious."

Ruby picked up her cup. "I'll get another cup of coffee to take with me," she said. "I wonder what McQuaid does to it to give it such wonderful body."

"He cracks an egg in it, shell and all. And if you think it has body today, come back for another cup tomorrow," I added, as I stood up. "It'll have legs and arms and a punch that'll knock you over."

Twelve

Christine Utterback, in an article entitled "Indigo: Mystic Blues" [*The Herb Quarterly*, Winter 1991], writes that women indigo dyers on the Eastern Indonesian island of Sumba transmit the craft secrets of the "blue arts" only along female bloodlines. It is thought that the spirits and deities assist indigo dyers and herbal healers to perfect their skills. This knowledge, mixed with practices of witchcraft and divination, are passed along, woman to woman, to the next generation.

The bulging clouds unzipped and the rain began to pour out just as we reached the cabin. Ruby, who meditates for thirty minutes every morning, draped a red shawl over her shoulders, lit some of her special handcrafted meditation incense, and settled herself on her blue zafu, facing one corner of the room, her feet tucked against her thighs in a lotus posture. She claims that the diffuse state of awareness she achieves in meditation is essential to the strengthening of intuition, something like push-ups for the right brain, and that she gets her strongest intuitions when she's meditating. I say that, at the least, it looks like a relaxing way to start the day. Unfortunately, I've never been able to sit still long enough to test the truth of her other claims. I'm afflicted with what she calls "monkey mind." The minute I sit down and try to get quiet, my thoughts leap aimlessly from here to there, and I start fidgeting.

"See you later," she said cheerily, but in a minute or so she had turned around again. "Oh, I almost forgot to mention it, China — I heard something in the night that woke me up."

"Something like what? Spiders stalking? Bats bumbling? Shangrilama humming?"

"Something like footsteps crunching on the gravel path. Like a door shutting and somebody trying to be quiet, but not being very good at it."

"A door shutting? There aren't any doors around here to shut, except for the door to the cabin." I paused. "Are you sure it wasn't me? You woke up when I came in and we had a conversation, but you were pretty sleepy. Maybe —"

"Of course it wasn't you. You were in bed, cutting z's. I checked the clock. It was three-thirty." She turned around to face the wall again, straightening her shoulders, adjusting her spine, tucking her feet. "Oh, well. It could have been my imagination. Maybe I dreamed it." Her speech began to slow. "If I dreamed it, I wonder what it means. Dreams are the language of intuition. Dreams . . ." Her voice trailed off.

It makes my back ache just to look at Ruby sitting like that, and since I've never been able to meditate for more than about four minutes, there wasn't any point in my joining her. I might have gone back to Sandberg's book on indigo, but I couldn't settle down. I couldn't prowl around the cabin, either, because I didn't want to disturb Ruby.

Anyway, it was now almost eight and the initial downpour seemed to have slacked off a bit, so I decided to run to the house to see if Allie was awake yet. I'd been putting off telling her what I had overheard in her bathroom, and it was making me feel guilty. I threw a sweatshirt over my head and dashed up the path to the house.

Allie was up and sitting at the kitchen table, finishing a bowl of shredded wheat. She was barefoot and dressed in ragged cutoffs and a T-shirt. Lucky lay beside her, chin on paws. Both of them looked up as I came in and wiped my sneakers on the rug in front of the door.

"Good morning," I said, draping the sweatshirt over the doorknob. "Nice weather for amphibious creatures."

"But not for an outdoor festival," Allie replied ruefully. "However, the radio says that the front should blow past in a couple of hours. It's supposed to clear up completely by noon."

"It won't break my heart if people stay away until afternoon," I said. "Sales were better than we expected last night, and our stock is kind of low. If it looks like the rain's going to let up, I might drive back to Pecan Springs and pick up a few things."

She nodded. "Breakfast? There's cereal or toast, whichever you prefer."

"Thanks, but I've eaten. McQuaid made camp pancakes — before it started raining." Allie had brewed a pot of green tea, not coffee, which was fine with me. I poured myself a cup and came back to the table. "Brian couldn't be bothered to eat. He was too busy catching fish." I held up my thumb and index finger, spread apart. "About as big as a minnow."

A smile ghosted across her mouth. "He might catch something worth keeping out there. Derek says —"

She stopped. Her eyes had a bruised look and her face was pale and puffy, as if she hadn't gotten a lot of sleep. On good days, Allie's energy and spirit can make her look almost attractive. This was not a good day.

When it became apparent that she wasn't going to finish her sentence, I said, "I have a confession to make, Allie. Something's been bothering me for over twenty-four hours and I have to tell you about it."

"A confession?" She got up and rinsed her cereal bowl, then picked up a long Navajo spindle — the shaft was nearly three feet long — and a basket of carded fleece. She sat down at the table and began getting ready to spin, and I thought again that spinning was a kind of therapy for people who otherwise might be chewing their fingernails. I hadn't ever seen Allie quite so nervous, but this was obviously a difficult time for her.

"So what do you have to confess?" she asked, sitting forward on her chair, adjusting to the length of her spindle.

"I was stuck in your bathroom night before last, when you and Derek came in and went upstairs. I overheard the whole thing. Your discussion, I mean."

"Don't be polite," Allie muttered. Her

face hardened, and whatever attractiveness her energy usually brought to it was lost in the bleakness of her expression. "It wasn't a discussion. It was a fight. We could have sold tickets." With the tip of the long spindle on the floor, she rolled the shaft up her right leg, from knee to thigh, then caught the turning shaft so that it spun in the circle of the thumb and first finger of her right hand, while the thread seemed to spin itself out of the fleece in her left. She watched the emerging thread intently.

"I'm sorry," I said, contrite. "I didn't want to listen, but I couldn't get dried off and into my clothes fast enough to —"

"Don't worry about it, China." Allie turned the spindle up her bare leg again, setting it spinning. "I'm glad you heard, actually. I've been wanting to talk things over with you, and that makes it a little easier. So I guess you know that Derek isn't . . . staying here right now."

"He's not sleeping in his camper?"

She shrugged. "If he is, he didn't get back here until after three. I thought I heard a vehicle coming down the lane, but when I got up to look, I couldn't see anything. His truck wasn't here when I got up this morning, so either he left before dawn, or I was dreaming."

"If you were, you and Ruby had the same dream." It must have been the camper door she had heard shutting, and Derek's footsteps on the path.

Allie turned the spindle again, harder this time. "Maybe he went over to Pecan Springs last night." She made a face. "To be with Ellen Holt. I saw her at the play."

I sighed. "I feel sort of responsible, since she's staying in my cottage."

"That's silly," Allie said shortly. "It's not your fault. It doesn't matter where she's staying — the Hilton, Motel 6, wherever. If Derek wants to see her, he'll go wherever she is." She stood the spindle upright on the floor and began turning it clockwise, winding the spun yarn onto the shaft. It bobbled and slid and she gave it up, going to the refrigerator to pour herself a glass of orange juice. She closed the fridge and stood there a moment, resting her arm and forehead against the door, breathing as if she'd been running.

When she finally came back to the table, she was more composed. "Anyway, it's not Ellen Holt that's really bothering me, China."

I gave her a sharp look, not quite believing her. Allie might like to think she could control her jealousy, but it wasn't that easy. I had seen it written across her face the day before.

❀ She sat down and went on. "For all I know, Derek might have been telling the truth when he said they were just talking. Brenda always has some sort of personal agenda. She likes to stir things up, to make everything seem worse than it really is." Her laugh was brittle, half-bitter, half-resigned. "And I suppose I can even understand what happened between him and Marie." She gave me a look to see if I knew who she was talking about. I nodded and she continued. "Marie was my friend, but she throws herself at every man who smiles at her. Derek isn't the first man she's used that way, and I don't suppose he'll be the last."

"Is it the lack of commitment?" I asked quietly. "Is that what's bothering you?"

"That's a big part of it." She studied her orange juice glass as if it were a crystal ball that might reveal the long-sought answer to some secret personal riddle. "At first I thought it was just a matter of time. Derek seemed to mean it when he said he loved me, and I thought maybe all he needed was for me to relax, not put any pressure on him. I thought he'd eventually want to get married, especially after he understood how important that kind of stability is for me. I don't need much money to get along on, but to me, marriage is . . ." She made a nervous gesture. "Well, if you're married, it means you've got a future together. A future you can both count on."

I would like to have said that marriage couldn't guarantee anybody's future, but I didn't want to interrupt the flow of her thoughts. She turned the glass in her fingers, as if she were wondering whether there was anything more to be learned by looking at it from other angles — or as if she were still debating how much she wanted to share with me.

At last she said, "But I began to realize that there's something inside Derek that kept him from making any commitments. Something from his past. Something he doesn't want me to know. Another woman, maybe. Maybe even a wife."

I frowned. "What makes you say that?"

She raised her shoulders and let them fall. "I don't know. Maybe because he's always so . . . secretive. He's taken a couple of trips during the time we've been together, and he never tells me where he's going. He has his mail delivered to a post office box in Taylor, even though he has to make a special trip into town to pick it up.

He keeps all of his personal papers — his writing, letters, stuff like that — in a lockbox he's built under one of the seats in his camper. I know, because I went out there one day when he was clearing stuff off the table and putting it away." She colored briefly and dropped her eyes. "I'm ashamed to say that I'd have sneaked out there and opened it if I could, but he keeps the key on his key ring, in his pocket."

"That doesn't have to mean he's hiding something," I remarked. "Maybe he just needs a private space that's all his own. A part of his life where you're not invited." I understand about this, because privacy and identity and independence are important issues for me, even more important since McQuaid and I married. I work hard to create and maintain areas in my life — thoughts, feelings, ideas, activities — that have nothing to do with my husband and what we have together. I just need that separate space, that's all. I'm healthier and happier when I know it's there.

Allie's mouth quirked. "I know it could mean that, and I certainly respect his need for privacy and a place of his own to write and think. But there's more to it than that, China. He's hiding something. I don't know whether it's a big, important thing —

like maybe he's got kids stashed some-where, or even a wife — or just a lot of stupid little things, like bad debts or an old drug record. But it's *something*. And what-ever it is, in my mind it's become like a wall between us. It keeps me from knowing who he is, and without knowing that, I can't fully trust him." Her face was taut and set, her voice fierce. She looked as she must have felt — angry and unattrac-tive. "So I focus on all these trivialities. The post office box. The lockbox. Marie. And now Ellen Holt, who is so damned *young*. Silly stuff, really. I hate myself for being so petty."

"But if you love him —"

Her mouth twisted painfully. "Well, that's the thing, you know? I *did* love Derek. I thought he hung the moon and the stars and made the sun come up in the morning. But in the past few months, that's changed. The little things — all the betrayals of trust — have begun to add up. They've made me doubt him." She straightened her shoulders and sat up stiffly. "They've made him seem . . . lacking, somehow. Not worthy of being loved the way I want to love him."

"Are you sure that anybody could be worthy of being loved in that way?" I asked gently. "After all, nobody's perfect. And the more you expect from someone, the more you set yourself up for disappointment when he fails to deliver." I paused, and put into words something I hadn't said out loud before, even to Ruby.

"At one point in my relationship with McQuaid, I imagined that he was the perfect Boy Scout: honest, loyal, trustworthy, and utterly incapable of betrayal. It was painful to learn that there were some parts of his personality that didn't match this ideal."

Painful. Such an inadequate word. It couldn't begin to tell the truth. I swallowed.

"But that image of him was only in my mind," I said. "When I began to see him the way he really was, he began to seem more . . . more *real,* somehow. I felt closer to him."

I don't think Allie heard a word I said. She was looking past me in an unfocussed way, as if she'd forgotten I was there. When she spoke, her voice was sharp-edged. "And now, this thing with Ellen — it makes me glad I don't love him any longer. It —"

She broke off and brought her eyes back to me, lifting her chin defiantly. "It's easier this way, China. Derek can go, if he wants to, and I won't miss him."

I looked at her sadly. It's one thing to decide to break off a relationship because you no longer love someone. It's quite another to rationalize a breakup by lying to yourself. And that's certainly what it sounded like to me.

She pushed the glass away and picked up her spindle again. "Yes, I hate to say it, but it's a relief to have it over. Like Casey's death, almost. The end of something." She was changing the subject, deliberately. "It's terrible to think that a couple of dozen people are glad because Casey managed to blunder into his own trap, but it's true." She spun the spindle up her thigh again, setting it whirling in the circle of her thumb and finger, steadily, without a wobble.

I watched her. "So what's next?"

"I guess I'll have to talk to Shirley about the funeral. Maybe we should just have graveside rites. Casey was big on God and the devil, but he wasn't much on going to church. And I don't imagine there'll be a crowd — unless they've come to cheer." Her voice was steady, like the spindle, without a wobble. There was no sadness, no bitterness in it.

Feeling restless and uneasy, as if there were something more here that I was supposed to understand, I got up and poured a second cup of tea. As I glanced out the window, McQuaid's blue truck came up the lane from the direction of the campsite and kept on going. Brian was with him. They must be on their way to Indigo for the day — McQuaid to give Sheriff Montgomery a hand with the investigation, Brian, no doubt, to connect with Diana and check out those baby rabbits.

I turned. "Is it true that Shirley was Casey's legal ward? Last night, when you went to answer the door, she said that Casey told her he needed her to sign some papers for the mining rights sale. If a court appointed Casey her guardian, he could sign for her — that is, if her signature was necessary. I'm wondering whether some of the Indigo property actually belongs to her."

"I have no idea," Allie said, winding another length of spun fleece onto the spindle. "As far as her legal situation is concerned, I've always assumed that what Grandpa Ford told us was true."

I sat back down, cradling my mug. Allie seemed much more comfortable with this subject. "What did he tell you?"

"That he was legally responsible for her and that she couldn't do anything without his say-so."

"Do you recall any mention of a court hearing on her guardianship?"

She shook her head. "That was a long time ago. I was teaching in Dallas then, and Mom was living up there too, so we weren't around here very much. There could have been a hearing, and nobody happened to mention it."

"You said that Shirley went to prison because she shot a man. What do you know about that?"

"Only what Mom told me. Shirley was always as wild and skittish as a deer, and about as undisciplined. She got pregnant when she was about fourteen, although I guess she miscarried or something, because so far as I know, there wasn't a baby. After that, she got into drugs, and the guy she was living with cheated on her. The way I heard it, she waited for him outside the other woman's house and shot him." Her mouth tightened. "Didn't kill him, although the way things turned out, it would have been a mercy. A year or two later, he got drunk and rammed his pickup into a car loaded with teenagers on their way to a prom. Wiped himself out

249

and took two of the kids with him."

"Sounds like she was hanging out with some pretty violent people," I said. "But she couldn't have been considered incompetent when she was tried for shooting the man, or she would have been sent to a state hospital instead of prison. Her incompetence would have to have been determined after she got out, when her stepfather petitioned to have himself appointed her legal guardian."

"After she got out. That's what Mom told me, anyway."

"And when he died, the court appointed Casey in her stepfather's place?"

"I wouldn't know about that," Allie said. She propped her spindle against the table and looked at me. "I guess I just assumed . . . Why are you asking all this, China?"

"Because the appointment of a guardian isn't something that just happens. A competency hearing is a big deal and the courts take it seriously, because an individual's right to make decisions is being taken away and given to somebody else. For this to happen, Shirley would have had to appear in court, with a lawyer. A social worker is usually involved, as well, and there's a psychological evaluation." I hesitated. "Shirley certainly seems competent enough now, although her mental condition may have been completely different during the years she was on drugs, or after she was released from prison. In any event, assuming that she was her stepfather's legal ward when he died, her new guardian — that is, Casey — would have to have been appointed by the court."

"So now that Casey is . . . now that he's managed to blow himself away, Shirley is supposed to have another —" Allie stopped, biting her lip. "Oh, Lord. I'm all she's got." Her voice became a wail. "But I don't want . . . I can't possibly . . ." She stopped and took a deep, shuddery breath. "China, Shirley never even learned to *read*. I just can't be responsible for her."

"I understand." I put my hand on her shoulder, feeling her tremble. "But let's not cross that bridge just yet. A friend of mine — Justine Wyzinski — specializes in family law. She's planning to come to the festival today. If she makes it, maybe we could sit down together and see if we can sort things out."

Allie seemed to pull herself together. "I'd appreciate that. I wish Mom was alive," she added in a lower voice. "She'd know what to do about Shirley. And how to handle Casey's funeral." She smiled wryly. "She'd probably have advice for me about how to handle Derek. Mom always had opinions on what I should do with my life."

I hesitated. "What you were saying a minute ago, about your uncle blowing himself away. Ruby and I had breakfast with McQuaid this morning, and he seemed to think that might not be true."

Allie's head snapped up. "Not true?" Her voice was sharp. "What do you mean?"

"When Casey told you about setting up the booby trap, did he say anything about his intentions?"

"Intentions?" she repeated. She reached for her spindle.

"I mean, did he say whether he was aiming to scare intruders off, or do some actual damage?"

She spun the shaft up her bare thigh, but the spindle escaped and rolled across the floor. She dove after it. "No, I don't think he said," she replied, returning to her chair. She bent to rewind the spun fiber, keeping her eyes on her work. "But he must have set it up to do real damage," she added, "or he wouldn't have been killed."

I felt a mild prickle of misgiving at the back of my neck. Something about this didn't feel right to me. "Maybe so," I conceded. "But if he set a lethal trap, it's even more curious that he would forget and walk right into it."

She gave the spindle another turn. "I told you last night, China. He must have thought he'd disarmed it. Anyway, Casey had lots on his mind. I can see him getting all involved with something else and forgetting about the trap." She didn't look up. "Or maybe he was drunk. Casey could put away a six-pack in an hour, easy. Ask Shirley, she'll tell you how much he drank. Or check out his record. He had at least one drunk-driving arrest."

The prickle of misgiving became a tingle. What Allie said sounded plausible enough, but something in her tone told me that she didn't believe it herself. Had she seen something she hadn't mentioned? Was she shielding someone? Shirley, maybe? Les, possibly? Or one of the many other people who had wanted her uncle dead?

"In fact," she went on, turning away again. "I'm sure that's exactly what happened." Her voice edged up a notch, the relief in it unmistakable, and troubling. "He got drunk and forgot all about —"

"Hey, guys," Ruby said, opening the screen door and coming into the kitchen, her indigo shawl draped over her head. "I figured I'd find you here."

"Has it stopped raining?" Allie asked, obviously glad for a change of subject. I felt apprehensive. Of course, she'd be upset at the idea that someone she knew might be a murderer, but —

"Mostly," Ruby said. "I've brought something to show you." She held out her hand, her palm open. On it lay a silvery hair clip. "I found it on the path behind the cabin."

"Behind the cabin?" Allie asked.

Ruby nodded. "This morning, around three-thirty, I thought I heard a door shutting and feet crunching on gravel. Just now, I went out to see if I could discover whether I really heard what I thought I heard, or whether it was a dream. The footprints, if there were any, were washed out by this morning's rain, but I found this in the middle of the path to Derek's camper." She glanced at Allie's boyish haircut. "It's not yours, obviously. And neither China nor I wear hair clips. So who do you suppose dropped it?"

Allie was staring at the clip, frowning, as if she were trying to remember where she had seen it before. But I didn't have to suppose, I *knew*. I had seen that silvery clip last night at the play, when it had been holding back Ellen Holt's honey-colored hair.

Ruby looked down at it, frowning slightly. "There's something about this clip that really bothers me. I'm getting strange vibes from it, as if —" She paused, wrinkling her forehead uneasily. ". . . as if there's danger connected with it. Danger for the person who owns it, I mean."

Recognition dawned on Allie's face. She reached out and took the clip, turning it over in her fingers. "It belongs to Ellen Holt," she said flatly. "I saw her wearing it last night. So what was she doing here, in the middle of the night?" She stood up. "I'm going out to Derek's camper."

"But he's not there," I said.

"I know," Allie said darkly. She was already halfway to the door. "That makes it a good time to have a look around."

From the look on her face, I'd say that Ruby's intuition was right. There was definitely danger ahead for the person who owned that hair clip.

Thirteen

Red is the color of fire, blood, danger, anger, passion, and desire. It is associated with Mars, the god of war, and with the heart.

The famous red coats of British soldiers were dyed with madder, as were the uniforms of French soldiers. According to Rita Buchanan, in *A Weaver's Garden*, madder's most important use was Turkey red dyeing, which was developed in India and transmitted through Turkey to France. Turkey red was a ritual color, full of magic and mystery, and was thought to evoke a fiery passion in the hearts of those who wore it or saw it. This made it a good color for military uniforms; however, it also made for a good target. Red combat uniforms were discontinued in the mid-1800s.

"The Symbolic Meaning of Color"
— Ruby Wilcox

Derek's red-and-white camper was parked about fifteen yards behind the cabin, set up on hydraulic jacks that allowed him to unload and load it easily onto his pickup truck. From the path that had been worn to the steps at the back, I guessed that he visited it regularly, and then remembered that he used it as a writing studio.

"They must have come here together," Allie said, in a taut, hard voice, striding forward. "They probably parked somewhere along the lane, hoping I wouldn't hear them."

I had to trot to keep up with her angry steps. "It wouldn't make sense for Derek to bring her here," I objected. "If they wanted to be together, they could go to Pecan Springs. The cottage would have been a great deal more . . . well, comfortable." If I had my choice, I'd much rather make love in a double bed than in the narrow bunk of a camper.

"You're saying he didn't bring her?" Allie demanded.

We reached the camper and stood, looking at it. "Maybe she came alone," Ruby ventured.

"What for?" I asked.

"If she did, it took a lot of chutzpah," Allie muttered, and I gave her a sideways look. So much for not being jealous, although I certainly couldn't blame her. By coming here without Allie's permission, Ellen was invading Allie's personal space. After all, Indigo Farm was Allie's home.

"Do you suppose she thought Derek was here?" Ruby asked.

"Maybe she knew he wasn't," I replied slowly, thinking that Ellen had been absent from the workshop during lunch the day before. Had she come out here then, too?

"That's it!" Ruby exclaimed, snapping her fingers. "She came here snooping!"

"Well, if you ask me," Allie said, "I think she and Derek got their signals crossed. She thought she was supposed to meet him here last night, and he thought she'd gone back to Pecan Springs." Hands on hips, she looked from me to Ruby, her mouth a thin line. "Why are we out here, anyway? I don't give a damn what those two were doing last night."

"Why are we out here?" Ruby narrowed her eyes in an imitation of Jessica Fletcher. "Well, now that I know it was Ellen who woke me up last night, I want to know why she was here. I wonder whether she tried to force her way in." She went to the door at the back and studied the lock for a minute. "There are no tool marks," she reported, stepping back. "I'll check the windows."

I went to the door and pulled smartly on the handle. The door popped open. "She didn't need any tools," I said. "It wasn't locked."

Allie seemed startled. "But Derek almost always locks the camper," she said uneasily. "I don't think we should go in," she added, as I put one foot on the step. "He'll be really upset if he finds out that we were messing around in his writing studio."

"I don't intend to do any messing around," I said, "but I think we should look inside. For all we know, this might have been a burglary or —"

Ruby pounced on my dangling sentence.

"Or somebody might be dead in there," she said in a dramatic tone.

"Dead!" Allie exclaimed, her face suddenly anxious. "You can't possibly mean —" She took a step forward, but Ruby put a hand on her arm, restraining her.

"I'm sorry, Allie," she said, penitently. "I get carried away sometimes. No, of course I don't mean that." She looked at me. "Go ahead, China. Take a quick look, just to make sure."

So while Ruby and Allie stood by, I pulled the door open wide and climbed the steps. The camper — which looked like it might be only a few years old — was cozy and well-equipped, just the right size for one person. It had a small stove with an oven, a refrigerator set into a paneled wall, a table with built-in seats and overhead compartments, a bunk in a raised alcove at the far end, an air conditioner built into the ceiling, a closet built into one wall. To my left was a narrow door, and when I opened it, I saw a compact bathroom: sink, toilet, shower, medicine cabinet. Everything was clean and well cared for and extraordinarily neat. A typewriter sat on the table and three pencils lay beside it, lined up like soldiers on a pad of yellow paper. The towels were folded just so on the racks, the books on the bookshelf were precisely arranged, the bunk made with military exactness. The whole place was as meticulously tidy as a monk's cell.

Given all this careful order, the few careless odds and ends stood out like signal flags. A drawer wasn't quite closed, and when I pulled it open, I could see that the neatly stacked contents inside had been disarranged. A couple of papers lay on one of the built-in seats, and as I opened the overhead compartment, more loose papers fell out, as if they'd been hurriedly thrust inside and the door shut. In the bathroom, the medicine cabinet door hung slightly ajar and a bottle of iodine had fallen into the sink and broken, leaving a rusty stain, still fresh and damp. And on the floor beside the door lay a small black plastic pen, one of those miniatures that you find in a pocket notebook-and-pen set. It was stamped OHIO NEWSPAPER ASSOCIATION.

I turned around and went back down the steps. "The place has been tossed," I said. "The tosser was reasonably careful, but not expert. If the tossee pays even the slightest attention, he'll almost certainly realize that someone has gone through his things." I held up what I'd found. "She even left her calling card. A pen from the Ohio Newspaper Association — and I happen to know that Ellen Holt is on leave from a newspaper job in Ohio."

"Damn!" Allie's eyes blazed.

"I don't know where the lockbox is, so I couldn't check it out," I said to Allie. "Maybe you'd better go in there and see if she found it."

"The lockbox?" Ruby asked.

"A secret compartment where Derek keeps his private papers," I replied.

Allie had disappeared into the camper and was back out again in a few minutes. "The lockbox is under one of the seats, hidden behind a piece of plywood," she said. She closed the door carefully. "I moved the plywood and checked the box, which doesn't look as if it's been damaged. I can't open it, but I doubt that Ellen even realized that it was there."

"But what in the world was she after?" Ruby asked, puzzled. "What did she *want?*"

I shook my head. "Not a clue," I said.

"Derek is very neat," Allie said. "I'm sure he'll notice that someone was in there." She looked up, startled. "You don't suppose she was trying to make it look like *I* did this, do you?"

"Why would she want to do that?" Ruby asked.

But there wasn't any answer to those questions, either.

Ruby and I went back to the cabin, and after a brief conference, came up with a game plan for the morning. It was just after nine. The rain had stopped and from the looks of the benevolent patches of brilliant blue sky to the north, it was gone for good. We planned to go back to Pecan Springs after the festival closed this afternoon, so we'd strip the beds and pack our clothes, drive into Indigo and unload, and set up our tables on the plaza. Ruby would take care of the booth while I drove back to the shop and picked up the items we were low on. On the way, I'd call Laurel with the list of things we needed, so she could have everything boxed and ready to go when I got there. And if Ellen Holt was around, I planned to have a quick chat with her and find out, if I could, why she had such an interest in Derek Cooper's camper. With luck, I'd be back in Indigo about twelve-thirty.

So we changed our clothes — Ruby into her indigo tie-dyed dress, I into my khaki wraparound skirt, a red plaid blouse, and sandals. After we left the cabin, we stopped at the house to let Allie know what we were planning, but she was gone, probably out seeing to her animals, so we left her a note, got back into Big Red Mama, and drove into town. On the way, I filled Ruby in on my conversation with Allie this morning. I also reported Allie's story about Shirley's guardianship, so that if the Whiz showed up, Ruby could give her some background.

"Tell Justine," I said, "that I suspect that Casey never bothered to go to court to have Shirley's guardianship transferred. She'll probably want to talk to Shirley and look over any documents she can dig up. Including Casey's will, if there is such a thing. Tell her to make sure that Allie is in on this discussion, though — she's Shirley's closest relative, now that Casey is dead."

Ruby tapped her fingernail against her teeth. "It's difficult to believe that in this day and age a grown woman can be fooled into thinking that some man has legal authority over her when he really doesn't."

I shifted down for the stop sign, looked both ways, and pulled out onto the highway. Off to the left, I could see the dragline, looming like a giant predator behind the trees. "Maybe not so difficult," I said. "Allie says that Shirley can't read. I can imagine that she might be confused and bewildered enough to accept whatever her stepfather told her, especially right after she got out of prison."

"I suppose her self-confidence must have been terribly low, too," Ruby replied. "If she can't read, she probably doesn't have a driver's license." She sucked her lower lip between her teeth and was silent for a moment. "I can't imagine not being able to read. It's an absolutely basic survival skill!"

I glanced into the mirror and was astonished to see a huge coal hauler riding on my tail, trying to pass. I sucked in my breath and could almost feel Big Mama cringe. It was like being chased by a tyrannosaurus with an attitude. The twisting two-lane road wasn't designed for such monsters. No wonder so many people were up in arms about the mine.

When the truck finally passed, I let out my breath in a long sigh of relief. "Where were we? Oh, yes, Shirley. Maybe it isn't any great surprise that she's willing to stay home and keep house — or at least she was, until she met Les. If she can't read and she can't drive and she has no self-confidence, what could she do to help herself?" Except to latch onto a man who promised to take her away from it all, which might be exactly why Les was important to her. How important had he been? And how willing to help her get out of a hopeless situation?

"She couldn't do *anything,* of course," Ruby said, replying to my question. "And when her stepfather died and Casey took over, she'd never guess that they were supposed to go back to court."

"And even if she suspected that her step-father and stepbrother didn't have legal authority over her, where would she get the courage to challenge it? After a while, taking orders might get to be a habit, to the point where she's no longer capable of thinking for herself — especially if Casey is knocking her around or abusing her sexually."

"And then that biker comes along on his Harley." Ruby wore a dark frown. "Out of the frying pan and into the fire." She turned in the seat to look at me. "I suppose you noticed that Shirley didn't give Les an alibi for the time of Casey's death. You told me last night that he came back to the motorcycle *after* Casey was killed."

"I noticed," I said. "But if Casey was killed by a booby trap, an alibi for the time of death doesn't mean diddly. The trap could have been rigged hours before it went off. Days, even. That's the beauty of these things. You can set the trap and be miles away when it goes off. All you have to do is make sure that your victim is there when it happens."

We were approaching a low-water crossing — a place where the road dipped and water flowed over it after a heavy rainstorm. I slowed the van and glanced at the wooden gauge beside the road, the levels marked at foot intervals. People die at low-water crossings in Texas, and I don't intend to be one of them. But the water here wasn't deep or swift enough to be dangerous, so I shifted into low gear and crawled across, water splashing halfway up the hubcaps.

"Duh," Ruby said. "Of course. Delayed death." She paused. "How did the killer manage that, I wonder. Did he — or she — make a date with Casey Ford to meet at the Bluebonnet? Did Ford agree because he knew that he'd disarmed his trap?" She turned to look at me. "This is going to be a complicated investigation, isn't it?"

I nodded. "I doubt that Sheriff Montgomery is doing back flips, but if you ask me, McQuaid enjoys these little complications. Makes the case more of a challenge. A war of wits with a killer who's standing in the bushes watching the police turn the town inside out."

Ruby was silent for a moment, chewing on her lower lip. "And then there's Allie's theory. That her uncle got drunk and stumbled into his own trap."

"The blood-alcohol content is routinely included in the autopsy report," I said, swinging Big Mama off the county road and onto Main Street, heading toward the plaza. "But even if Casey was drunk, it doesn't prove that Allie's right. Say, for instance, that Casey disarmed his booby trap on Wednesday and the killer came along on Thursday and rearmed it, then set up a date to meet Casey at the Bluebonnet on Friday. Casey could have been drunk as a skunk when he showed up for the meeting and it wouldn't prove a thing, one way or another. Except that he was feeling no pain when he went to meet his Maker." Not a bad way to die, maybe, given the painful alternatives.

"I suppose it's possible that the killer might even have set the trap for somebody else," Ruby said thoughtfully. "That would really complicate the investigation, wouldn't it? You'd have an unknown victim and an unknown killer. I wonder —"

But I never got to find out what Ruby was wondering. She bit off her sentence and pulled in her breath. My mouth fell open. Both of us stared.

A half-block ahead, Main Street was closed off by a brown sheriff's car parked diagonally across the right-of-way, the rotating flasher spilling red and blue light onto both sides of the street. A red volunteer fire truck from Lexington was parked in the street in the middle of a twisted spaghetti of hoses, tended by yellow-jacketed men in fire helmets and gloves. A little farther down, another fire truck was just driving away, followed by a sheriff's car. A large crowd of spectators lingered on one side of the street, silently watching. And on the other, where Sandra Higgins's Bluebonnet Coffee Shop had stood the night before, there was nothing but a pile of charred and smoking rubble.

Ruby recovered her voice first. "Good golly, Miss Molly," she breathed. "Somebody's torched the crime scene."

Ruby and I found McQuaid and Sheriff Montgomery staring at the burned-out building, their hands shoved deep into their pockets and gloom written across their faces.

"When did it happen?" I asked.

"Early," McQuaid growled imprecisely.

"Shouldn't have happened at all." Charlie Montgomery was tight-lipped. "*Wouldn't* have happened if Pete had done his job the way he was 'sposed to. He was in charge of the crime scene — all he had to do was keep an eye on the place. If it'd been me screwed up like that, Sheriff McFarland would whip my butt so bad I'd have to stand up to sleep."

McQuaid put a comforting hand on his shoulder. "Don't be too hard on Pete, Charlie. These things happen. I'd've done just what he did, parked out in front with the radio going to keep me awake. Even if

Pete checked out that alley every ten minutes, it wouldn't have been good enough. It only took thirty seconds for somebody to pour gasoline into that trash bin and toss in a match. From there on out the building was history."

"Excuse me," I said, more loudly. "What time did this happen, exactly?"

Charlie Montgomery turned, noticing me. He dredged up a smile. "Oh, g'mornin, Miz McQuaid. How're you this mornin'? Sorry to take your husband away from the fishin' trip." He doffed his hat to Ruby. "Mornin', ma'am."

"The *time*," I said.

"The deputy radioed it in at six," McQuaid said. "It took the fire truck about a half hour to get here from Lexington, but by then the building was gone."

"And everything in it," Charlie added in a sour tone. "Losin' the crime scene is gonna make a tough job a damned sight tougher."

Ruby nudged me. "Six," she said in a low voice. "Which means that the fire was probably set about five-forty-five. And at three-thirty or thereabouts, Ellen Holt was tossing Derek Cooper's camper."

I nodded. On her way back to Pecan Springs, had Ellen taken a detour to torch

270

the scene of Casey Ford's death? But the timing was off by a couple of hours, and anyway, why would she have done it? The Bluebonnet meant nothing to her.

"I suppose," I said to the sheriff, "that you've already had a good look at the area around the trash bin."

"Yep," Charlie said regretfully. "Didn't turn anything up. That time of the morning, don't reckon anybody saw anything, either. If they did, they haven't come forward."

I glanced across the street and saw Sandra and her daughter Diana standing together, with Brian next to Diana. Brenda was not far away, one hand on her hip and a sarcastic smile on her face. Betty was with her, hair still in curlers, as if she'd just gotten out of bed. Jerome and Carl stood in front of the door to the Indigo Café, shoulder-to-shoulder, faces grim, as if they were security guards blocking intruders. Maxine and Stella were arranged in a mother-daughter duo, Maxine in black shirt and pants, Stella wearing a loose, flowing red dress with a gold-printed red vest and that gold turban on her head — costumed for more fortune telling, probably. The tall, stoop-shouldered man standing behind Maxine, bald head gleaming, worry twisting his thin features, must be Harry. He looked pretty much the way I had expected. A man Maxine could tolerate because he knew how to say, *Yes, ma'am.*

It was quite a lineup. There was no point in adding a doubtful name — Ellen's — to the list when McQuaid and Montgomery already had a whole town full of suspects to interview, including one apprentice witch and God only knew how many other weird folk. I wondered briefly if gasoline and matches were ever used to cast a protective spell, and how many people might have the idea that fire purifies.

"Well, it's too bad," McQuaid said. "Without the evidence we might have discovered in there, this thing certainly isn't going to be a piece of cake." He paused. "China and Ruby are acquainted with some of these folks, Charlie. They gave me the names of seven or eight who might have something to gain by Ford's death. I guess we can start with them." He glanced over at the crowd of tight-lipped spectators, which by now must have included every citizen of Indigo. "And if we run out, it looks like there's plenty more. How many people live in this town?"

"Thirty-seven," Jerome said. He had left

Carl to hold the fort in front of the Indigo Café and come up behind us, quietly. We turned, startled, as he held out a piece of paper. "I thought you'd need a list, so here it is. Everybody's names and phone numbers. We're all eager to cooperate, of course. I have also listed the buildings that Mr. Ford owned. You might want to check them and see if he set any other booby traps."

"Thanks, Mr. Buchanan," Sheriff Montgomery said. He pocketed the list. "Sure appreciate your efforts."

"Right," Jerome said. "Just let me know if there's anything I can do personally to assist your investigation." He glanced at the smoking rubble. "I know that I speak for everyone in Indigo when I say that this morning's accident is extremely unfortunate."

"Accident?" McQuaid replied shortly. He leaned forward, his jaw jutting. "Is that what you think this is? An accident?"

"Why, what else could it be?" Jerome's smile was bland and ingratiating. "Just like last night, when Mr. Ford got killed. You can ask anybody — we all knew that booby trap was just an accident waiting to happen. To tell the truth, we're just glad that Mr. Ford tripped it himself, and not some innocent child. Poetic justice, if you will." He pulled himself straighter. "I'll be in the café all day, if you need me, gentlemen. And if you would like to drop in for lunch, Carl and I would be honored to have you as our guests — on the house." He backed away, then turned and crossed the street.

"Thirty-seven," McQuaid said disgustedly. "Hell, is *that* all?" He turned to the sheriff. "How many deputies do you have, Charlie?"

"Ten, including the night shift."

"Better get three or four of them over here," McQuaid said. "This is going to take some work. The hell of it is, these folks aren't going to tell us a damn thing. Why should they? They all wanted him dead."

"Yeah," the sheriff said, "and now we've got two crimes. Murder and arson." He paused. "Could be the same person, though. The killer fired the crime scene to keep us from finding important evidence."

McQuaid shrugged. "Could also be two different people," he replied. "Somebody else fired the crime scene to keep us from identifying the killer."

The sheriff shook his head mournfully. "I been sittin' around for six weeks with nothin' to do but chase cows and lock up drunks, and now this."

Contemplating the charred wreckage of their crime scene and the prospect of interviewing thirty-seven citizens of Indigo, the two men lapsed into a gloomy silence. Neither of them looked as if they especially welcomed these challenges. I couldn't say that I blamed them.

Fourteen

HERB QUICHE
/ (A THYME AND SEASONS FAVORITE)

3 eggs, slightly beaten
2 cups evaporated milk
salt and pepper to taste
3/4 cup grated Swiss cheese
9-inch unbaked pie shell
1/2 cup cooked, drained,
    chopped spinach
1/2 cup sautéed mushrooms
3 tablespoons fresh snipped chives
1 teaspoon fresh thyme leaves, minced
1 teaspoon fresh parsley, minced
1 tablespoon butter or margarine

garnish: leaves of fresh greens (kale, arugula, lettuce) and fresh chive blossoms or other edible flowers

Preheat oven to 350 degrees. Combine eggs, milk, salt, and pepper. Spread the grated cheese evenly in the bottom of the pie shell. Mix the spinach, mushrooms, and herbs and spoon over the cheese. Pour the milk-and-egg mixture over all. Dot the top with butter or margarine. Place the pie plate on a cookie sheet and bake until set, about 30–35 minutes. Remove when the outside is set and the middle still jiggles when shaken. Let stand 10–15 minutes before you cut it. Set each slice on a few leaves of fresh greens and add chive blossoms. For a spectacular brunch, serve with sliced melon, strawberries, or orange sections.

Forty minutes later, Ruby and I had finished setting up the booth, Ruby was waiting on our first customer of the day, and Big Red Mama and I were heading back to Pecan Springs. On the cell phone, I punched in the number of the shop and gave Laurel the list of items we needed. I also asked her to knock on the door of Thyme Cottage and if Ellen Holt was there, to tell her that I'd be there inside an hour and would like to have a brief chat.

Thyme and Seasons was having its usual Saturday, a half-dozen customers strolling through the gardens, a few more browsing in the shop, and a larger group in the tea-room, enjoying the herb quiche garnished with chive blossoms that is Janet's popular brunch specialty. People have been known to call up and ask when she plans to put it on the menu, just so they won't miss it. And she always bakes extra, so customers can buy one to take home and put in the freezer. Janet says it's not quite as tender after it's been frozen, but still a treat.

Laurel and I loaded Big Mama with the boxes she had filled and a half-dozen plastic trays of potted herbs — rosemary, thyme, Saint-John's-wort, and some scented geraniums. I stopped in the tearoom to check with Janet (as usual, she had everything under control in the kitchen) and to say hello to her cousin Rachel, who was waiting tables for us today. The tearoom, with its green wainscoting, chintz place mats and chair seats, and baskets of philodendron and ivy, looked fresh and pretty — exactly the right place to sit down, enjoy a brisk cup of tea and a piece of Janet's quiche, and take a rest from the labors of shopping and garden-viewing.

When Ruby had suggested, some eighteen months before, that we use her lottery winnings to finance the tearoom, I wasn't very keen on the idea. I didn't want to depend on her financially or feel responsible for the money she proposed to sink into the project. But now that Thyme for Tea has been in operation for a year and I've seen the way the business has grown, I'm delighted. Janet's a superb cook, and Ruby and I have been discussing how we can use her skills more effectively. We've started picking up occasional catering jobs, and they've been profitable enough that we've decided to do more of it. I'm not a Martha Stewart wannabe and I'm not looking to make a killing in the restaurant business. But the fact is that small herb shops are having a hard time of it these days, now that the big guys — Walmart, Kmart, even the grocery chains — have jumped onto the herbal bandwagon. If I want to stay in business and make a decent living at it, I'll need to diversify — if I can do it without spreading myself too thin. Ruby feels the same way, so we make a good team.

I sampled the quiche, wished Janet and Rachel a good day, and headed down the path to the guest cottage. Out in the alley, I saw Mr. Cowan walking his yappy little dog, Miss Lula. Mr. Cowan, who is nearly ninety and looks even older, is the unofficial neighborhood watchman. Nothing escapes his notice, and Lula, who must be pushing ninety herself, in dog years, is equally nosy.

"Hello, Mr. Cowan," I said with a

pleasant smile. I like the old guy, even if he is inclined to be contrary.

Glowering at me, he ran a skeletal hand over his shiny bald head. Lula bared yellow teeth and advanced on me. I took a step back. My liking for Mr. Cowan does not extend to his dog — and she feels the same about me.

"You tell that flibbertigibbet blonde who's staying in yer place that folks in the neighborhood don't 'preciate trucks tearin' up an' down the alley at two in the a.m.," Mr. Cowan growled.

Mr. Cowan is always complaining about something — trucks, cars, kids on their Rollerblades, but I could see his concern. "Two in the morning!" I said sympathetically. "That's terrible."

"Damn right it's terrible," he grumbled. "Woke up poor little Miss Lula. Took her a whole hour t' git back t' sleep."

Poor little Miss Lula, looking none the worse for losing an hour's sleep, went over to Ellen's car and nonchalantly peed on one tire.

"How do you know that the person who's renting my guest house has anything to do with trucks in the alley?" I asked curiously.

" 'Cause the truck pulled in right there,

where that little white car is parked." He pointed to the space occupied by Ellen's Honda Civic. "I hadda git up t' see what was makin' the racket. Put the fear o' God in 'im, too." His chortle was nasty. "When I come out with my flashlight and shined it on the fella, he jumped right straight back in his truck and vamoosed."

"Thank you for being so alert," I said. "Everybody in the neighborhood appreciates your keeping an eye on things."

"Durn tootin'," Mr. Cowan muttered. "Gotta have somebody watchin' all the time."

"By the way," I said, "when you came out with your flashlight, did you happen to notice whether that little white car was parked there?"

"Nah, it wudn't," he said.

"And what time was that?"

"Long 'bout two a.m. Like I said, took Miss Lula a whole hour to git back to sleep, poor thing." He put his fingers between his lips and gave a piercing whistle that made me want to put my hands over my ears. "Come on, Miss Lula. We gotta git home. It's time fer yer pills." He glared at me. "You tell her, y'hear? No more trucks!"

"Sure thing, Mr. Cowan." I raised my

hand in a farewell wave and turned to go around to the cottage door. As I walked past Ellen's Honda, I glanced down and noticed that the Ohio license plate began with a pair of Zs — one of those oddly random things you just happen to see and remember. I couldn't have guessed that it would ever have any significance. But afterward, when everything was over, I was to wonder how things would have turned out if I hadn't noticed that license plate. Was there some fate at work that I couldn't understand? How long would it have been before anybody found —

But that's getting ahead of the story, and anyway, this particular mystery can never be resolved. In Ruby's version of things, the universe is full of random bits of information floating through the ether like radio signals, and if your receiver is in good operating condition and you're tuned to the right channel, you'll get the message. That explanation seems pretty far-fetched to me, but since I don't have a better one, it will have to do.

The cottage bears no trace of its earlier incarnation as a stone stable. The rough-plastered walls are painted white, the skylight spills sunshine into the comfortable living room, and the fieldstone fireplace and terra-cotta tile floor give the place a look of rustic simplicity. Most of the people who stay there enjoy keeping it neat, but when Ellen answered the door and invited me in, I could see that her carelessness in Derek's camper was symptomatic of a general sloppiness. The sofa and chairs were draped with dirty clothes, the sink was full of dishes, and a surreptitious glance into the bedroom showed that the bed hadn't been made. On the kitchen counter, beside her open laptop computer, was the key to the cottage on its usual yellow plastic smiley-face key fob, an untidy litter of notebooks, file folders, and papers, along with a stack of microcassettes and a small cassette recorder.

But Ellen looked much neater than her surroundings, and if she was tired after staying up late to search Derek's camper, there was no sign of it. She was freshly showered, her face was scrubbed, and she was dressed in crisp white pants and a clingy red halter blouse, her honey-gold hair flowing loosely over her shoulders. Looking at her fresh young prettiness, I felt like Methuselah's mother. But that feeling might just give me an advantage.

I gave her a maternal smile. "You need something to hold your hair back, my dear.

How about this?" I held out my hand, flat. On it was the large silvery hair clip that Ruby had found.

"My clip!" Ellen exclaimed happily, reaching for it. "Where did you — ?"

She stopped, her hand out, her hazel eyes widening as she remembered where she had lost it.

"Oh," she said softly.

"Indeed." I closed my fingers over the clip and tucked it into my shoulder bag. "The next time you trespass on private property and enter a dwelling without the owner's permission, you should be careful not to leave your calling card." My tone was sharper, no longer motherly. I stepped forward.

"But I didn't —" She stood aside to let me in, her cheeks turning pink. Flustered, she looked even younger and prettier. "I don't know what you're thinking, Ms. Bayles, but you're wrong. I would certainly never —"

I took the plastic pen out of my bag and held it up. "And when you toss a place, it is not — I repeat *not* — cool to advertise. If you'd been more careful, Mr. Cooper might not have known you were there. You would have preserved the element of surprise."

She pulled in her breath. "Does he . . . does he know?"

I put the pen in my purse. "You'll have to ask him that question."

She turned her head away, her cheeks blazing. "Did you come here to lecture me?"

"Lecture? Let's just call it a word to the wise." I went to the wingback chair beside the fireplace, removed the filmy bra, and draped it over the lampshade. I sat down, crossed my legs comfortably, and gestured to the opposite chair. "Have a seat, won't you?"

To sit, she had to remove pantyhose, a pool coverup, and a pair of bike shorts from the chair. She dumped them onto the floor, arranged herself in a studiedly casual pose, and fixed me with a challenging stare.

"What do you want?"

"Information."

"Well, you're not going to get it," she said haughtily. "I'm a member of the press, and I don't have to —"

"Ah," I said, as if I had been enlightened. "Press privilege. Perhaps that explains why you felt free to ransack someone's house."

The challenge turned sullen. "It wasn't a

house. It was only a camper. Nobody actually lives there."

"Better bone up on your law, hon. The structure is used for the overnight accommodation of Mr. Cooper, and as such is defined in the Texas Penal Code, Chapter Thirty, Section Two, as a habitation. Your burglary is a second-degree felony. You can also be charged with two counts of criminal trespass." This method of intimidation — citing chapter and verse of the code — doesn't usually work with somebody who's older and wiser, but Ellen was neither.

She tried for insolence. "You're some kind of lawyer, I suppose."

"You got it, sweetie." I turned up the corners of my mouth in a smile. "Second-degree felony earns you two to twenty, plus a hefty fine. And the judge won't be impressed by your newspaper affiliation. Quite the contrary. Texas courts love to throw the book at the media."

That got her attention. She pushed back her hair and gave me a wild glance. "But I didn't take anything, honest! I couldn't find what I was looking for!"

"What makes you think that all burglaries are successful? The fact that you failed to find what you were after reduces neither the charge nor the penalty." I paused, tenting my fingers under my chin and pursing my lips. It's a gesture I don't use very much these days. "What *were* you after, Ellen?"

Ellen twisted her hair around a finger, looking away from me. In the kitchen, the faucet dripped into the silence.

"Well?" I asked. I opened my purse and took out my cell phone. "My husband, who is a former homicide detective, is a close friend of the sheriff of Dalton County. I can assure you that Sheriff Montgomery has zero tolerance for —"

"If I tell you," she broke in, "will you forget about the . . . burglary?"

"It depends on whether you decide to tell me the truth or try to fork over another lie."

"You have to *promise*."

"Sorry, babe," I said regretfully. "I don't do promises." I flipped the cell phone open, but just as I began punching in numbers, it chirped at me. The caller was Ruby, who wanted to tell me that Justine had arrived and that she was going to leave Diana and Brian in charge of the booth while she and the Whiz went over to the Indigo Café with Allie, to discuss Shirley's situation. But Ellen didn't know that.

"McQuaid!" I said. "I was just about to

call. Is Sheriff Montgomery there with you?"

"China?" Ruby asked uncertainly. "China, what —"

"Good. Will you tell him that I've identified the person who burglarized Derek Cooper's camper last night? Her name is Ellen Holt. I'll be glad to hold on while you —"

Ellen scooted forward on the edge of her chair. "All right!" she said tersely. "Turn off that phone, damn it. I'll tell you what you want to know."

"China," Ruby said, "I don't know what's going on there, but I also need to tell you that —"

"Thanks, McQuaid," I said. "Listen, something's come up here. Tell the sheriff I'll get back to him on this matter, okay?"

"China," Ruby said hurriedly, "wait, China! I also wanted to tell you that McQuaid and the sheriff are having trouble here."

"Really?" I paused. I might lose Ellen if I gave her time to think, but I wanted to know what was going on. "What kind of trouble?"

"Somebody got into the sheriff's car, stuck a key partway into the ignition, and snapped it off. He can't start it, of course.

Looks like he'll have to get it towed."

"Mercy," I said, deadpan. That was a particularly dirty trick, and not hard to do, either. Coming on the heels of the crime scene arson, it was beginning to seem that the good citizens of Indigo were dead set on throwing multiple monkey wrenches into the sheriff's investigation. "Everything else going okay there?"

"It's hard to say. McQuaid and the sheriff are interviewing people in the old Dalton County Jail. It's kitty-corner from our booth on the plaza, so I've got a good view of the door. They must be sending a deputy around to pick up the people they want to talk to, because every now and then a deputy escorts somebody else inside." She giggled. "It's like a casting call for potential heavies. The only trouble is that none of the players look the part very well."

I heard the cottage telephone ring. Ellen stopped glaring at me, sprang out of her chair, and dashed down the hall to take the call in the bedroom, where I couldn't hear the conversation. I frowned, not liking the interruption. But while Ellen was occupied, I might as well find out what was happening in Indigo.

"Who else have they interviewed so far?" I asked.

"Stella and her mother. Jerome and Carl. Oh, yes, and Sandra. It looks like they're working on that list we gave McQuaid this morning." Ruby laughed a little. "They also have the thirty-seven names that Jerome gave them, in case they run out of people before they run out of time."

"I wonder if they're having any luck."

"I don't think so. I talked to Betty, the woman at the candle shop, and she says that nobody knows a thing about the arson — or at least anything they're willing to tell the sheriff. I talked to Stella, too, and as far as the killing goes, apparently everybody is sticking to the same story, that Casey Ford tripped his own booby trap. But her mother was with her, so she wasn't able to talk freely." She paused. "It's the town bully syndrome, China. People are glad that the guy is dead, and they want to see the killer go free. And without evidence or an eyewitness, I don't see how the sheriff is going to pin this on anybody."

It sounded like the investigation was getting nowhere fast, and I could imagine that McQuaid's frustration level must be going through the roof. I said good-bye, turned off the phone, and put it back in my purse. Ellen was still in the bedroom, talking on the phone, her voice low, so I took the opportunity to go into the kitchen and get myself a glass of water, pausing to glance at the research materials spread out on the counter next to the computer.

A newspaper clipping headlined *Wilder Search Enters Third Week* lay on top of a second folder marked *James White, Kent State* and a third with *Texas Towns* written on the tab. The top tape on the stack of microcassettes was labeled *JW Interview.* And the text displayed on the laptop monitor seemed to be an interview with someone named Jane Wilder.

In my present life as an ordinary citizen, I'm not much of a snooper. Privacy is one of my personal issues, and I wouldn't take it kindly if somebody browsed through my personal papers. But by this time, I was intrigued. William Wilder was a Canadian writer who had turned up missing a few years ago. I was intensely curious about Ellen's interest in the case, but my snooping was interrupted by the sound of her steps coming down the hall. Carrying the glass of water, I went back to my chair.

"Sorry to keep you waiting, Ellen," I said cheerfully. "Let's see — when we were interrupted, you were about to tell me why you searched Derek Cooper's camper."

Ellen settled back in her chair. "All

right," she said shortly. "It's none of your business, but since you insist, I'll tell you. Derek Cooper is my father's brother."

This was *not* what I had expected to hear. "Your uncle?" I asked, so startled that my hand jerked and the water slopped out of my glass. So much for Brenda's romantic version of their relationship.

"That's right. Uncle Derek and my father were never very close. Dad didn't even know where he was, and to tell the truth, my sister — my twin, Elizabeth — and I didn't much care."

A twin? What would it be like to be in the same room with the pair of them? Overwhelming, probably.

"But Dad died about six months ago," Ellen went on, "and Liz and I thought Uncle Derek ought to know. It took a while to locate him, and when I finally managed to track him down, he wasn't . . . well, he wasn't exactly thrilled to see me."

"Okay," I said dryly. "So your uncle isn't the family type. Is that why you ransacked his camper?"

"The thing is that he —" She gnawed on her lip. "He's got some important family papers that my grandfather gave him. Old land grants, letters, stuff like that. When I asked him if I could have a look, he told me to go fly a kite. So I decided —" She paused, twiddling her hair.

I gave her a boost to get her started again. "You decided to search his camper for the papers?"

She looked down. "I don't see any reason why Uncle Derek should have them. They're as much Liz's and mine as his. So I thought I'd look for them." Her head came up and she gave me a repentant smile, flashing those delicious Barbie doll dimples. "I'm sorry, Ms. Bayles. I won't do anything like that, ever again. It was obviously a mistake in judgment. You've put the fear of God into me."

I eyed her. If her story about the family papers was a lie, it was unusually full of details. Most people who counterfeit a story stick to a more general sketch. "If you were trying to locate your uncle, why the cover story about a book on small towns?" I gestured toward her laptop, open on the counter. "You *are* obviously writing."

"Of course I'm writing," she said, tossing her hair back over her shoulder. "And I *am* working on a project about Texas towns. I have to make a living somehow, don't I? I thought that since I was coming to Indigo to talk to Uncle Derek, I could do some research and write the trip off." She pushed herself forward on the edge of the chair. "Excuse me, but that telephone call was from someone I've been trying to interview for the book, and I need to drive back to . . ." She hesitated just slightly. "I have to drive to Austin, and I'll be there all afternoon. The person I'm seeing lives west of the city, actually, not far from Lake Travis. So if you have no more questions, I really need to get started." She stood.

I stood as well. Her story about Derek didn't quite ring true to me, but I was out of time and patience. I needed to get back to Indigo, and I'd clearly gotten as much from Ellen as she was willing to give, at least at the moment. Perhaps later I might be able to persuade her to tell me more. And if she was telling the truth, Allie would be comforted to know that there was no sexual connection between Derek and this young woman.

I said good-bye and left. But I've wondered many times since what would have happened if I had pushed Ellen a little harder to tell me what was really going on. Would it have changed the way things ultimately turned out? Or was the direction of those events already so fixed, the momentum so powerful, that nothing I said or did could have altered it?

I'll never know the answer to that question, of course. But I'll always wonder.

Fifteen

I would rather wear my own indigo wrapper than a rich red cloak that isn't mine.

— African proverb

"Hi, Mom." Brian greeted me as I struggled to the booth, loaded with the boxes Laurel had packed. "We've had a great morning. Business has been really *bad*."

"Bad?" I thumped the boxes on the brick pavement and surveyed the half-empty tables and displays. "But a lot of our stuff is gone. What happened? Did you *give* it away?"

"Bad means really good," Brian said in a pitying tone, as if I were someone who needed special instruction in the language. "Bad is awesome. Bad is *beast*."

"And we've raked in bags of booty," Diana put in enthusiastically. A cluster of earrings sparkled along the curl of both ears. "People say this booth is choice. They come over here before they go anywhere else."

"Oh, yeah?" *Booty* and *choice* I understood. I began opening boxes. "I'm sure you guys have done a terrific job. Ruby and I appreciate —" I glanced into the cash box. "Yikes! You really have taken in lots of money! You sure you haven't robbed a bank?"

The kids exchanged knowing glances, giggling in unison.

"Want me to show you our special technique for attracting customers?" Brian asked. Without waiting for an answer, he ran out in front of the table and let out a whoop, beginning what looked like some sort of primitive tribal dance. "Yeeehaw! Come and getcher Texas herbs here! Cool stuff, awesome prices, finer than frog hair! Bring your ducats and boogie on over." He stopped dancing and beamed at me. "How was that, huh, Mom? Want me to do it some more?"

I ducked down behind the display stand as people turned to gawk at Brian. "Thanks," I said. "I get the picture." I dipped hastily into the cash box. "Have you guys had lunch yet?" When they shook their heads, I gave Brian a ten. "Take your time," I said. "Treat yourselves."

"You sure?" Diana asked, with a respectful glance at the ten.

"Oh, absolutely," I replied.

"Wow, that's so *bad!*" She punched Brian on the arm. "Come on, Brian. Want to have another look at those bunnies before we eat?"

"We'll be back in an hour, Mom," Brian promised. As he turned to go, he said, "Oh, yeah, Dad's in the jail. He's been interviewing suspects all morning."

"Well," Diana said in a superior tone, "your dad and the sheriff can interview as many as they want, but it won't do them any good."

"Oh, really?" I said, setting out the tray of potted rosemary plants. "Why is that?"

Diana's look suggested that I ought to be able to figure this out. "Because he killed himself," she said, and added, "and if somebody else did it, he ought to get a medal instead of going to jail. That's what my mother says." She put on a knowing look. "That's probably why the Bluebonnet got burned down."

I frowned at her. Something in the way she said that made me think — "Do you know anything about the building being torched?" I asked.

She opened her eyes wide. "Who, me? Of course not. I don't know who threw the smoke bomb, either." She punched Brian on the arm. "Come on, Brian, let's beagle."

"Wait a minute," I said. "What smoke bomb? When?"

"The one that went off under the deputy's car about a half-hour ago," Brian said. He threw up his arms as if he were describing a mushroom cloud. "There was lots of smoke. Dad and the sheriff came running out of the jail with fire extinguishers. They thought the car was on fire." He giggled. "They looked pretty funny."

I tried to keep my voice low and even. "Brian, throwing a smoke bomb under a policeman's car is a criminal offense. Whoever did it could get into a lot of trouble."

"Yeah, sure," Diana said. "But they have to catch them first." She tugged at Brian's arm. "Come *on,* Brian!"

I gritted my teeth as they rambled off. A snapped-off key in the ignition, a smoke bomb — McQuaid and Charlie must feel as if they were under siege. When Ruby got back, I'd run over to the jail and see what I could find out about the status of the investigation.

I finished arranging items I'd brought, waited on a couple of customers, and sat down to catch my breath. But I hadn't been sitting long when Ruby, Justine, and Allie came across the plaza. They weren't exactly a matched set. Allie was wearing cutoffs and her Indigo Farms T-shirt, Ruby was in that skinny tie-dyed blue dress, and the Whiz, who is shaped something like the Little Engine That Could, was wearing a wrinkled beige jacket missing one button, a brown skirt with the hem hanging loose, and a cream-colored blouse hand-decorated with taco sauce. She had combed her hair the previous Thursday morning, and her tortoise-shell glasses were askew as usual, the lenses filmed with dust. Justine Wyzinski is smarter than your average Supreme Court justice, but she certainly gives new meaning to the phrase "careless dresser."

"Hi, China," Ruby said. "How'd your talk with Ellen go? Did you get her to confess?"

I was about to tell Ruby and Allie the story I'd gotten from Ellen, but the Whiz stepped forward, glancing impatiently at her watch.

"Hey, Hot Shot, good to see you." Justine is the only person in the world who remembers my law school nickname, coined in the days when she and I were competitors. "Let's not hang around here too long. If we're going to talk to Shirley, we'd better get a move on." Justine, who idles at impulse power and forges ahead on warp drive, has a disconcerting habit of arriving ahead of the appointed time. When you arrive, on time to the minute, she behaves as though you are late. This used to infuriate me when we were in law school together. Now it's amusing — more or less.

"Hello, Justine." I smiled. "Kind of you to spare us a whole five minutes and thirty seconds."

The Whiz has absolutely no sense of humor, and she takes everything literally. She pursed her lips. "I can do better than that, I suppose. However, I do need to be back in San Antonio by four. If we're going, let's go."

"I told Justine that I'd like you to come along, China," Allie said. "Shirley knows you. She seems comfortable with you."

"But I just got here a few minutes ago," I said, "and it's not right for me to run off and leave Ruby again. Why don't you and Justine go? I can hear about it later."

"I really wish you'd come with us," Allie said in a low voice. She shot an uneasy glance at Justine, and I understood. The Whiz can be genuinely sympathetic and generous, but when you first meet her you may feel as if you're standing in front of a herd of stampeding elephants. Shirley might get the idea that she was about to be trampled.

"I think you should go, China," Ruby said. She looked around. "Where are Brian and Diana?"

"Our intrepid entrepreneurs? I sent them to lunch. I thought they needed to take a break from their strenuous advertising efforts."

"Advertising?" Ruby asked, perplexed.

"You don't want to know," I said. "They'll be back in an hour."

"I'll stay with the booth until then," Ruby said. "After that, they can work and I'll take a break. There are one or two more people I want to talk to about last night."

"Talk to?" Allie frowned. "Like who? Why?"

Ruby wrinkled her nose. "You don't think these townspeople are going to tell the sheriff the truth about what really happened last night, do you? But they might just open up to somebody who isn't quite so . . . well, threatening. I thought I'd do a little snooping around."

The Whiz nodded approvingly. "Good idea, Ruby." To Allie, she said, "These two have collaborated with me on one or two criminal cases in the past, Allison, and I am pleased to say that they are patient, meticulous, and disciplined in their investigative techniques. Imaginative, as well. They think outside the box. If anyone can ferret out any significant information about Casey Ford's unfortunate demise, they can."

I smiled. Allie looked taken aback, but that's because she's not used to Justine's style. Ruby was pleased.

"Thanks for the compliment, Justine," she said. "To be specific, Allie, I want to talk with Jerome. I have a theory."

Allie's eyes went back to Ruby. "A theory?" she asked uncomfortably.

Ruby leaned forward, her face intent. "I've read that some killers are fascinated by police work, so they hang out at the scene of the crime. Some of them even offer to help. Last night, Jerome was right up front, helping with the crowd, and this morning, he gave the sheriff a list of all the townspeople's names. Very helpful."

"But Jerome is Indigo's unofficial mayor," Allie replied. "I'm sure that's why he's trying to help. I can't believe that Jerome would have anything to do with what happened to Casey." She sounded very positive.

I could have told Allie that no matter how strongly she might feel about Jerome, there was no point in trying to raise a fact to dispute Ruby's theory. When Ruby gets an idea into her head — particularly when it fits in with her image of herself as Nancy or Kinsey — you might as well just get out of her way. The devil of it is, though, that Ruby is often right.

Ruby tossed her head. "Unofficial mayor, huh? All the more reason for him to want to protect Indigo by getting rid of the threat that Casey obviously posed. I haven't had a chance to speak to Brenda yet, either. I thought I'd drop in at her antique store this afternoon." She nodded toward the booth where Stella was telling fortunes, her gold turban bent over the outstretched hand of a dumpy, anxious-faced woman who didn't look very happy about the future that Stella was reading in her palm. "I also intend to talk to Stella, when her mother isn't around to correct everything she says. I'll bet I can dig something out of her."

She probably will, too. People *do* talk to Ruby, and they are usually much less guarded than they are with men who wear uniforms. When she's talking to you, Ruby is all ears and eyes. She says "uh-huh" and "oh, my" and "isn't that amazing?" at precisely the right places, and her gaze is fastened on you as if she were spellbound by your words. Before you realize you've opened your mouth, she has all your dirty little secrets.

But Justine had something else on her mind. She looked at her watch again. "This is all very provocative, Ruby, but it doesn't forward our efforts to achieve some clarification of Shirley's legal situation." She pressed her lips together. "I'm afraid I really must get this expedition underway. I need to —"

"Be back in San Antonio by four," I said with a sigh. I picked up my purse and slung it over my shoulder. "Okay, you guys, you talked me into it. Let's beagle."

"Beagle?" the Whiz asked, her eyes slitting. She hates it when somebody uses a word she doesn't understand.

But before I could answer, somebody hailed us and we turned around. A uniformed deputy, a short, stocky young woman, was coming across the plaza from the direction of the old Dalton County Jail.

"Ms. Selby," she said to Allie, "Sheriff Montgomery would like to talk to you now. Please come with me."

Allie looked suddenly apprehensive. "But I —" She swallowed. "Can't it wait? I was about to —"

"The sheriff would like to see you *now*, please." The deputy was firm and businesslike. "If you don't mind."

The look Allie turned on me was frightened, as if she were appealing for my support. I was puzzled. Why should Allie be afraid of talking to the sheriff? But the look was gone in an instant.

"I guess you two will have to go on without me, then," she said. She glanced at the Whiz and lowered her voice. "Just don't hassle Shirley, that's all. She's not as simple-minded as she seems, but she kind of checks out when things get complicated."

Justine put out her hand, smiling. "Just do what you have to do, Allison. We'll take care of the rest."

Justine doesn't always use big words.

When we pulled up in front of the old farmhouse, I was relieved to see that Miss Mayjean's car was gone and Les's red Harley was nowhere in sight. This was a conversation that would probably go better with just the three of us.

Shirley answered my knock by opening

the door on a chain and peering apprehensively through the crack.

"Hi, Shirl," I said, in a friendly tone. "Allie asked me to come over and see you. I've brought somebody who wants to talk to you."

"Somebody who?" Shirley was suspicious. "I already told the sheriff I don't know nothin' about how Casey got killed."

The Whiz stepped forward. "My name is Justine Wyzinski. Allison asked me to give you a little help."

"What kind of help?" Shirley asked, narrowing her eyes. "I got Miss Mayjean and Les, too, and Allie. What do I need somebody else for?"

Justine and I exchanged glances. I said, "Ms. Wyzinski is a lawyer, Shirley. She can help you understand about your legal situation. How about if we sit down and talk for a few minutes?"

"Lawyers." Shirley snorted. "Seems to me that's how I got into this perdicament in the first place." But she took the chain off the door, opened it, and stepped back. She was wearing the same jeans, but her blue cotton shirt was clean, her hair was parted in the middle and braided in two thick braids, and the bruise on her face was beginning to fade.

A moment later, we were all sitting around the kitchen table. And five minutes after that, the Whiz had established with two or three questions that Shirley had no recollection of ever appearing in court for a competency hearing.

"The only times I was ever in a court-room," she said in a gritty voice, "was when I took a gun to Marty Higgins 'cause the jerk was cheatin' on me. That was when I got sent to prison."

For all her impatience, the Whiz can be very gentle. "So you don't remember being in court when a judge said that your step-father was responsible for you and was now your legal guardian?"

"No, ma'am," Shirley said, earnestly. "But I remember sittin' in this very chair when Daddy Ford come right through that door and *said* that's what the judge said." She threw a furtive glance in the direction of the door as if she half-expected her step-father to materialize on the threshold. "He said I wasn't s'posed to do anything ever again without his sayin' so, or I'd go back to prison quicker'n a sneeze through a window screen. Showed me the paper, too. It had my name on it, and his, and a bunch of official stuff." Her long, heavy sigh was resigned. "Casey went to the judge and got a paper like that, too, after Daddy Ford died. No use in me arguin'. It's all there in black 'n' white. All legal." She touched the bruise on her face. "It says he can make me do whatever he wants." Then she smiled. "But he can't do that no more, can he?" Her voice held a vibrant note of exhilaration.

I leaned forward. "Do you know where that paper is now, Shirley? Ms. Wyzinski and I would like to have a look at it."

"I s'pose it's in Casey's room. He's got a box where he keeps papers and legal stuff. The room's locked, though, and I'm not s'posed to go in there." Shirley straightened her shoulders and added, in a serious tone, "But he's dead now, so he cain't tell me what to do." She stood up and motioned to me. "Come on. There's a key hid over the door."

The door to Casey's room bore a bold red-and-black NO TRESPASSING sign and a heavy gray padlock. Shirley stood on her tiptoes and ran her fingers above the door frame until she found the key. "He didn't think I knew where it was," she said, putting the key into the padlock, "but I saw him take it down once." She turned the key, tugged the lock open, and we went into the small room.

Casey Ford was not a neat person. The air was filled with the stench of cigars and dirty clothes. The bed was unmade, underwear and socks were scattered around, and NRA literature and survivalist magazines littered the carpet, which was the color of barnyard mud. A scarred wooden table was shoved against the wall. In addition to a half-bottle of cheap red wine, an opened can of peanuts, and a couple of empty pork rind bags, I saw a pile of empty shotgun shells, a soup can half-filled with gun powder, a box of cartridge reloading tools, and a sack of rock salt. A shotgun was leaning against the table. My eyes went back to the rock salt.

"Whew," Shirley said. "Stinks in here." She went to the window and raised it with some effort. "That's where Casey loads shells for his shotgun," she added, noticing my glance.

"Uh-huh," I said. Rock salt. The stuff you load into a shotgun cartridge if you aim to injure, rather than kill. "You said you talked to the sheriff this morning. Did he come up here?"

She shook her head. "All he wanted to know was where was I last night, and did I know anything about how Casey mighta got hisself shot." She opened the closet door and pointed. "There it is."

The gray metal box — a cheap one, the sort of thing you buy at Office Depot to store file folders — was shoved against the wall, half-hidden under a pile of old camouflage gear. It was locked.

"Do you know where Casey kept the key?" I asked.

She shrugged. "Guess it's on his key ring."

"If it's okay with you, I think we can open it without a key. We might have to jimmy it, though."

"Sure." A sly smile ghosted across her face. "Guess it's my box now." She glanced around the room, her eyes beginning to shine. "Think I'll clear out this trash and make me a place to sew. Miss Mayjean says she's got an old sewing machine I can use till I get one for myself. I've always wanted a sewing machine."

We carried the box back to the kitchen, and Shirley went out to the shed to get a hammer and screwdriver. When the door had closed behind her, Justine leaned forward.

"There's no competency issue here, in my opinion," she said decisively. "Shirley may need assistance in making certain business decisions, but she certainly ap-

311

pears to be capable of taking care of herself. I doubt that any judge would find it necessary to place her under the control of a guardian — and I'll bet she's never had one, either. What she's had is a tyrannical stepfather who was determined to keep her under control, and a stepbrother who carried on the family tradition."

"What a tragedy," I said sadly. "All those years of her life, wasted. With education and training, she could have made something of herself."

"Yes, but look at it this way, China," the Whiz said, practical, as always. "If her stepbrother hadn't been killed, a lot more years would have been wasted. In fact, she might never have gotten out from under his thumb. This woman may not have had much of a past, but she has a future."

Justine was right, of course. But I couldn't help thinking that Shirley's future might have provided a very powerful motive for murder. And while I found it hard to believe that she had been involved in her brother's killing — she struck me as a transparent, guileless woman, with nothing in her manner to suggest guilty knowledge — her boyfriend was quite another matter. Les *Born to Raise Hell* Osler wanted to marry her, and Casey had forbidden it.

Did Les love Shirley enough to kill for her? But something other than love might have been involved. Greed, for instance.

"There's apparently some property," I said. "According to Allie, Casey inherited quite a bit of real estate from his father. That's the land that he was about to sign over to the mine. I suppose it will go to Shirley now. Although —" I frowned. "Although there was no blood relationship between Shirley and Casey, so maybe she won't inherit. Allie was his niece. She's actually more closely related to Casey than Shirley is."

"What was the relationship between Shirley and Casey Ford, exactly?"

"Shirley's mother married Casey's father — that's the man Shirley calls Daddy Ford — when Shirley was a teenager. I don't know the details, and Allie doesn't seem to, either. Miss Mayjean might, though."

Shirley was back with the hammer and screwdriver. A few sharp, well-placed licks popped the box open. It was stuffed full of papers.

The Whiz surveyed the stash. "Would you recognize the document Casey showed you, Shirley?"

"The one the judge gave Casey? It was in a yella envelope, with red writing on the front." Her lower lip caught between her teeth, Shirley riffled through the contents of the box until she found what she was looking for. Without a word, she handed it to the Whiz.

The large manilla envelope was fat and full of papers. The Whiz opened it, took out the documents, and began to scan them rapidly.

Shirley watched her, envy written across her face. "Seems like magic, you readin' so good," she said gruffly. "When I was a kid, I tried to learn, but the letters was all scrambled. Never could make no sense out of 'em. Miss Mayjean tried to help, but I fin'ly just give up. Somethin' wrong in my brain, I guess."

Dyslexia, I thought regretfully. Today, kids who suffer from this neurological disability are assigned to special education classes, with techniques and technologies to help them learn. Thirty years ago, in Shirley's small-town school, it would have been a very different story. Dyslexic kids were labeled dumb, stupid, feeble-minded, even mentally retarded. Those who didn't learn to read were required to repeat the lower grades, until it became obvious that they couldn't learn — and were then simply promoted to the next grade, where the teachers turned their backs on the problem. As soon as they could, they dropped out of school. The next step for many, as it had been for Shirley, was a teen pregnancy, drugs, violence, prison. Most grew up with the despairing belief that they were hopelessly dull-witted.

The Whiz leafed swiftly through a few more pages, pausing to read one or two, then held out the one that had been on top. "Is this what Casey showed you to prove that the judge put you in his custody?"

"That's it," Shirley said with satisfaction. "It's got that round, bumpy thing at the bottom." She pointed to the embossed notary stamp. "And my name, right there. Shirley Ann Rosser. I can read that much, anyway. I can write it, too." Her face darkened. "Cain't write anything else, but I can write that."

"Rosser?" the Whiz asked. "So your name isn't Shirley Ford?"

Shirley shook her head. "Rosser was my real daddy's name. When Daddy Ford married Mama, he wanted to make me change it and be a Ford like his two kids, but Mama wouldn't have it. She said I was born a Rosser and I oughta stay a Rosser, 'cause my daddy was a good man."

She frowned down at the paper, putting her finger on the top line. "Casey read me this. Told me it was somethin' I should remember, 'cause it was what the judge said. Don't recall 'xactly, but it was about him assumin' the duty of takin' care of me."

"Affidavit of Assumption of Duties by Successor Trustee," Justine read out loud.

"That's it," Shirley said, obviously pleased that she had remembered some of the words. "Duties."

"Successor Trustee?" I asked in surprise. "But that's not —"

"Exactly," the Whiz said, handing me the affidavit. "See for yourself."

The document was dated and officially notarized. In it, Casey Leland Ford affirmed that the Declaration of Trust creating the Janece Rosser Ford Living Trust provided that upon the deaths of Janece Rosser Ford, grantor, and Franklin Ford, trustee, he had become successor trustee, entitled to act on behalf of Shirley A. Rosser, sole heir and beneficiary of the Janece Rosser Ford Living Trust.

Sole heir and beneficiary? I looked at the Whiz, who wore a deliberative look. "And what other surprises do we have in that envelope?"

The Whiz began to tick the items off, in

a you-are-not-going-to-believe-me-but-I-am-not-making-this-up tone. "An original Declaration of Trust, with a list of the property to be placed in the trust. Mostly real estate, and some blue chips: IBM, Exxon, AT&T, Kodak. Beneficiary: minor child Shirley A. Rosser. Original trustee: Franklin Ford. Successor trustee: Casey Leland Ford." She thumbed through several other sheets of paper. "Here's an appraisal of the trust assets, as of the date of the grantor's death." She held out the appraisal. The list was almost two pages long, and the bottom line was over a million dollars.

I whistled. "And that was twenty-some years ago. Real estate, blue chips — the value could easily have tripled by now." There must be multiple millions involved, a powerful incentive for keeping Shirley in the dark about this trust, and under what amounted to house arrest. And no wonder her stepbrother refused to allow her to marry. If she ever got out from under his control, she — or her husband — might find out how much she was really worth.

The Whiz pushed her lips in and out, considering. "In my opinion," she said judiciously, "what we have here is an unambiguous instance of fraud. Felony theft, first degree. If Shirley's stepbrother were convicted on this one, he'd be in jail for the rest of his wretched life."

"Don't forget false imprisonment," I said. "Restraint without consent, by means of intimidation and deception, so as to interfere substantially with the person's liberty." I shook my head. "But when you start tallying up how much it would've cost the system to apprehend, prosecute, and punish this bozo, whoever blew him away ought to get a reward."

"It might also be worthwhile to check out the income tax situation with the Feds," Justine said thoughtfully. "Sounds like tax fraud is a definite possibility. This is one for the books."

"Right," I said. "And remember that Casey didn't invent this bizarre situation. He inherited it from his father. This has been going on for over twenty years." I looked around at the kitchen of the old farmhouse. "I wonder where all the bank accounts are and where the money went. Casey sure as hell didn't sink it into this place."

Shirley had gone to the refrigerator and taken out a pitcher of lemonade. "I made this for Miss Mayjean," she said, "but I don't mind if you have some, since you're doin' all that readin'. Must be thirsty work." She poured three glasses and put them on the table. "Those big words — I didn't understand a one of 'em. What's this about my mama's property?"

The Whiz took off her glasses, rubbed the bridge of her nose, and put them back on. "To make a long story short, the paper that Casey showed you has nothing to do with guardianship, Shirley. It's related to real and financial property that your mother left in trust for you when she died."

"She means," I translated, "that your mother has left you some land and money."

Shirley frowned. "But Daddy Ford said she gave it all to him when she died. Wasn't much left, neither. Just this old house and the garden and the place where Allison lives, and a building or two in Indigo. The rest, it went to pay Mama's doctor bills. She was sick for over a year, and in the hospital a lot of that time. Daddy Ford said it cost ever' nickel the two of 'em had, her an' him both."

"Your mother had property when she married him?" I asked.

Shirley lifted her chin. "Well, I reckon she did, before she got sick." She smiled proudly. "There was land in our fam'ly, way back. Indigo Dobbs was Mama's daddy's mother, y'see."

The Whiz looked to me for explanation, and I added an explanatory note. "The town of Indigo is named for Indigo Dobbs. Her father was the major landowner around here back at the turn of the century. This was prosperous country until the twenties, when the boll weevil ate up the cotton and everybody went broke."

"The fam'ly near went broke, too," Shirley said, sitting down with her lemonade. "I've heard Gramma Dobbs tell many a time 'bout how poor they got, couldn't buy no shoes nor schoolbooks. But Gramma, she worked hard. The men folks were ready to give up lots of times, but not her. And the bank never took Gramma's land, the way it did the neighbors'. She was right proud of that."

"I see," the Whiz said. She put her glasses back on. "Well, Shirley, I'd have to review all of these papers before I could say anything for sure, but it appears that the man you call Daddy Ford did not tell you the truth. When your mother died, she left her property to you, not to him. And there was plenty of land."

"To *me?*" Shirley's mouth had dropped

open. "But Daddy Ford said —"

The Whiz raised her hand. "However, since you weren't eighteen, she appointed him your trustee. He was supposed to take care of the property, manage the income, and turn everything over to you when you came of age."

Shirley frowned. "Come of age. That'd be when I was twenty-one?"

"Right," I said.

"Well, I reckon that's why he didn't do it," she said darkly. "When I was twenty-one, I was in prison. Folks in prison cain't own nothin' was the way Daddy Ford told me."

"But that's not true," I objected. At the look on her face, though, I decided not to go into it.

"Whatever the reason," the Whiz said quietly, "your Daddy Ford didn't do what he was supposed to do when you became twenty-one. Instead, he pretended that there was no property or money, and kept it all for himself. And he invented a story about being your guardian, to keep you from finding out the truth."

"He made it up?" Shirley was incredulous. "You're tellin' me that Daddy Ford and Casey, they never had the right to tell me what to do?"

"Yes," the Whiz said gently. "That's what I'm telling you, Shirley. I will check the county and state records to be sure." She held out the Affidavit of Assumption of Duties. "But if this is the only means by which Casey claimed his authority as your guardian, there *is* no guardianship. You are free to do as you please."

Outside, I heard the slam of a car door and a moment later Miss Mayjean opened the screen and came in. She was carrying a portable sewing machine.

"Hello, everyone," she said cheerfully. "Shirley, I've brought you that sewing machine. I've got fabric out in the car and —"

"Miss Mayjean!" Shirley cried, jumping up from the table. "You ain't never gonna guess what I just found out! My mama left me somethin', after all. And Daddy Ford and Casey, they —" She stopped, frowning. "You're a lawyer, you tell her," she appealed to the Whiz. "I don't know all the words."

Justine introduced herself, then recapped our discoveries. Miss Mayjean seemed to hold her breath, and when the Whiz was finished, let it out in an amazed *whoomf.*

"I always knew there was something funny going on," she said. "But those

Fords, they wouldn't let me get close enough to guess what it was." She shook her head, her mouth looking pinched. "I blame myself, Shirley. I should have insisted on seeing your mother's will. I should have hired a lawyer for you. If I had only looked after you better —"

Shirley threw her arm around Miss Mayjean's shoulders. "Now, don't you go gettin' down on yourself," she said, consoling. "You got nothin' to fault yourself for, Miss Mayjean. Not a thing, y'hear?" She looked up, a range of emotions crossing her face: happiness, joy, release — and apprehension and anxiety. "Does all this mean I can marry Les if I want?"

The Whiz put on her magisterial face. "In my opinion, it would be prudent to postpone marriage until you have achieved a more comprehensive understanding of your financial circumstances, and until the judicial standing of your relationship to the deceased has been finally determined."

Shirley eyed her suspiciously, then turned to me. "What did she say?"

"She said that you and Les should hold your horses until you know for sure how all this is going to pan out."

"And until," Miss Mayjean said with some asperity, "you've had a chance to get out and see some of the world." She put the sewing machine on the table. "I thought we might make up a couple of dresses, and you could go over to Linda Anne's beauty parlor and get your hair fixed."

Shirley considered this for a moment. "Well," she said finally, "I don't mind waitin', Miss Mayjean, if that's the right thing to do. And I don't see nothin' wrong with gettin' my hair fixed. But I also don't mind tellin' you that I love Les Osler, and that it don't matter none to him whether I got money or a new dress or my hair curled, though I guess maybe that'd be nice, now that you mention it."

She got up from the table and looked into the little mirror that was hanging beside the refrigerator, her fingers touching her cheeks, her mouth, her hair. Then she turned to face us.

"Les loves me for me, not for how I look or what I got, and he was willin' to take me when I didn't have a dime. So I guess all this stuff won't matter much to him." She glanced around the kitchen. "But it sure won't hurt none to have a little money. Right after I get that tee-vee, I could buy me one of those microwave ovens, and a sewing machine of my own." She thought for a moment. "Or maybe instead of a microwave, I could get Les a new clutch for his pickup. That's why he's ridin' that Harley, 'cause his truck's laid up." She smiled happily. "Yeah, that's what I'll do with the money. I'll get a new clutch for his pickup. He'll be real pleased."

The Whiz folded the list of appraised properties and put it back into the envelope. "I think," she said, "that there might be enough money for a microwave *and* a clutch. Plus a little something left over."

Sixteen

HOW BLUE WAS DISCOVERED

Different cultures offer different explanations for the discovery of indigo dye. Storytellers in western Africa relate how a young mother goes to the river to make a sacrifice, taking her infant daughter. The baby falls asleep on a white cloth spread over a cushion of indigo leaves. While her mother is making her sacrifice of rice and salt, the little girl wets herself, then rolls over onto the leaves and suffocates.

The mother finds her dead daughter and begins to weep and wail, throwing ashes from her fire over herself. She notices, though, that the cloth has turned blue where the baby's urine has wet the indigo leaves. The gods, taking pity on her grief, show her how to mix indigo leaves with salt, urine, and ashes, to make the color blue.

The mother returns home to teach the wise women of her tribe how to make blue. But she does not teach the men, because not even the wisest among them would be able to understand.

"Well, China," Justine said after we'd gotten back into Big Mama and were driving back to Indigo, "did you have any idea how that situation was going to turn out?"

"Absolutely not," I said. "You know, now that I come to think of it, Shirley's probably lucky to be alive. Once she'd signed away those mining rights, Casey wouldn't have had any more use for her. He could have finished her off, cleaned out the trust, and vamoosed. Few people would have missed her, given the fact that she'd been a virtual prisoner in that farmhouse since she got out of prison. Hardly anybody knew she was there."

"Except for this guy who wants to marry her. Les." The Whiz gave me a significant look. "What kind of man is he?"

I shifted down for the corner, hardly sparing a glance for the dragline behind the trees — no threat to the town, now that Casey Ford was dead. I hadn't asked Shirley what she was going to do about the mining rights, but I doubted very much that she would sell them. The land, the town, the wild things — would all be safe.

"Les is rough around the edges," I said, in answer to Justine's question. "He's the kind who works hard, makes his own breaks, and doesn't take to being shoved around."

"The killing kind?" she asked sharply.

"I suppose I'd give you a qualified yes," I conceded. "He was plenty angry about the way Casey was beating up on Shirley." And for all Les knew, Casey was the only thing standing between him and the woman he'd chosen. "He had both the motive and the opportunity," I added, "the means having already been provided by Ford himself."

And Les had worked for Ford, so presumably he knew about those booby traps. Maybe he had even helped Casey set them up. If so, he knew that they weren't rigged to kill — that they'd been aimed low and loaded with the rock salt I had seen on the table in Casey's bedroom — and that Casey had subsequently disarmed at least one of them. It would have been easy for him to change the trap setup, then invite Casey to a powwow at the Bluebonnet, ostensibly to discuss Shirley's situation.

But even as I mentally ran through this scenario, I realized that the idea that Les Osler was a killer did not appeal to me at all. This dissatisfaction had very little to do with Les — I don't particularly fancy men in black tank tops with tattoos on their biceps — and a great deal to do with Shirley. I'd been enormously moved by her declaration: *Les loves me for me, not for how I look or what I got.* How many people in the world feel loved simply for who they are? How many women could look forward to marriage with that kind of trust? Maybe it wouldn't work out for them — life throws all kinds of curve balls and sliders and sometimes we strike out — but Shirley deserved the opportunity to find out for herself, even if her discovery included a broken heart. That's what freedom is all about, isn't it? Maybe it was my liking for Shirley, or my old instincts popping to the surface — whatever it was, Les might be guilty as sin, but I was rooting for his innocence.

The Whiz was silent for a few minutes, looking out the window. "Changing the subject," she said, "how's McQuaid these days? Everything okay with him?"

Justine had been one of the people who'd helped to see me through the difficult weeks after the shooting, when I didn't know whether McQuaid would live or die — or if he lived, what kind of disability he might have to live with. I'd always be grateful to her for her help.

"Physically, he's much improved," I said. "He only uses his canes when he's really tired. Otherwise —" I shrugged. "Well, I guess the plain truth is that he's bored with teaching, or maybe it's just departmental politics getting him down. I don't think he likes the academic life as much as he thought he would when he left Houston Homicide."

"Maybe he misses the risk-taking," Justine observed. "I suppose people take chances in the academic world, but they aren't usually life-and-death."

"Maybe," I agreed ruefully, although I don't much like the idea of life-and-death risks when the life we're talking about is my husband's. "Anyway, he's enjoying working on this case with Charlie Montgomery. It's given him something to think about, other than Sally."

"Oh, Sally." The Whiz's eyebrows went up. She knew about McQuaid's ex-wife, because she'd helped me search for her a couple of years ago, when Sally turned up missing. "What's happening in Dingbat's life these days?"

I slowed up to let a tractor cross the road, a hay bale the size of a minivan impaled on a rear-end fork. "She's planning to get married."

Justine's "Oh, yeah?" was sarcastic. From time to time, she has ventured the opinion that Sally is an air-brained bimbo.

"Right," I said. "And if you ask me, this guy she's engaged to is an abuser. The jerk whacked Brian's backside hard enough to raise some serious bruises. Brian says he's overheard them arguing, and I wouldn't be surprised if Sally's been knocked around, too. But the man is a stockbroker and drives a Lexus, and she probably thinks she can redeem him. McQuaid is doing a background check to see if Henningson —"

"Henningson?" Justine gave me a penetrating glance. "That wouldn't be Arthur Henningson, would it?"

"That's him. One of your clients?"

"Nope, never met the rat. Just his lawyers." She chuckled darkly. "But I did represent his wife Raissa in her divorce action."

"You're kidding." The tractor gone, I speeded up again.

"Why would I kid?" She shrugged her hefty shoulders. "It was a mean divorce, brimful of animosity, anger, and angst. And I'm not one whit shocked to hear that Artie baby is up to his old tricks."

"Meaning —"

"There's no record of it in the divorce papers, of course, but Raissa's secret weapon was a broken jaw, a dislocated thumb, and some pretty ugly bruises."

"Her *secret* weapon? She didn't press charges, I take it."

"Oh, hell, no. Raissa's too smart for that. She taped the argument that led up to the assault and dropped the cassette off in my office on her way to a private clinic for repairs. After his lawyer listened to it, he did the prudent thing and advised Henningson to settle."

"I take it that there was a fair amount of community property," I remarked dryly, "and no prenuptial agreement."

"Exactly. Stocks that he'd bought with her money, in a market rising faster and higher than my grandma's biscuits. Raissa is smart, but she was blinded by love." Justine grinned. "When the decree was granted, she remarked that a broken jaw was a small price to pay for getting out of that marriage with her portfolio intact."

"I see," I said thoughtfully. "If it's money he's after, I wonder why he's bothering with Sally. She doesn't have any —" I stopped. "Oh, hell, of course she does. Her father died last year. That's how she could afford to move into that high-rise condo."

"She'd better hang on to her checkbook. According to Raissa, Artie's a snake in a silk suit."

I turned off the county road onto Main Street. "Would you be willing to tell Sally what you know?"

The Whiz narrowed her eyes. "What? You're asking me to divulge the tragic personal events that led up to a secret divorce agreement?" She sounded aggrieved. "You're suggesting that I should set aside lawyer-client privilege just to keep McQuaid's dim-bulb ex-wife from making a mistake she'll live to regret?"

"Well, yes," I said. "Would you mind?"

"Of course I wouldn't mind." She shook her head grimly. "I tell you, China, I wouldn't wish that sonovabitch Artie Henningson on anybody. Not even on Little Miss Brain-dead."

"McQuaid will be glad to hear that," I said. "Let's drag him out of that jail and tell him."

"You drag him out of that jail," the Whiz said. She looked at her watch. "I've had enough fun and games for one day. I need to get back to San Antonio. I've got a brief to prepare for a hearing on Monday." She heaved a long, heavy sigh. "No rest for the gifted."

* * *

I checked in at the booth to see how everything was going. Brian and Diana were there, but I had just missed Ruby, who had gone off to talk to Brenda. The kids reported that it had been a pretty slow afternoon so far, especially since Ruby had told them that they couldn't do any more advertising.

"How are you supposed to get people's attention if you can't yell at them?" Brian grumbled.

"It's called the soft sell," I said, rearranging a stack of handmade herb candles. "Shoppers don't like strong-arm tactics. They prefer to walk around and enjoy the festival, and if they happen to see something they like, they'll stop and buy it."

"It's cool with us if you don't want to make any money," Diana said cheerfully, as I pulled out one of the plastic tubs and began restocking the potpourri display. "We're having a blast." She looked starrily at Brian.

Ah, young love, the sweetest love of all. Whether it lasts for six hours or six months, every minute of it is new-minted and miraculous.

"Oh, I forgot," Brian put in. "Dad was here a couple of minutes ago, looking for you."

I rearranged a couple of cellophane bags of rose potpourri and stepped back to admire the effect. "Oh, yeah? What did he want?"

"He wanted to tell you that he and the sheriff got their man."

I turned to stare at him. "Their what?"

"The guy who killed Casey Ford."

Diana put her hands on her hips. "Your dad and the sheriff don't know their heads from a hole in the ground," she said heatedly. "It wasn't him. Casey Ford killed himself. Everybody knows that."

"Well, somebody doesn't know it," Brian retorted in a superior tone, " 'cause somebody fingered the killer. That's what Dad said."

"Fingered *who?*" I demanded. "Who did they arrest?"

"They did not arrest him," Diana replied, with emphasis. "They just took him in for questioning, that's all." She scowled at Brian, the stars fading from her eyes. "*That's* what your dad said. Don't you ever listen?"

"Use your brain, girl." Brian was stung. "They wouldn't waste time taking somebody in for questioning if they didn't think he —"

"Will you *stop?*" I yelled. "You kids are driving me crazy!"

Across the plaza, a large woman in a frilly pink dress turned and gave me a frown, to show that she disapproved of moms yelling at their children. I lowered my voice.

"Okay, you guys," I said fiercely. "I want to know who they took in for questioning, and I want to know *now.*"

Brian spoke with mild reproof. "Well, you don't need to blow a fuse. His name is Les somebody. Rides a red Harley." He turned his fist up and down and made vroom-vroom noises, as if he were revving a motorcycle. "Big sucker," he said admiringly.

Brian could have been referring to either Les or the motorcycle, but either way it was bad news for Les — and for Shirley, too. Had Sheriff Montgomery uncovered some sort of physical evidence to implicate him?

"Where's your dad?" I asked.

Brian jerked his thumb over his shoulder in the direction of the Indigo Café, across the street. "He went over there. I'll walk you." He glanced quickly at Diana. "Be right back. Okay?"

Diana tossed her hair back. "Pardon

moi," she said, "but I was just wondering, like whether we're gonna get any money for this. For taking care of the booth, I mean. After all, we're spending hours and hours just sitting here."

"That's fair," I said, although just moments before, being together had been its own sweet reward. "Five bucks an hour, split between the two of you. How's that?"

"Sure," Brian replied.

"Five-fifteen is minimum wage," Diana said astutely.

This girl would go far. "Okay, then. Five-fifteen," I replied.

Brian and I angled across the brick plaza. When we reached the street, he said, in a low voice, "Mom, I gotta tell you something. But you have to promise not to let it get back to Diana that I was the one who told, or she will be super pissed off at me. She made me swear I wouldn't say a word to Dad about this — but she didn't think of making me promise not to tell you."

I stopped at the curb. I'm wary of making agreements like this, but there was something in the boy's voice that told me it was important. Anyway, I'm a pushover for anything prefaced with "Mom."

"Okay," I said. "What's up?"

"Diana saw the guy who set fire to the

Bluebonnet this morning," Brian said, his face unusually sober. "She set her alarm clock and went out to see how Ethel and her babies were doing, and she saw him throw something — gasoline, she thinks — into the trash bin. Then he must have tossed in a match, because the whole thing went up in flames."

"I see," I said, keeping my voice carefully neutral. "Did Diana recognize this firebug? Does she know who he is?"

"Yeah," he said. "Some bald guy named Harry. She said he runs the Emporium and that his wife is a gargoyle and his daughter is a witch." He squared his shoulders, an adult anxiety written on his features. "I know this is serious stuff, Mom. You have to tell Dad and he has to tell the sheriff. But I don't want to get Diana in trouble with her mom or anybody." He turned down the corners of his mouth, obviously unhappy. "Although I guess I don't have any control over that, do I? The minute I tell, it's out of my hands."

"Thank you, Brian." I ruffled his hair with my hand. Kids surprise you sometimes with how much they understand about the ethical dilemmas they face. "I'll ask your dad to do his best to keep Diana out of it."

I started across the street. So Harry had torched the crime scene. Did that suggest that he was a killer, too?

Seventeen

FRIJOLES DE OLLA
(BEANS IN A POT)

1 lb. dry black beans, washed, picked,
   soaked overnight, and drained
4 quarts water
2 onions, sliced
12 whole cloves garlic
salt to taste
2 teaspoons fresh minced oregano,
   or 1 teaspoon dried
1 1/2 teaspoons cumin
2 sprigs fresh minced epazote,
   or 1 teaspoon dried

garnish: sour cream, chopped cilantro, tomato, green onion, jalapeño pepper, grated Monterey Jack cheese

In a large pot, bring four quarts of water to a boil. Add soaked beans, onion, and garlic. After an hour of cooking, add salt, oregano, cumin, and epazote. Cook for another half hour, or until beans are done. (Beans are cooked when you can easily mash one against the roof of your mouth with your tongue.) Puree about 1 cup of the beans (you can use your blender for this); return pureed beans to the beans in the pot. Serve in pottery bowls, garnished with sour cream and chopped cilantro, tomato, green onion, or jalapeño pepper. Sprinkle with grated cheese.

You can find Indigo Café look-alikes in dozens of small Texas towns. It occupied the first floor of a narrow two-story brick building that in an earlier incarnation had been a saloon. Its interior walls, also brick, were hung with rusty implements, Texas license plates from the '20s and '30s, and photographs of cowboys, bluebonnets, and longhorn cows — Texas's national treasures. Underfoot was a scuffed wooden floor; overhead, baskets of dusty Boston ferns that looked like they could use a drink, a bath, and a haircut. A long wooden bar with a polished brass foot rail and leather-topped stools — a genuine antique, from the looks of it — took up one side of the long, high-ceilinged room, while the rest was crowded with wooden tables and chairs. The festival was apparently bringing in quite a bit of business, for almost every table was occupied by tourists: families with kids in strollers and high chairs; senior ladies with blue hair, their husbands in those one-piece zip-front jumpsuits that always remind me of prison garb; trendy-looking DINCs — double-income, no children — out to spend as much as they could. I caught sight of Jerome scurrying out of the kitchen with a loaded tray on his shoulder, while Carl was taking an order from a table of eight. The place was not only packed but noisy, with a jukebox in the back playing Gary P. Nunn's all-time big hit, "I Wanna Go Home with the Armadillo." True Texas.

McQuaid was perched on a stool at the near end of the bar, a plateful of enchiladas, a plastic basket of chips, and a frosty mug of beer in front of him.

"Late lunch, huh?" I said, taking the stool next to him.

"Charlie and I didn't get around to eating." He forked a chunk of enchilada into his mouth, the yellow cheese stringing across his chin. "You know how it is when you get busy," he said, in an all-in-a-day's-work tone.

I certainly knew how it was, since I'd neglected to eat lunch, too. But I had several items on my agenda. I went straight to the first one.

"Brian tells me that the sheriff took Les Osler in for questioning a little while ago."

"Yeah, that's right." McQuaid picked up his beer and took a swig. It had a couple of slices of lime in it, Mexican style. "Want something to eat, babe?" He took the menu out of the rack in front of him and handed it to me. "They've got chicken flautas."

I'm a pushover for flautas — tortillas filled with boned cooked chicken, then deep-fried and served with salsa, sour cream, and grated Monterey Jack — and now that I was here, with the sights and smells of Tex-Mex food all around me, I was ravenous. I hooked my finger at Carl, who had come around the bar and was heading in my direction with a questioning look.

"Flautas," I said, not bothering with the menu. "Frijoles with double guacamole, and a Corona with lime."

"You can put that on my tab," McQuaid said, as Carl slid a basket of blue-corn tortilla chips and a bowl of salsa in front of me. Today, he was wearing a pink-and-green tropical print shirt, shorts, and sandals, with sunglasses propped on top of his brown buzz cut. If he was trying to look like a bartender in Cozumel, he was succeeding. He flashed a grateful grin at McQuaid.

"On the house," he said. "Congratulations. You guys work fast."

"Thanks," McQuaid said, over the rim of his beer mug. "So you heard, huh?"

"Yeah. Jerome told me that Les Osler's been arrested. No big surprise, I guess."

McQuaid put down his mug and picked up his fork. "You had your suspicions, huh?"

"Yeah." Carl swiped the bar in front of me with a damp cloth. "He was in here the other day, telling Jerome and me that he wanted to marry Ford's sister. He said Casey'd told him no, but that was bullshit and he was going to do something about it. Guess he already had it all figured out. Reckon it wasn't too hard, since he probably gave Casey a hand setting the trap up." He lobbed the bar rag into a sink. "Be right back with your beer, ma'am."

"Brian said you got a tip on Osler," I said, dredging a chip in the salsa. "Somebody fingered him." I smiled slightly. "That was his word for it, anyway."

"Yeah. She saw him slipping into the back door of the Bluebonnet, about twenty minutes before Ford was shot. We tried talking to him, but he's your basic uncooperative type. Charlie thought he could squeeze him harder if he questioned him at the sheriff's office."

The salsa probably wasn't hot enough for McQuaid, who has an asbestos tongue and a firewall all the way down to his stomach, but it was just fine for me. "Twenty minutes before the gun went off?" I asked. "That makes it almost ten, and pitch-black. As I recall, that alley's not lighted, and the old cotton gin blocks the light from the plaza. So who's this she-person with the see-in-the-dark eyes?"

He bent over his enchilada. "The apprentice witch. But she didn't come running in to accuse him, if that's what you're thinking. She was reluctant to tell us what she'd seen. Like everybody else in town, she started out by insisting that Ford stumbled into his own trap and got exactly what he deserved. It was a while before she loosened up and told us what she'd seen."

"A generous act of public service," I remarked ironically, as Carl arrived with my beer. I squeezed the lime into it and took an appreciative swallow. Light and malty. Some people like salt with Mexican beer, but I'm not one of them. "I don't suppose you or Charlie just happened to mention to She-Who-Can-See-in-the-Dark that her very own father might be on the suspect list," I went on. "That might have helped to loosen her a bit."

"Absolutely not," he replied indignantly. "She volunteered it herself, without a word of prompting, after we'd been talking for a few minutes. So you can forget the idea that we scripted her."

"Could have been her mother's script," I replied. "In the Mason family, Maxine is the one who gives the orders. According to Diana, she is a gargoyle."

"A gargoyle?" McQuaid looked puzzled. "What's that?"

"Ask Diana," I said, and got to my second item, which made a great deal more sense now that I knew who had identified Les Osler. "And speaking of Diana, did you know that she lives right behind the Bluebonnet? On the other side of the alley?"

"Yeah?" McQuaid put down his fork. "Interesting, but what's your point, Sherlock?"

"My point is that when she went out to her backyard early this morning to make sure that Ethel and her bunny babies were okay, she happened to see Stella's father Harry torching the Bluebonnet."

That got his full attention. He swiveled

his stool to look at me, both eyebrows raised. "Harry Mason?"

I nodded. "What's more, Diana didn't volunteer the information. She told Brian, but she made him promise not to tell you. So he told me instead. He hopes that Diana won't get into trouble, and he particularly doesn't want to be identified as the snitch, if that's possible." I took a swig of beer. "It certainly seems to me that this new and totally unsolicited information casts some doubt on Stella's identification of Les."

McQuaid rubbed his chin reflectively, discovered the cheese, and scrubbed at it with his napkin. I took his silence for confirmation.

"Well, then," I said, "do you have anything else? Any corroboration of Stella's story? Any other reason to hold Osler?"

He motioned with his head in the direction of Jerome, who was hurrying back to the kitchen with an empty tray. "Jerome said he saw Osler's red Harley parked on the street right after the shooting."

My plate of flautas arrived, sizzling hot, with a pottery bowl of beans on the side, redolent with comino and the slightly resinous epazote, a traditional Mexican herb traditionally used to reduce flatulence. It

347

makes the enthusiastic bean-eater more so-cially acceptable.

"We already knew where he parked his Harley," I replied. "Shirley told us. So other than Stella and Jerome, you've got nothing, I take it." I spread the guacamole and sour cream over my flautas and dug in. "What does Osler say?"

McQuaid sighed. "Claims it's a case of mistaken identity. Says he spent the eve-ning knocking on the doors of people he knew, trying to find a place for Shirley to hang out. Says he was at a buddy's house at the time Stella saw him going into the Bluebonnet." He gave me a narrow look. "What's going on, China? You're the one who told me that Osler had a strong mo-tive, and you also seemed to think he had opportunity, as well. Have you changed your mind?"

I sighed. "Not . . . exactly." I hadn't changed my mind. It was my heart that was asking the questions. Or as Ruby might have put it, my right brain. It was beginning to seem to me that too many people wanted to nail this thing on Les Osler. Stella, Jerome, Carl —

"Well, then, what's your problem?" McQuaid tossed his napkin onto the bar and pushed his empty plate away. "It won't hurt Osler to cool his heels in custody for a few hours. In the meantime, Charlie's got a couple of deputies checking his alibi." He frowned at me. "What *is* the problem?"

"Oh, I don't know," I said, savoring my flautas. "It's just that — well, I've been with Shirley this afternoon. I hate the idea of her getting hurt, especially when it's beginning to look as if she'll have a chance at straightening out her life." I gave him a quick report about what Justine and I had found in the metal box, concluding with, "It looks like there was no basis for Casey's claim of guardianship — and that he and his father had been embezzling the assets from Shirley's trust. There appear to be substantial assets in the estate."

McQuaid whistled. "That's what I call an ingenious fraud."

"Yeah. The lawyers and accountants are going to have a field day with this one. If Ford wasn't already dead, he'd be spending the rest of his life in prison. But none of this strengthens Osler's motive," I added in a cautioning tone. "If he'd known what Ford was up to, he would simply have blown the whistle, rather than go to the trouble of killing the guy." I paused. "You're absolutely sure that Casey didn't get drunk and blunder into his own trap?"

"I'll never be a hundred percent sure of anything. But the autopsy report came back a couple of hours ago. Ford had one, maybe two beers, probably about the time he ate supper. No way was he drunk."

I thought of the rock salt I had seen in Casey's bedroom, and went to the third item on my agenda. "Did you check out the other buildings on the list Jerome gave you — the ones Ford claimed to own?" Only Ford didn't own them, I knew now. Shirley did.

McQuaid nodded. "I found one other shotgun trap. The gun was empty but the trap was still in place, and aimed low. Charlie's getting the gun and the shell checked out for prints. They'll probably belong to Casey."

"When I was at Shirley's this afternoon, I found something else that belonged to Casey. A bag of rock salt, some empty shotgun shell casings, and another shotgun. The rock salt and casings are on the table he used for reloading, in his bedroom. You might want to send somebody out to pick them up, just to add them to your collection."

"Hot damn!" McQuaid exclaimed. "Rock salt! You realize what that means, don't you?"

"Yeah," I said. "It's pretty solid evidence that the trap Casey set was nonlethal — although it would be a lot more conclusive if the Bluebonnet hadn't burned and you still had the murder weapon."

"Oh, yeah?" He hoisted his beer with a grin. "So who says we don't have the murder weapon, Counselor?"

I fixed him with a penetrating look. "Excuse me, McQuaid, but you seem to have something up your sleeve."

"Right. A murder weapon and an empty shell casing."

"I should have known," I said, my mouth full of flautas. "So you took the shotgun out of the Bluebonnet before you left last night."

"Right again. You don't think that I'd leave a murder weapon lying around unattended, do you? I put it in the trunk of Charlie's car, and he took it back to his office and locked it in the evidence room. This morning, one of the deputies lifted several clear prints off the gun, and one off the empty casing."

"Very tricky," I said in an admiring tone. "Bet you haven't told a soul."

He laughed. "You're the first to know. It didn't seem like a good idea to spread the news around town. Better for the killer to

351

think that there's no way of making a print match. A little confidence makes some folks careless." He gave me a serious look. "If those prints belong to Osler, China, that's all it will take to charge him. *And* to convict him."

"And if they don't?"

A shrug. "Then we're back at square one. But not quite. As soon as we can, we'll lean on Harry about the torching of the Bluebonnet. And of the thirty-seven people who live in this town, we've printed thirty-six of them. Charlie's getting the prints run as we speak."

I took a swallow of beer. "Thirty-six out of thirty-seven. So who's the missing person?"

"Who do you think?" The corners of McQuaid's mouth quirked. "Harry. According to his wife, he went to Waco this morning, supposedly to look at some inventory he's planning to buy."

"No foolin'." I grinned. "Does that tell us something?"

"Maybe," McQuaid replied cautiously. "But it's entirely possible that Harry's the arsonist and Osler's the murderer. If Shirley's as well-off as you think, maybe she ought to get her boyfriend a lawyer."

"I'm not convinced Osler killed Casey Ford," I said.

"That's because you don't want to be," McQuaid replied. "You may act tough on the outside, but inside, you're a softie. You fall for a love story every time. You need to remember that not all love stories have a happy ending, though."

"Here's another one that may not have a happy ending," I said. While I polished off my lunch, I told him what the Whiz had told me about Henningson's divorce from Raissa.

McQuaid looked somber. "Well, it doesn't surprise me — but it doesn't make me jump up and down for joy, either. I feel sorry for Sally." He shook his head gloomily. "At least it'll get Henningson out of her life, and Brian's." He turned on his stool, put his hand on my shoulder, and dropped a kiss on my forehead. "Thanks, babe. I would have uncovered the divorce eventually, but I doubt that I'd have dug up those grisly details."

"You're welcome." I drained my beer. "So now what?"

He stood and took out his billfold. "I'm going to give Charlie a call and report what Diana told Brian. He'll probably ask the Department of Public Safety to keep an eye out for Harry. Then I thought I'd pick up Brian and go back to the tank for some afternoon fishing." He put a tip on the bar. "What time are you and Ruby closing the booth?"

"The festival closes at four-thirty," I said. I looked at my watch and was surprised to see that it was after three. No wonder I'd been hungry.

"Want to go fishing with us?" He frowned, remembering. "No, you said that you and Ruby were driving back to Pecan Springs this evening, didn't you?"

I nodded. "I also need to find Allie and let her know what's going on with Les, so she can break the news to Shirley. When the festival closes, we'll pack up and head back home, where I intend to climb into a hot bath." I gave him a sexy smile as I got off the stool. "You're sure you won't join me? There's room in the bathtub for two." I know this, because we've tried it out. It's a tight fit, but that just makes it more fun.

He slipped his arm around my waist. "I'd love to, but I promised the kid we'd —"

"I'm looking for the sheriff," an urgent voice said. "I need to talk to him. Do you know where he is?" I turned. It was Brenda.

"Sheriff Montgomery has gone back to his office," McQuaid said, "but I'll be talking to him by phone. Can I relay a message?"

"I need to tell him something," Brenda replied. "I probably wouldn't have thought of it, but I just heard that Les Osler has been arrested for killing Casey Ford, and I remembered —"

"Nobody's been arrested," I interrupted sharply. "He was taken in for questioning, that's all."

Brenda's "Oh?" was colored with an unmistakable disappointment, and her raised eyebrows asked why this was any of my business. "Well, at least he's a suspect," she amended. She turned back to McQuaid. "I wanted to tell the sheriff that I saw Les Osler having an argument with Casey Ford a couple of days ago — a real shouting match."

McQuaid obligingly took out his notebook. "What day did this happen?" he asked, and wrote down the details of the story that Brenda repeated for him. She had come out of the back door of the cotton gin, where she'd been helping to paint the stage set for the play. Ford and Osler were toe-to-toe and eye-to-eye, as she put it, in the alley behind the Bluebonnet. She arrived on the scene just in time to hear the tail end of their shouted conversation: Casey's "If you don't stay away from her, I'll have your sorry ass in jail," and Osler's "Try that, you filthy bastard, and you're a dead man." She got the distinct impression that the two men would've traded punches if they hadn't looked up and seen her. Red-faced and furious, Osler had stalked away, and Ford opened the back door of the Bluebonnet and disappeared inside.

"As I said," she added, "I didn't think much of it at the time. Casey Ford was always getting into arguments, although most people were afraid to stand up to him. But after what happened last night —" She let the sentence trail off. "I just thought the sheriff would want to know," she added smoothly, with a so-there-you-are glance at me. "I'd be glad to make a statement, if he thinks that would be useful."

McQuaid took down her name and phone number and thanked her politely for the information. When she was gone, he turned to me, his dark eyebrows pulled together in a questioning look.

"Does it look to you as if the good citizens of Indigo are ganging up on Osler?" I asked archly. "I wonder if they're picking on him because he's an outsider. Not really one of them."

McQuaid put away his notebook. "Could be because he's guilty," he said, but he was half-smiling, and I had the feeling that he agreed with me. But before I could say anything else, we were interrupted again.

"Excuse me," Jerome said loudly. He was standing beside the door, reading from a slip of paper. "Does anyone here own a white Honda Civic, Ohio license plate ZZP 7234, parked beside the old school? If it's yours, you need to go turn the lights off."

It's probably Ruby's influence, this questioning of the universe. But later, when I thought about the sad events of that long and tragic afternoon, I would wonder about the synchronicity of experience, as Ruby calls it. Or maybe it's just the sheer randomness of the world, the multiple what-ifs of the way things happen. If Jerome had been handed that slip of paper two minutes later, I would have already been across the street, heading back to the booth, and after that, home to Pecan Springs and a long, hot self-indulgent bath and —

And then what? If I hadn't heard that message, or if somebody hadn't noticed that the lights were on, or if they hadn't been left on in the first place, how would

357

things have turned out differently?

But the lights *were* left on, and somebody did happen to notice and write down the license plate number, and then happened to bring it to the café, where Jerome read it off while I was still there. I heard it, and I frowned. That Honda had to belong to Ellen Holt — I'd seen that Ohio ZZ plate on the car that was parked next to my cottage. But Ellen had told me that she was going to Austin for an interview.

Of course, people lie all the time, and for all kinds of reasons, good, bad, indifferent — and often entirely trivial. But somehow I had the feeling that this lie had some important significance. What was it? What was going on?

Eighteen

In Egyptian tombs of the third millennium B.C., archaeologists have found mummies wrapped in funeral cloths with indigo-dyed borders, and indigo was the dominant color in the funeral clothing of Pharaoh Tutankhamen. In central Asia, mourning robes were dyed with indigo. Fabrics found at the site of the Sutton Hoo burial in England were dyed with indigo and woad. For many cultures, the color blue, the color of the sky, was associated with death and the after-world.

"Okay, babe, I'm outta here." McQuaid hooked an arm around my neck and brushed his lips across my forehead, which is as close as he usually comes to a display of public affection. "I'll meet you back at the booth in five or ten minutes?"

"Right." I am less inhibited. I rose on tiptoes to kiss the corner of his mouth. He is, after all, my husband. I'm entitled.

I followed McQuaid out, but instead of going across the street to the booth, which

I had every intention of doing, I found myself lingering on the sidewalk in front of the café. I had more important things to think about than Ellen Holt's comings and goings, and a great many more important things to do than check out her car. But she was staying in my guest house, which made me feel sort of responsible, and I was undeniably curious. The old school was only a block down the street. It would take just a minute to walk over there and see —

See what? Okay, so the little blonde dingbat had left her lights on, and probably locked the car, to boot. I do it, too, from time to time, especially when I'm in a hurry or preoccupied. When I'm anxious to get somewhere or see somebody or —

"Oh, there you are," Ruby said breathlessly. "The kids told me I'd find you here. I just heard something from Stella that the sheriff ought to know."

"Uh-huh," I said. I could almost see the old school from where I stood. Not much of a detour. "You haven't seen Ellen Holt this afternoon, have you?"

Ruby shook her head. "I just saw Allie, though, as I was crossing the street. She looked really upset and angry. No, more than angry, furious. Mad enough to bite bullets. I called to her and I know she saw me, but she ducked into the theater. I wonder what's wrong."

Allie? Angry? Furious? Mad enough to — I frowned. Had Ellen come to Indigo to meet Allie? That might be natural enough, given that Ellen's uncle — if that's who he was — lived with Allie. But why lie about it?

Ruby was staring at me. "What's up, China? Why are you looking like that?"

"Nothing's up," I said, starting off. "I'm not looking like anything. I'm going back to the booth."

She took a few hurried steps to catch up to me. "Then you're going in the wrong direction." She caught my arm and pointed across the street. "The booth is over there."

"Oh." I stopped. "So it is. Well, don't mind me. I'm just taking a little detour. You don't have to come if you don't want to."

"Detour? Detour where?"

"To find out what Ellen's doing in Indigo, when she told me she was going to Austin." I started walking again. "Justine interrupted me earlier, when I was about to tell you that Ellen is Derek's niece — or at least, that's what she says. She went to his camper last night looking for some family papers he's supposed to have."

"So that's the story," Ruby said, shaking her head. "It's amazing how facts can get bent out of shape." She frowned. "Speaking of distorted facts, have you heard what Stella told the sheriff?"

"About seeing Les Osler going into the Bluebonnet? Yes, McQuaid told me."

"Well, it's not true."

We stopped at the curb, waiting for an SUV full of festival-goers to pass, then stepped out into the street. On the far curb, I stopped and looked at her. "You mean, Stella didn't really see him? Does she know that Les Osler was taken in for questioning on the strength of her statement?"

"Yes, and she feels bad about it, down deep." Ruby made a face. We started to walk again. "At first she gave me the same story she gave the sheriff. But after we talked for a while, she told me that she wasn't sure. She saw *somebody*, but it was pretty dark and she didn't see him very clearly. She'd like to think it was Les Osler, but —"

"Why in the world would she like to think it was Les Osler if it wasn't?"

"Because he's . . ." Ruby shrugged. "Well, Stella didn't say this in so many words, but I got the idea that she and the others don't like him. After all, he worked for Casey Ford, tearing down some of the buildings. And he doesn't live in Indigo, and he isn't one of the people who are trying to revive the town." She was getting a little breathless, trying to walk fast and talk fast at the same time. "The folks here would rather believe that Casey Ford killed himself when he tripped his own booby trap. But if it turns out to be murder, they'd certainly prefer that the murderer wasn't one of them."

"Especially Harry Mason," I said grimly, "who didn't stay around today to be fingerprinted."

"Yes. Stella says her dad went to Fort Worth to see his sister. He won't be back for several days."

I laughed shortly. "Fort Worth? Maxine told the sheriff he went to Waco on business. Mother and daughter had better coordinate their stories, or somebody will accuse them of lying." I paused, recalling how anxious Carl and Brenda had been to implicate Osler — and no doubt there would be others, if the need arose. "There's obviously a conspiracy in Indigo, and Les Osler is being set up to take the rap for somebody else."

363

For one of *them*.

For Harry Mason, who had been seen torching the crime scene by a witness without an ax to grind.

Who might have been acting under the direction of his wife, who loved to give orders and who had railroaded the HIRC members into passing a motion that Casey Ford should be stopped at all costs.

"Exactly," Ruby said. "As soon as we get back, I'll let the sheriff know that he'd better talk to Stella again. I think she'll tell him the truth, now that she realizes how serious this is." She stopped and bent over to refasten the strap of her sandal, which had come loose. "Did you and Justine learn anything interesting when you talked to Shirley?"

"You wouldn't believe," I said, "but it's a long story. It'll have to wait until we find what we're looking for."

We were at the end of the block by now, in front of a square, two-story red brick building. INDIGO ELEMENTARY SCHOOL, according to the sign across the front. Once, this had been one of the most important buildings in town. It was the place where everybody's kids attended all eight grades, in an era before middle and magnet schools were invented and teachers had to have a minor in computer science in order to teach third grade. This was where Miss Mayjean must have taught, back in the days when the blackboard was the teacher's favorite technology, and she could count on the Room Mother to send chocolate chip cookies and grape Kool-Aid every Friday afternoon.

But that was all in the past. Now, the play yard was overgrown with grass, yellow dock, and sunflowers; the windows were covered with water-stained plywood; and the derelict old building had a sadly wistful look, as if it longed to be once more at the center of community life.

The parking lot beside the school was almost full, though. As we stood on the sidewalk, a noisy group of kids and parents passed us and began unlocking a minivan, as another car and truck drove in. People attending the festival were obviously using it as a place to park.

Ruby was looking around. "Well, why *are* we here, China? What are we looking for?"

"Ellen Holt's car," I said, starting through the parking lot, the gravel crunching under my feet. "Jerome announced her license number in the café. She left her lights on. I thought I'd see if I could find it."

"Why?" Ruby asked reasonably. "It's probably locked, so you won't be able to turn the lights off."

"I'm not sure why," I said. "I just have this funny feeling, that's all."

It was the wrong thing to say. "A funny feeling?" Ruby turned to me with interest. "That's your intuition speaking to you, China. Relax and pay attention to it. Don't let your mind get cluttered up with anxious thoughts — just be receptive to whatever comes. Welcome it, don't push it away."

"I am being receptive," I said, feeling irritated. "I don't have any anxious thoughts." Now wasn't a very good time for Ruby to give me a lesson in how to be psychic. It was hot, and I was tired, and I was already beginning to regret this wild-goose chase. What did I expect to accomplish, anyway?

We had reached the end of the parking lot. Back here, there were fewer cars.

"Yes, you do have anxious thoughts," Ruby replied, looking at me narrowly. "I can tell by the way your jaw is clenched. Loosen up, China, or you'll never be able to hear what your intuition is telling you."

"It's not intuition, it's suspicion," I said. "When I talked to Ellen this morning, she made a point of saying that she was going to Austin. If she came here instead, she must have been lying to me. But why would she go to the trouble of making up a story? Why not just tell me she was coming to Indigo?"

And as I said this, I saw it — a white Honda with Ohio plates, parked next to the building, between a green Dodge truck and a little red VW with a BABY ON BOARD sign in the rear window. If it hadn't been for the lights being turned on, the Honda wasn't a car you'd look at twice.

"That's it," I said, pointing. "That's Ellen's car."

Ruby tried one door and I tried the other, but both doors were locked. "It's weird that she'd go away and leave the lights on," she said, stepping back to regard the car thoughtfully. "She must have had her mind on something else."

"I think Ellen always has her mind on something else," I replied. "She's a very pretty young woman, but if you ask me, she is *exactly* the kind of person who would get out of a car and accidentally leave the lights on."

"Or maybe she did it deliberately, as a signal," Ruby said. Wearing a slight frown, her head cocked as if she were listening to a voice I couldn't hear, she stepped forward and placed both hands on the hood of the car, thumbs touching, fingers spread wide, lightly resting on the metal.

"Oh, yeah?" I made a skeptical noise. "A signal? What does it say? *Call the police, I'm being held for ransom?*"

"Hush, China." Ruby closed her eyes and spread her fingers wider apart. Her voice dipped. "I'm trying to listen."

I frowned. After a few years of hanging around with Ruby, I have learned to be impressed with her intuitive capabilities. But I seriously doubted that even the most skilled psychic could learn anything worth knowing from a Honda Civic.

Ruby's eyes opened, wide and startled. "China, something is wrong. Really wrong, I mean. I am sensing a terribly dark aura. An aura of death."

"Well, you've definitely got that right." I pointed at the lights, which seemed dimmer than they had when I first noticed them. "In a few minutes that battery will be deader than a three-day-old corpse." I looked around the parking lot. "While you're communicating with the Honda, why don't you ask it what Ellen is doing here? We might as well learn something useful."

But Ruby wasn't listening to me. Instead, she had turned away from the car and was walking resolutely toward the old school building. When she reached it, she began to walk along the back wall, her left arm outstretched, fingers lightly brushing the bricks, her head down, as if she were following a trail of invisible footprints.

"Ruby?" I asked. "What are you doing? Ruby?"

She didn't answer. As I watched, puzzled, she reached the back door a dozen paces away and stopped, her hand on the door handle. She stood for a moment, her head tilted to one side, then began to pull. I expected the door to be locked — after all, the windows were boarded up and the building was obviously deserted — but it opened easily.

That's when I got alarmed. "Hey!" I said sharply. "Don't go in there."

She turned her head to look at me. "I have to. Ellen's inside." Her eyes were unfocused and vague, her voice tinny, pitched up a half-octave. The light reflected off the gravel at her feet, making her face look shadowed, masklike. "Something's awfully wrong. Can't you feel it?"

And suddenly I could feel it, a chilly wave of danger and menacing peril that seemed to ripple like icy water around my ankles and rise rapidly to my knees and my hips, while I stood motionless in the parking lot, the bright October sun warming my shoulders. And then the sun itself, still bright, lost its warmth and grew cold, and I was embraced, shivering, in a wintry white light that froze me in place, unable to move, almost unable to breathe.

But I couldn't just stand there like a statue and let Ruby walk into God-only-knew-what. With a shuddery effort, I shook off the paralysis.

"Don't be silly, Ruby," I heard myself saying as I went toward her. "Even Ellen would know better than to go poking around in that old building." Walking felt like wading through a frozen lake, mushy with ice, like walking in a dream. My voice sounded like a dream-voice, too, remote, not mine, but the words were real enough. "Don't go in there. Somebody might have rigged a booby trap. Anyway, the windows are boarded up and the electricity's been turned off. It's pitch-black."

"I have a flashlight." Ruby reached into her purse and took out one of those little plastic pocket torches that barely give enough light to read your watch. And then, without a single backward glance, the woman who can be scared silly by a spider the size of a button squared her shoulders and stepped into the dark, deserted building.

"Well, *hell*," I muttered. I stood still for the space of several breaths, thinking that the last time I followed Ruby through an unlocked door into a strange building, it had turned out to be a greenhouse filled with something close to a million dollars' worth of lush, green marijuana plants. As we stood inside the door gawking, we'd been nabbed by the South Texas Regional Narcotics Unit, who meant business. Escaping from their inconsiderate custody had required the help of the Adams County sheriff — a humiliating experience I certainly didn't intend to repeat.

But this building was abandoned, and there was no telling the condition of the interior. Booby traps aside, a stairway might have been removed, or a floor could have caved in. I couldn't let Ruby go prowling around in the dark all alone. She might fall down and break a leg, or something might fall on her. *This is dumb,* I thought. *Dumb, dumb, dumb.* But I pushed the door wide open, propped it with a rock, and went after her.

The light from the open doorway spilled

like gray paint down four scuffed concrete steps and into two long, narrow hallways that disappeared into the darkness, one straight ahead, the other off to the left, like two passageways into some ancient crypt. The building was heavy over my head, a lightless mausoleum populated by the spirits of restless children, and the air inside was cold, much colder than it had been in the parking lot. It had a stale, oppressive taste, thick and sour with the mingled, memorable scents of chalk, dirty tennis shoes, and pine oil cleaner. The smell of all school buildings, old and new. But there was the smell of something else, as well. The smell of danger and fear. The faint, rich smell of warm blood.

I shook my head. *Get hold of yourself, girl. Ruby has you spooked, has you carrying this intuition thing too far. Dirty tennis shoes, yes. Ghosts, maybe. Blood, definitely not.* I blinked and looked around, wanting to fasten onto something commonplace, something ordinary.

There was a closed door to my right. It bore a sign in large, hand-printed block letters: MISS MAYJEAN CARTER. FIRST GRADE, and a cork bulletin board on the wall next to the door was filled with crayon drawings of houses and trees and stick figures. So this had been Miss Mayjean's room, ordinary enough, certainly — but the spectral presence of those long-ago children, who must be grown now, with children of their own, seemed suddenly strong and real. I stared at the door, imagining that behind it I could hear the echo of their light, childish voices obediently chanting the alphabet, reciting numbers, reading aloud about Dick and Jane and Spot. Shirley must have gone to Miss Mayjean's first grade here, but she wouldn't have read as easily as the other children. Perhaps Miss Mayjean was the first person to realize that something was wrong.

There was a light switch beside the door, and my hand automatically went out for it, but when I flicked it nothing happened. I dropped my hand. I had been right. The lights had been turned off long ago. If the ghosts of restive children studied here, supervised by a ghostly replica of Miss Mayjean, they studied in the dark.

Two hallways, both as black as the inside of a cow. "Ruby," I called, reluctant to leave the patch of light beside the open door. "Hello, Ruby. Where did you go?"

My call was swallowed by the utter silence, as if it had been soaked up by a thick sponge, but tiny bits of dust, set in motion by my breath, danced on the pale, silvery air. Somewhere outside, a car alarm erupted into a belligerent cacophony of shrill wails and raucous hiccups, like a child having a temper tantrum. The noise seemed far away, as if it existed somewhere in the future, in the country we had come from.

By this time, part of me was thoroughly and foolishly frightened, although of what, I couldn't have said. My forehead was damp with sweat, my palms were clammy, my heart was pounding. The other part was thoroughly pissed and totally out of patience with Ruby. She had the flashlight, for Pete's sake. She could have waited until I caught up with her, instead of leaving me to grope my way in the dark. What was she thinking?

I stepped into the dimness of the long straight-ahead hallway, running my fingers along the cement-block wall. At that moment, my improvised door prop gave way and the heavy door closed behind me of its own weight, clanging shut so loudly that I gave a small shriek. Of its own weight? Or was it pushed? The dark was absolute and terrifying, like the dark inside a coffin.

"Ruby!" I yelped, hearing the fear in my

words, tasting it on my tongue. "Ruby, where the devil are you?"

"I'm back here *here here*," Ruby replied, from somewhere down the hall. She might have been calling from inside an echo chamber. "I'm in the second-grade room *room room*." Her voice seemed to be fading away, as if she were moving away from me, into an even darker distance. Then it was loud again, and closer, and stronger.

"I've found her, China. Come here." *Come here here here.*

"Found her? Found *Ellen?*" But that was nonsense. What was Ellen doing in the basement of a deserted school building, in the dark? For that matter, what was *I* doing here, acting like some brainless woman in *Tales from the Crypt?*

In the blackness, I began to make out a very faint yellow glow, seven or eight yards ahead and to the right. In total darkness, even a tiny light can call attention to itself, just as complete silence seems to magnify the slightest sound, a cracking twig, a dying breath. I shuffled slowly toward it the way you walk through a strange bedroom in the dark, not lifting my feet to keep from stepping on a sleeping dragon.

"So you've found Ellen," I made myself say. I sounded unnaturally brisk and cheery, like a nurse telling a dying woman that she'll feel better any minute now. "Well, good. Wonderful. Now we can all sit down and talk. But let's go outside, shall we? It's dark as a tomb in here." I had reached the open door. It was cold as a tomb, too, colder here than in the hallway, even.

"Ellen can't go outside." Ruby was standing a dozen paces inside the room, holding the flashlight so that it illuminated her feet. Her voice was flat, without inflection. "She's dead, China."

"Dead?" I said stupidly. "What are you talking about, Ruby? She can't be —"

Ruby lifted her tiny flashlight and the feeble light fell on a crumpled body. It was Ellen. She seemed to have dived headfirst into the room, arms outstretched to break her fall. It took only one quick glance to see that the back of her skull had been horribly crushed. She was lying motionless on the cold cement floor, her honey-colored hair loose and swirling over her shoulders and into the pool of rich, red blood under her head, blood that had sprayed into an arc across the floor, splattered with the impact of the blow that killed her. She was wearing close-fitting blue jeans, a striped top, sandals. Her purse was spilled beside her body — lipstick, a coin carrier, a pencil, a notebook, a minirecorder. Not far away lay a two-foot piece of metal pipe, covered with blood.

The smell of blood rose up around us like a coppery fog, so thick and strong that it was furry on my tongue. I tried to take a deep, steadying breath, but the taste caught at the back of my throat and I gagged.

"I'm going to be sick," Ruby said in a strangled voice. She thrust the flashlight into my hand and turned and bolted for the door. She didn't make it very far, though. I could hear her retching in the hallway.

I wanted to pick up the minirecorder and check to see whether it held a cassette tape, but there might be prints on it. I left it where it lay and went to find Ruby. She was leaning against the cement-block wall, wiping her mouth with the back of her hand. There was a puddle of vomit on the floor, and vomit was splashed on her shoes. Her face was bleached white.

"Go get McQuaid," I said quietly. "I'll stay with Ellen."

"You can't, China." Ruby glanced apprehensively over her shoulder, as if she were seeing shadows in the dark. "It's too dangerous. The killer might come back."

I doubted it. Whoever had murdered Ellen would not be hanging around waiting for the victim to be discovered. And anyway, the murder weapon had been left behind, there on the floor. The killer would be unarmed.

But who was I to argue with Ruby, who had been irrefutably right ever since she had laid hands on that Honda? And I suddenly realized that I didn't much like the idea of waiting beside Ellen's body in this tomb of a building, with only a flashlight battery between me and the silent menace of the dark.

"Go get McQuaid," I said. "I'll wait outside."

Nineteen

On the island of Sumba, the art of indigo dyeing is part of a larger traditional practice involving the mysteries of divination, magic, and herbal medicines. This complex body of occult knowledge is possessed only by a few Kodi women who understand the dangerous practices of *moro,* or "blueness," and are known as the "blue-handed women" (*warico kabahu moro*). Because of their association with indigo dyeing, they are viewed by the Kodi as intimately associated with death.

Adapted from
"Why Do Ladies Sing the Blues?"
— Janet Hoskins

"What I want to know," McQuaid said, in his sternest cop tone, "is what the devil you and Ruby were doing in that school building in the first place." His voice rose. "And I want to know the *truth.*"

Ruby and I exchanged glances. "It was the lights," I said. "The car lights. Ellen Holt — the victim — left them on." At

379

McQuaid's mystified look, I added, "Don't you remember Jerome reading off her license plate number when we were in the Indigo Café?"

McQuaid frowned. "I remember something about a car with its lights on, but I didn't pick up on it." He paused, very serious. "So how did *you* know, China? Was this Ellen Holt a friend of yours?"

Behind McQuaid, I could see the sheriff's car pulling into the parking lot and Charlie Montgomery getting out. One deputy had taped off the entrance to the parking lot, and as festival-goers straggled in to pick up their vehicles, he was taking their names and phone numbers before allowing them to drive out of the lot. Most of them hadn't driven very far, however. They parked out on the street and walked back to stand outside the cordoned-off area, jiggling their children on their hips, pushing a grandmother in a wheelchair. They stood silently, watching.

"How did you know it was Ellen Holt's car?" McQuaid asked insistently.

"I saw it at Thyme Cottage this morning," I said. "When —"

Surprised, McQuaid stopped me. "Thyme Cottage? The victim was staying in your guest house?"

The victim. The last time I had seen her alive, Ellen had been cute and pert and sure of herself, a sexy, flirtatious young woman. Now she was dead, that pretty head dreadfully battered. Now she was a *victim*.

"She's been at the cottage for four or five days," I said, trying to keep my voice level. "When Jerome read the license number, I recognized it as hers."

"Lucky she left the lights on," McQuaid muttered. "If she hadn't, that car might not have been spotted for quite a while."

I wanted to say, Oh, yeah? Well, maybe it wasn't just luck. Maybe she knew that she was going into a dangerous situation and she wanted to leave a signal. Or maybe something else intervened, some force that none of us understand, except perhaps Ruby. But there would never be any way of knowing, one way or another, so all I said was, "Yeah. Lucky."

McQuaid frowned at me. "Okay, so you recognized that it was Ellen Holt's car. So why did you come looking for it?"

I shrugged. "I had a hunch, I guess." If I'd said, *I had a flash of psychic insight,* I'd have lost him immediately. But having a hunch was acceptable. Cops know about hunches — they have them all the time, sometimes they even act on them. They'd never think of themselves as psychic, though.

"I dropped in to talk to Ellen at the cottage this morning," I went on, "and she told me that she was going to be in Austin all afternoon. In fact, she even told me where she planned to go, somewhere west of town. So when I heard Jerome read off the license plate —" I shrugged. "I guess I was just curious. Then I bumped into Ruby and we came here together."

McQuaid was not satisfied. "Was it curiosity that sent you into that deserted building?" When I didn't answer that rhetorical question, his face darkened. "For Pete's sake, China, didn't you and Ruby give one single thought to the danger involved? A man was killed last night when he walked into a booby trap in an abandoned building. Didn't it occur to you that the same thing might happen to you?" His voice was rising. "What in the name of God made you open that door and go inside?"

Beside me, Ruby shifted uncomfortably. She opened her mouth to speak but closed it again, and threw me a plaintive look that said, plain as day, that she wanted McQuaid to know what had happened but she didn't want to be the one to tell him.

I sighed. "Do you want to know the truth? Or would you rather hear something you can believe without stretching credulity?"

"Oh, shit," McQuaid said. He glanced from one of us to the other with the look of someone who suspects that you have a terrible disease and doesn't want to get too close for fear that it's catching. But his need to know overcame his skepticism. "Okay," he said with a long sigh. "Shoot."

"Ruby put her hands on Ellen's car," I said.

McQuaid has known Ruby a long time, too, and while he hasn't seen much direct evidence of her aptitudes, he's heard about them from me.

"That Civic?" He swiveled to stare at it. The lights had faded, and the VW beetle with the BABY ON BOARD sign was gone, driven away by a frazzled woman with twin toddlers. He turned back to Ruby. "So you put your hands on the Honda," he said, trying to suppress his skepticism. "So what happened then?"

Ruby looked at me, then back at McQuaid. "I knew she'd gone into the school," she replied simply. "I knew she was dead." Her eyes were bleak, her mouth was frightened.

"I see," McQuaid said flatly. "So why didn't you come to get one of the deputies, instead of going in there to find her yourselves?"

Ruby answered his question with one of her own. "Would the deputy have come, just on my say-so?" When McQuaid didn't answer, she said, "I didn't think so. That's why I went in." She reached for my hand and held it tightly. "China followed me because she was worried that I'd fall down and break a leg, or that something would topple over onto me."

I stared at her. She was saying exactly what I had thought, but had not put into words.

"You two." He looked from one to the other of us, shaking his head as if he were baffled. "I'll tell Charlie," he said. "Lord knows what he'll make of all this."

"Yeah, well, while you guys are picking holes in our story," I said hotly, "you might just give some thought to just how long she might have lain there if we *hadn't* gone in."

"We will." He gave me a long, sober look. "I'll go see if Charlie wants to ask you two any questions."

I put my hand on his arm. "I saw her

minirecorder lying on the floor beside her body. Could you check to see if there's a tape in it?"

Five minutes later, he was back. "Charlie says he'll take your word for it," he said, unsmiling. "You two can go." He looked at me. "The tape recorder is empty," he said. "No cassette. Does that answer your question?"

"Yeah," I said with a frown. "It does. I don't suppose you have the keys to her car, do you?" I added. Maybe she'd left the cassette in the car.

He frowned at me. "The car is part of the crime scene, China. Off limits. You know that."

"Right." I smiled thinly, turning to go. "But it doesn't hurt to try." If Ellen's killer had taken the cassette tape, it might have something to do with her murder. But what?

"Hang on a sec," McQuaid said. "Charlie will probably want to have a look through Ellen's things at Thyme Cottage." He frowned. "You stay away from the cottage, d'you hear? We'll want to give it a good going-over."

"If I'm not there you'll need the key," I said. "It's on a yellow plastic smiley-face key fob. I didn't see it on the floor beside her, so it must be in her purse."

"We'll look," McQuaid said. He put one arm around Ruby and the other around me, and bent to kiss my ear. "I guess I haven't said thanks, but it's a good thing you did what you did." He grinned awkwardly. "Even if it wasn't such a great idea." He frowned. "Well, you know what I mean."

"Right," I said.

Ruby gave him a small smile. "You're welcome."

Ruby and I were walking past Ellen's Honda on our way out of the lot when something occurred to me. I turned, registering something I'd noticed and forgotten. The green truck next to the Honda had a bale of hay in the bed and a gun rack across the back window.

"That truck," I said, pointing. "Isn't it Allie's?"

Ruby studied it. "You're right," she said. She looked at me, her eyes widening. "And just before I caught up with you in front of the café, I saw her running down the street, away from the school. She looked really angry."

We stared at one another for a long moment.

"You don't suppose that Allie —" Ruby began.

"I can't believe that Allie —" I said, at the same time.

We both stopped.

After a minute, I asked, "Do you want to put your hands on her truck?"

Ruby bit her lip and gave me a look that was half-hurt, half-afraid.

"I'm not being sarcastic," I said hastily. "I mean it, Ruby. The last time you did that, you found out —"

Ruby shuddered. "I know what happened the last time," she said, dropping her eyes. She turned away and started walking, her shoulders hunched. "And I don't want to do it again. I don't *ever* want to do it again."

By the time we got back to our booth on the plaza, it was nearly four-thirty. Closing time.

"Where have you been?" Brian demanded. He looked at his watch. "We've been here four hours."

"Five," Diana said, "counting this morning." She nodded at the tables. "Doin' good, too. Sold lots of stuff. Real boss."

"Five hours," I said, making a quick mental calculation. "That makes around twenty-six bucks, right? Ruby and I are glad you could give us a hand." I gave them each fifteen dollars out of the cash box. "Will this cover it?"

"Yeah!" Brian said enthusiastically. He pocketed the money, his irritation gone. "Where's Dad? Diana's mom says she can come fishing with us."

Fishing? Oh, good Lord. "Your dad's down the street," I said carefully, "but I don't think he's quite ready to go fishing just yet. Why don't you two just hang around here and —"

"It's that woman that got murdered in the school basement, isn't it?" Diana asked excitedly. "We, like, heard people talking about it. Come on, Brian, let's go see what's happening!"

"I don't think your father —" I began, but they were already gone.

"I suppose McQuaid can cope," Ruby said, pulling the empty tubs out from under the tables.

"He copes better than I do, actually," I replied. "I guess it's the cop in him." I scanned the bare tables and displays. "Looks like we did pretty well, wouldn't you say? We've sold nearly everything we brought."

But Ruby wasn't smiling at the success of our sale, and neither was I. Silently, we packed up what little was left of our merchandise, folded up our tables and displays, and loaded everything into Big Red Mama, while around us, other vendors were doing the same thing. Usually, this is a pleasant time, when vendors can relax and talk among themselves about the festival, comparing it to others they've gone to, complaining about poor sales or celebrating a full cash box.

But the vendors' voices were muted and they looked over their shoulders as they worked and talked. Some of them were watching us, too, with barely disguised interest. They had obviously heard about Ellen, and they probably knew that we'd been the ones who discovered her body. They were curious, but nobody would come up and ask us about it.

When Mama was mostly loaded, I left Ruby to finish up and walked back to the site of our booth, checking to make sure that we hadn't left anything behind. I couldn't blame the other vendors for wanting to know what had happened. Murder is the ultimate breach of the social contract, the very worst crime we can imagine. When it touches us, directly or even indirectly, we feel vulnerable, apprehensive, threatened. Because I had known Ellen, however slightly, I was filled with pity and sadness at the thought of the young woman who would not live to fulfill the promise of her life. Those who didn't know Ellen had to feel excitement, intrigue, curiosity. There had already been two killings in two days in this small town, where death came mostly to the old. Were these random murders? Or were they connected?

I bent over to pick up some loose pieces of paper and absently tossed them into the trash can. Before we found Ellen's body, I'd believed that somebody in Indigo — Harry Mason, probably, since he had torched the crime scene and then fled — had killed Casey Ford. But now that there were *two* killings, I had to question that conclusion, for the second cast the first in an entirely different light. The two had taken place within a few hundred feet of one another, in the same twenty-four-hour period. There had to be a connection between them — but what? What threads could possibly connect two such disparate deaths?

I went over what I knew. One victim had lived in the Indigo area, the other was a visitor from somewhere in Ohio. One was an older man, the other a young woman, and there was no indication that the two had ever met. Casey was shot when he walked into a trap that he himself had originally rigged in the Bluebonnet, while Ellen was bludgeoned when she went into the abandoned school.

I shook my head and started back to the van. This collection of facts suggested that the crimes weren't related. In most of the multiple homicides I've known about, killers don't mix their MOs. They're consistent. They may kill with guns, or with knives, or with blunt objects — but not with some combination of the above.

Back at Big Mama, I climbed into the driver's seat, rolled down the window, and waited for Ruby, who was talking to Stella. It wasn't just a question of method, either, but of motive. Plenty of people in Indigo had a reason to kill Casey, but who could have wanted Ellen dead, and why? And who had a motive to kill *both* of them?

I chewed the corner of my lip and drummed my fingers on the steering wheel. I might not like the thought, but there were two people who knew both Casey and Ellen, and there was a strong possibility that one of them was the murderer.

Ruby climbed into the van. "Okay, China," she said, "everything's packed and ready to go." She rolled down the window and put her head out. " 'Bye, Stella," she called. "Stop by the shops the next time you're in Pecan Springs."

I turned on the ignition. One of the two people, of course, was Derek Cooper. I hadn't entirely bought Ellen's story that Derek was her uncle — and even if he was, murder can happen in the best of families. Most family murders, however, are crimes of passion, sparked by a wild family argument. This was a premeditated homicide that took place at a prearranged meeting place, where the murderer, weapon in hand, had lain in wait for his unsuspecting victim. Why? What possible motive might he have? What might Derek gain from Ellen's death?

But to answer these questions, I'd have to know a great deal more than I did about their relationship, something that wouldn't be easy now that Ellen was dead, and would certainly involve a great deal of detective work. I couldn't even hazard a guess at this point.

I put Mama into reverse and backed her out of our parking place and into the alley. To make the whole thing even more puzzling, Derek had no motive, as far as I could see, to kill Casey Ford. He stood to gain nothing from Casey's death, especially since he and Allie had already broken off their relationship.

I shifted into first gear and started down the alley, steering to miss the potholes. Ruby was talking, but I could scarcely hear her over the urgent dialogue going on inside my head, an argument I couldn't quiet. If the two homicides were related — and they had to be, didn't they? — I didn't see how Derek could figure in both of them.

But Allie, unfortunately, was an entirely different story.

Allison Selby had plenty of compelling reasons to kill Casey Ford. The man had put her farm at risk, and her livelihood, and the lives of the wild things she loved so deeply. He was about to put an end to the resurrection of Indigo, and he was abusive to Shirley. All these reasons added up to a large plus in the motive column. And Allie had opportunity, as well, for she knew about the traps Casey had set and could easily have arranged for him to have gone to the Bluebonnet on Friday evening, perhaps on the pretext of meeting her there.

And Allie had almost as much reason to want Ellen Holt dead, believing, as she did, that there was something between

Ellen and Derek. Sure, she'd told me she was ready to let Derek go, but how did I know she was telling the truth? If she was planning to kill Ellen, wouldn't she have contrived some such story to tell me when she realized that I had overheard her argument with Derek? For all I knew, everything Allie had told me that morning in the kitchen could have been a lie, fabricated to keep me from believing that she still cared about Derek and to hide the fact that she wanted Ellen out of the way. She certainly had opportunity, too, for Ruby had seen her only five or ten minutes before we discovered the body, running frantically down the street, away from the abandoned school. And perhaps, having set up Casey's death and seen him lying in the street with a hole ripped in his chest, hitting Ellen over the head with a piece of pipe might not seem like such a big deal.

I didn't want to think these things, for I had known Allie for over twenty years. But these ugly, repulsive thoughts wouldn't crawl back into the dark corners of my mind, where they belonged. They had to be acknowledged, confronted, questioned. Who can say what someone might do when she's threatened with losing her place, losing her town, losing someone she loves?

Sometimes, the burden of too much loss can snap us, break us, make us lose sight of whatever moral compass we steer by. Sometimes, we can be driven to do things that would horrify us in saner moments.

And how well did I know Allie, anyway? It was true that we'd been undergraduates together, but except for a few close moments, when one or the other of us was having a romantic crisis, we hadn't shared a great deal. We hadn't stayed in touch, either — there were large gaps in our friendship over the years. And even when we were friends, Allie had struck me as a complicated, enigmatic person who never quite revealed all of herself. It's difficult to truly know someone like that, difficult to predict how she might feel, or what she might think, or what she might be capable of doing.

We'd come to the end of the alley, and I made a left turn.

Ruby stopped what she was saying and cleared her throat. "I hate to say this again," she said, "but aren't you going in the wrong direction?" She pointed over her shoulder. "The road to Pecan Springs is *that* way."

"We're going back to the school," I said. "I need to talk to McQuaid and the sheriff."

Ruby turned to face me. "It's about Allie, isn't it?" she asked quietly.

I nodded. Trust Ruby to read my mind.

"You think she did it, then?"

"What do you think?" I countered.

She was silent for a moment. "I'm not sure," she said finally. "You're the one she talked to about her relationship with Derek. You've known her for a long time. You'd have a better idea than I would."

"But you're the one who's psychic," I retorted, not smiling, thinking of Ruby putting her hands on Ellen's car.

Ruby shivered. "Don't say that," she replied in a low voice. "I don't want to go through that ever again, China. It was awful. I'd rather not have any power, than to have that kind. From now on," she added determinedly, "I'm going to tune out stuff like that."

I wanted to remind her that if you were truly psychic, you couldn't pick and choose the information you received — it just came to you, like it or not, and you had to choose how to act on it. But Ruby already knew that. This was a problem that she was going to have to sort out for herself. I had one of my own — a big one.

"Well, I'm not sure about Allie, either," I said grimly. "But she isn't likely to come forward with information that might incriminate her. I don't like doing it, but I guess I have to."

I thought of Brian and his dilemmas: whether to tell what Diana had told him in confidence, whether to tell what Henningson had done to him. My difficulty was no different than his, although it probably had more serious implications. What I was about to tell Sheriff Montgomery wouldn't make him run right out to Indigo Farm and arrest Allie, but it would certainly put her at the top of his suspect list. And once she was the focus of an intense homicide investigation, there was no telling what else would turn up. In my old life, if Allie had been my client, it would have been my job to keep inculpatory information like this from the police, as far as I could ethically do it, and further, if I thought I could get away with it. But that was then and this was now, and Allie wasn't my client, just a friend. The sheriff had two homicides on his hands and like it or not, I was still an officer of the court and duty-bound to assist his investigation. I certainly wasn't comfortable about this, but I knew what I had to do.

Ruby flashed me a brief, sad smile. "Well, if you're looking for consolations, here's one. Since Les was in custody when Ellen was killed, he's got to be in the clear. That is, if the two deaths are related. Which they might or might not be." Her smile faded and she let out her breath in a long sigh. "It's complicated, isn't it? And when you know someone, it's hard to imagine that she could . . ." Her voice trailed off.

"It's complicated," I agreed. "I'm just glad that I'm not the one who has to put all the pieces together and come up with an answer. That's what the sheriff gets paid to do."

Twenty

On the Indonesian island of Sumba, Janet Hoskins writes in "Why Do Ladies Sing the Blues?," death and the process of indigo dyeing were inextricably mixed. Shrouds were dyed with indigo. The smell of the fermenting indigo pot was like the smell of the decaying corpse. Death by violence was called a "blue death," where the soul escaped into the blue sky and could only be called back through special ceremonies. And on the nearby island of Roti, a pot of indigo dye was poured onto the grave of someone who had died a "bad death," the blue dye fixing the soul in the grave to keep it from wandering.

It was after eight by the time we finally got back to Pecan Springs, and indigo shadows were pooling under the overhanging branches of the large pecan trees that line the streets. McQuaid and the sheriff had been dealing with other matters at the crime scene, and we'd had to wait until they had time to talk to us. The telling of the story took a while, too, since I had to include quite a bit of background and since both the sheriff and McQuaid had numerous questions.

But finally the distasteful task was over. Charlie and McQuaid drove off to Indigo Farm to talk to Allie, and to Derek as well, although both seemed to think that Allie was the more likely suspect. Brian and Diana had gone to Diana's house for grilled cheese sandwiches and another look at Ethel and her babies; McQuaid would pick him up later and take him back to the camp. Having finished our dirty work, Ruby and I climbed into Big Mama and started home.

We were silent on the drive, each of us busy with her own thoughts. I don't know what Ruby was thinking, but I was going over things in my mind, still trying to make sense of the complex web of events and relationships that had ensnared Ruby and me this weekend. Usually, coming back from a successful festival, I'm relaxed and happy, pleased with our sales and thinking of the new friends and potential customers we've met. Tonight was different. It was one of those occasions when I realize just how much I have — love, good work, good friends — and feel sad that others can't have that, too. I still had a sour taste in my mouth, too, after listing for McQuaid all the reasons that he and the sheriff should have a serious talk with Allie. That hot bath was going to feel very, very good.

The shops were closed, of course, by the time we got back, so it would be a good time to unload all our stuff. I intended to park out in front, but the restaurant across the street — Casa de las Dos Amigas — was doing its usual brisk Saturday night business and all the on-street parking was taken. So I drove down Crockett past the shops, made a left turn onto Nueces, and another left into the alley, intending to back into the parking space next to the guest cottage. Since Ellen's car was still in Indigo, there'd be plenty of room.

But there wasn't any room at all. Parked diagonally in the parking place next to the cottage was a red pickup truck with a red-and-white camper on it.

Ruby clutched at my arm. "That's Derek's truck," she gasped, "and his camper! What in the world —"

Derek's truck? Turning the wheel sharply, I swung the van into the space behind Mr. Cowan's garage, where he keeps his compost heap and a couple of garbage cans. The blinds were closed in the cottage, but there was a light in the living room, and the shadowy shape of someone moving around. Was it Derek? Had he broken in? What was he looking for?

I opened the van door. "I need to find out what Derek's up to," I said in a low voice. "You stay here, Ruby."

"Not on your life," Ruby hissed, opening her door. It banged into Mr. Cowan's garbage can, sending the lid clattering into the compost bin. In the backyard, Miss Lula began a frantic yap-yap-yapping.

"Nuts," Ruby said disgustedly.

"Ssshhh," I said, but it was too late. As if he'd been waiting for us, Mr. Cowan popped around the garage, his plaid flannel bathrobe flapping around bare, skinny legs. In one hand, he brandished his cane like a sword, while the other clutched a plastic sack of garbage. Miss Lula added a cadenza of howls to her yaps.

"What's goin' on out here?" he demanded indignantly. "Who's trashin' my garbage can?"

"It's just us, Mr. Cowan," Ruby said in a loud whisper. She jumped out of the van. "I knocked the lid off your can. I'm sorry."

"Speak up there," Mr. Cowan commanded. "I cain't hear you for all the racket." He narrowed his eyes. "And how come you're parkin' on my side of the alley? Ain't you got 'nough parkin' on your own side?" He turned around. "Lula!" he yelled. "Lula, you stop that fool racket right now, you hear? Yer gonna make Miz Jenkins madder'n she already is."

I put my finger to my lips. "Please keep your voice down, Mr. Cowan." As if lowering our voices would help the situation any, with Miss Lula howling bloody murder.

To add to the confusion, the yard light came on next door. Mrs. Jenkins's screen door banged open and she shrilled at the top of her lungs, "Roy Cowan, is that stupid mutt of yours in my garbage again?"

"Keep my voice down?" Mr. Cowan snarled at me. "What good's that gonna do, with trucks racin' up and down the alley and fools bangin' the garbage can lids like they was the cymbals in the Dee-troit Symphony, and makin' Miss Lula bark and upsettin' Miz Jenkins, who's mad as a cow already?" He jabbed his cane in the direction of Derek's truck. "And that's the same fella who caused all the trouble last night. He's got a camper top on his truck now, but that's him, all right. Bet you a nickel he's a burglar."

Just at that moment, I saw Derek coming from the front of the cottage, heading for his truck. He was carrying a book bag over his shoulder and Ellen's laptop under his arm. Her laptop? Why would he —

"There he is!" Mr. Cowan crowed excitedly, hopping from one leg to the other. "There's the burglar!"

Derek picked up his pace as he realized that he had an audience, and as he reached the truck and opened the door, he turned and saw me. Surprise flickered across his face, mixed with anger, and he clutched the computer to his chest. And in that instant, I put the clues together, and realized who he was and why he needed that laptop.

"Hello, William Wilder," I said pleasantly. "Before you make off with Ellen's computer and research materials, don't you think we'd better have a talk?"

His face twisted. Wrenching the truck door open, he swung the bookbag into the truck and jumped in after it. But as he did, he dropped the computer. He didn't stop to pick it up. He slammed the door and hit the ignition, jamming the transmission into reverse and skidding into the alley, then into low, peeling out with a spray of loose gravel.

Ruby dashed for the laptop as I leapt back into Big Mama and started her. The van lurched forward as Ruby yanked the passenger door open and jumped in.

"I've got it!" she crowed, holding up the laptop, and something else. A key on a yellow smiley-face fob. The evidence that put Derek at the scene of Ellen's death.

Ruby recognized it, too. "He killed her, didn't he?" she asked, staring at the key. "But who is William Wilder?"

"Later," I grated. "Get on the cell phone, Ruby. Call 911. Tell them we're tailing a murder suspect. Give them a description of the truck and keep them on the line until we can get his license number."

Ruby braced her feet and punched in the numbers as we took off. Derek had only a few moment's head start, and we had the advantage of knowing the Pecan Springs streets. But his unfamiliarity with the neighborhood and the fact that he was driving a vehicle that had all the maneuverability of a Sherman tank didn't slow him down much. He made a fast left at Crockett, roaring down the quiet residential street as if it were the Daytona Speedway, as unwary joggers and dogs, out for an evening run, were forced to dive out of his way.

I stayed on his tail as well as I could, although I didn't have Derek's steely nerve or lack of reverence for crosswalks and stop signs. I lost some serious ground when a little old lady backed her old blue Mercury out of a driveway right in front of me, then slowed to a crawl down the middle of the street, as she checked out her hairdo and eyebrows in the rearview mirror. It was another block before I could manage to get around her.

❧ Meanwhile, Ruby was hanging on to the panic bar above the door with her right hand and holding the phone in her left, talking to the 911 dispatcher. "That's right. A red Chevy late-model pickup with a red-and-white over-the-cab camper. Texas QBZ 751." She paused. The dispatcher must have given her a hard time, because when she replied, her voice was sharp and hard. "Forget that. We're not letting him out of our sight. Don't you get it, lady? This isn't your ordinary burglar. We think he killed a woman this afternoon, over in Indigo."

"Two people," I said, suddenly grasping a possibility I should have thought of before. "Casey Ford's death might have been a mistake. He could have walked into a trap that Derek had set for Ellen."

Ruby stared at me, open-mouthed, then let out her breath. To the dispatcher, she said, "Make that two. Yes, two murders. The guy's name is Derek Cooper — or at least, that's the name he's been using." She glanced at me, her eyebrows raised. There was a pause. "Well, we don't know about armed, but he's sure as hell *dangerous.*"

Derek braked briefly at the red light at Comal, the first major four-lane cross-street we'd come to, then hung a sharp right, directly in front of fast-moving traffic coming from the left. I sucked in my breath as the camper tilted up on two wheels between a Domino's Pizza delivery car and a yellow convertible full of teen-agers.

"Tell the dispatcher that he's heading for I-35," I said tersely, negotiating the corner at Comal more slowly, with all four wheels mostly on the road. Even so, Big Mama rocked and the tubs and trays we'd packed so carefully slid from right to left, with loud crashing sounds. When this was over, we were going to have a mess to clean up. I could forget about that hot bath for quite a while.

"I-35," Ruby said into the phone. She listened a moment, then turned to me. "The 911 operator says we should abandon the chase. She says the cops will pick him up on the freeway."

"Assuming that he gets onto the freeway," I said. "He might be planning something tricky, like heading cross-country. Tell her we're keeping him in sight until we know which way he's going."

Keeping Derek in sight hadn't been all that difficult so far, since the streets were well-lit and the camper was light-colored and taller than most of the surrounding vehicles. Most, but not all. He was four or five vehicles ahead of me when he made a left off Comal and onto Rio Grande, two blocks from the access road, slipping neatly in front of a big silver-colored bus the size of a boxcar, with a Tour Texas! poster on the back. When I finally got a chance to make the same left, I was not only behind the bus but behind a big brown UPS truck, as well, and Derek's camper was effectively blocked from view.

I tried to pass the UPS truck, but a pair of girls with streaming hair on a motorcycle cut me off, yelling something rude as they flew past. The motorcycle was followed by a bumper-to-bumper string of fast-moving cars. Big Mama was sailing along at an uncomfortable speed, but we were stuck in the right-hand lane and there wasn't a damn thing I could do about it. And we were within a couple of blocks of I-35 and the access road. If he got into the left-hand turn lane, he'd go through the I-35 underpass, hang a quick left, and be northbound to Austin; if he took the right lane directly onto the access ramp, he'd be heading south, toward San Antonio.

"Tell 911 that he's coming up to the freeway," I said between clenched teeth. "But we can't tell yet whether he's headed north or south."

Ruby rolled down her window all the way. "Hug the curb, China," she commanded, unbuckling her lap belt. "Maybe I can see around this side."

It was our only chance. I pushed Big Mama sharply toward the right and put her two right wheels in the gutter, then bounced them over the curb. Ruby stuck her head and shoulders, and then her whole upper body, out of the van's window. All I could see was her indigo-dyed fanny. Hanging on to the steering wheel like grim death with my left hand, I reached over with my right and grabbed a fistful of cloth.

"Dear Lord," I muttered, "please don't let that door fly open." And please don't

409

make us come to a quick stop or hit a major pothole, or let Ruby whack her head against a signpost, or any of the hundred other calamities that loom when you're speeding along at fifty miles an hour behind a UPS truck with your right wheels up on the curb and your best friend dangling out of the window. Amen.

A few seconds later, Ruby wriggled back into her seat, her hair a wind-blown mass of coppery curls, her dress twisted, her freckled face red with exertion.

"He's making a right turn onto the access road!" she cried excitedly, refastening her belt. "He's heading south, China!"

"Tell 911," I said, jolting back off the curb and into the lane. "Once the black-and-whites have got a fix on him, we can drop out."

And not a minute too soon. I was shaking from tension and anger and fear, and relief that Ruby was safely back in her seat. My hands were superglued to Big Mama's steering wheel, my heart was in my mouth, and I could tell by the sour taste on my tongue that my stomach was headed there, too. If we didn't stop soon, I was going to throw up all over my lap.

"911?" Ruby looked at her hands. They were empty. "Omigod," she gasped, eyes wide. "I must have dropped the phone out the window!"

"Then we'll just have to stay with him," I said, swallowing my stomach back down where it belonged. The right-turn lane opened up as the bus and the UPS truck went through a green light at the access road, and I took it, fast and bouncy. We hit a pothole about the size of Canyon Lake, and I bit my tongue hard enough to bring blood. I could taste it, hot and salty.

"Shit," Ruby muttered, grabbing for the panic handle above the door.

"Oh, no, don't do that," I said, sailing left and onto the on-ramp. "We've got enough problems as it is."

Derek must have been pushing his pickup as fast as it would go, for he was already a dozen cars ahead of us, dodging and swerving from lane to lane. This section of freeway was lighted, but the lamp-posts were far apart and there were patches of blackness in between. I tried to keep my eyes on his taillights and the pattern of reflectors across the rear of the camper, but I was distracted by what Ruby was doing. She had unbuckled her belt again and wedged herself between the seat and the dash, groping on the floor.

"Get back in your seat and buckle up,

Ruby!" I yelled, as a green Toyota SUV pulled to the right in front of us and I had to brake hard. "If I run into something, you're dead!" Of course, at this speed, we'd both be dead, seat belts or no seat belts.

"I'm looking for the phone," Ruby said in a muffled voice. "Maybe it slid underneath." An instant later, flushed with triumph, she was back in the seat and buckling her belt.

"Found it," she said, punching in 911.

"Tell the dispatcher that we're coming up on Exit 192," I said, accelerating. "Ask her to get a cop out here, quick. I don't know how long we can stay with him."

Ruby connected with the 911 dispatcher as the Toyota, having finally put on its right turn-signal, took the off-ramp. I edged up my speed and began to close up on Derek, who was cruising down the right lane at nearly eighty miles an hour. The traffic was fairly light at this time of night, and as we passed the next couple of exits, I tried to loosen up, pulling my stiff fingers loose from Mama's steering wheel and wiggling them to get the circulation going again. I would have felt a lot better if it were daylight instead of dark, the strip of road ahead illuminated only by our headlights and the lights of northbound traffic on the other side of the median. But at least we were going in a straight line, with minimal interference from other vehicles, and I could breathe a little easier.

I breathed a *lot* easier after a northbound state patrol car skidded across the grassy median, put on his rotating light and siren, and nosed in behind Derek, just as the truck passed a row of orange-striped crash barrels at Exit 192. In the rearview mirror, I saw a southbound patrol car, lights flashing and siren wailing, coming up fast in the center lane, as traffic peeled right and left to get out of his way, like bowling pins falling away from a ball. As I watched the second trooper pull alongside Derek's truck, I sucked in my breath and blew it back out again in a loud *whoosh* of relief. I don't think I've ever been so glad to see the cops in my whole life. I took my foot off the accelerator and Mama slowed to a sedate seventy. It felt as if we had suddenly dropped out of warp drive.

"They're here!" Ruby exclaimed into the phone. "Two state troopers. It's over."

But it wasn't. Derek should have slowed, pulled onto the shoulder, and stopped. Within a couple of minutes, the two troopers should have had him out of the truck and searched, cuffed, and stowed for transport to the nearest lockup, where Sheriff Montgomery would show up to question him and the truth about the Indigo murders would eventually emerge.

But that wasn't what happened.

Instead of slowing, Derek held it at eighty, still in the right lane with two patrol cars on his tail. The next exit, to Seguin and I-10, was only a mile ahead, and I wondered if he might try to shake the car beside him by taking the off-ramp at the last possible moment — not a smart idea, but he probably wasn't thinking very clearly. But just then the two patrol cars were joined by a third, flying past at the speed of sound in the middle lane until he came up almost even with Derek. That's the end of it, I thought. He'll have to stop and surrender.

But Derek had one other card up his sleeve. What happened next, from my vantage point twenty car-lengths behind the four-vehicle entourage, seemed to take place in slow motion, illuminated by the headlights of the trooper behind Derek.

Thirty yards before the truck reached the overpass, it swerved to the right and headed, straight and true, for the concrete support pier. The impact was inevitable and head-on, followed by a fiery flash. A fountain of flame erupted into the darkness as the tailing patrol car swerved to the left to avoid the blazing wreck, narrowly avoiding another vehicle.

"Oh, God!" Ruby cried, and stuffed her fist into her mouth. I braked hard, yanked the wheel to the right, skidded to a stop, and jumped out. But there was nothing I could do except stand in the dark beside the freeway, watching in stunned horror as the pickup and camper were engulfed in flame.

It was over. Derek Cooper — William Wilder — was dead. And with him had died the truth of what had happened in Indigo.

Twenty-one

If in any dyed woolen fabric the color has been imparted to it while it was yet in the state of unspun wool, it is said to be wool-dyed, or dyed in the wool.
The Dyeing of Textile Fabrics, 1885
— J. J. Hummel

But truth does not always die with the one who holds the secret, for although the book bag full of Ellen Holt's notes and cassette tapes was lost in the fiery wreckage of Derek's pickup truck, Ellen's laptop was safe and she'd left other notes and an appointment calendar in the cottage. It didn't take a Bill Gates to open the files and read the complicated story behind the deaths of Derek Cooper and Ellen Holt, a story that began long before the two of them ever met, when the man we knew as Derek Cooper was somebody else entirely and Ellen hadn't even been born.

But there was yet another person who knew the truth, or most of it. Ellen had lied when she told me that Derek Cooper was her uncle — he was nothing of the sort

— but she hadn't lied when she'd said she had a twin sister. Elizabeth Holt's email address was in Ellen's computer, along with all the emails they had exchanged while Ellen was in Texas. When she was notified of Ellen's death, Elizabeth got on the next plane to Texas. Ruby and I picked her up in Austin on Sunday afternoon, the day after Ellen's murder. After the initial surprise of meeting her — she looked so much like her sister that we could almost imagine that Ellen had come back from the dead — we took her back to Pecan Springs and made her as comfortable as possible in Thyme Cottage. She was sad and grief-stricken, as you would be if your sister had been murdered, but telling Ellen's story to us and to the police seemed to help her a great deal. Since Ellen had been staying in my cottage and Ruby and I had discovered her body, Elizabeth seemed to feel that we were all connected. In only a few hours the three of us were speaking almost as naturally as old friends.

It was Monday before the details of what had happened in Indigo were completely sorted out. McQuaid and Charlie Montgomery learned from Ellen's emails to her sister and from a note in Ellen's pocket calendar that, indeed, Ellen had planned to meet Derek — William Wilder — at the Bluebonnet after the performance on Friday night, to get the interview he'd promised her. This information confirmed that Derek had intended the shotgun trap to kill Ellen. Then, after he'd failed to do away with her on Friday night, he had bludgeoned her to death on Saturday. The only unresolved question about the weekend's events was answered when Harry Mason confessed to torching the crime scene at the urging of his wife and several of the town's leading citizens. Obviously, Indigo had been delighted when Casey died, and — the town bully syndrome — nobody wanted the police to figure out who was really responsible for the death of the Man Everybody Hated.

But there's a great deal more to the story than the events that took place in Indigo over the weekend. Most of it was related in an article that Ellen had left on her laptop's hard drive, and Elizabeth, who knew the tale from the beginning, had filled in the rest. Now, all that was left was to tell Allie.

The four of us were sitting on Allie's front porch, Ruby and I in the swing and Elizabeth in a wicker rocker. Allie sat on the porch steps, reading the printout from Ellen's computer that we had brought. It had rained that morning, and the afternoon sky was still cloudy, the air smelled of rain-wet grass, and the pigeons in the dovecote murmured gently, their calls a tranquil lullaby that seemed to smooth away some of the violence and harshness of the past few days. Allie looked better, I thought, less anxious and more composed, although there were new lines around her mouth and a deep sorrow in her eyes.

She finished reading, gave a long sigh, and looked up. "Two years," she said sadly, dropping the pages on the step beside her. "I lived with this man for two whole years, and yet I never really knew him."

"He couldn't let anyone know him," Elizabeth said quietly. "He had something to hide." She was heading back to Ohio in Ellen's car that night, and she was dressed for travel in gray slacks and a black tunic. With her honey-colored hair pulled away from her face and twisted into a knot at the back of her head, she looked like a grownup, mature Ellen, and infinitely sad.

"If you ask me, he had quite a *lot* to hide," Ruby replied with asperity. "A couple of lifetimes, in fact. And just look at the wreckage he's left behind! You wouldn't think one man could be so deliberately cruel!"

Allie leaned forward, her elbows propped on her knees, her chin cupped in her hands. "But Derek — or William Wilder or James White, or whoever he was — wasn't cruel, Ruby, at least, not intentionally so. He was caught in a trap. All he wanted to do was escape, but the harder he tried, the more people he destroyed, until finally, in the end, he had to destroy himself." Her voice broke. "I don't think he had any choice but to drive into that highway pier."

I understood Allie's defense of Derek, but I couldn't agree with her. We all make choices every day, little ones and big ones, and we're morally responsible for the outcomes of those decisions. Over the course of the last three decades, Derek had continually chosen deceit and deception over truth and openness, and he was responsible for every consequence, down to his last suicidal moment. But Derek wasn't on trial here and I wasn't going to argue with Allie. She had enough pain to deal with as it was, and I couldn't blame her if she needed to think the best of someone she had cared for.

Allie covered her face with her hands.

When she dropped them, the tears were running freely down her cheeks and her mouth was twisted. She aimed her anger at Elizabeth. "If your sister had only left it alone, it wouldn't have had to come to this. She and Casey and Derek — they'd all be alive." Her voice became bitter. "I hate the idea that three people are dead because a crime writer was after a story."

"It's not that simple," I said — and yet, if you reduced everything to the essential, that was the core of it. According to Elizabeth, and to the nearly completed article we'd found in Ellen's computer, the story began back in the 1970s, at Kent State University in Ohio. James White was an undergraduate there, and already known for his extraordinary talent as a playwright. Several of his works — bitter, angry anti-war plays — had been staged to rave reviews by the university's drama department, and a New York critic who had happened to see one of them had written in some excitement that James White had a great future ahead of him in the American theater.

But the war in Vietnam changed the direction of the young playwright's life, as it changed the lives of so many others. He received his draft notice in February of 1970, but instead of reporting for induction, he and a buddy, who'd also been drafted, got in a car and headed for the Canadian border. Near Cleveland, they stopped at a convenience store. While James White waited in the car, his friend attempted a robbery, shooting and killing the clerk. Before he could flee, he was gunned down by the clerk's brother, an off-duty policeman who happened to be in the store. It was never clear how much White knew about the holdup, but that didn't matter to the authorities. As far as they were concerned, White was the driver of the getaway car, and the local prosecutor had him indicted as an accessory to murder — a charge for which there is no statute of limitations. For the rest of his life, until that charge was cleared, James White would be a wanted man.

There were many tragedies at Kent State that year, for in early May, four students were killed, one was permanently paralyzed, and eight were wounded when the Ohio National Guard opened fire on a group of student antiwar protestors. If White had been on campus that day, he would undoubtedly have been in the front ranks of the protestors and he might have been among those killed. But the man known as James White was already dead.

He had reached Toronto and, like so many other American draft evaders of that era, had begun a new life.

But unlike other Americans, who were only waiting out the war, White could never go back. He obtained identity papers under the name of William Wilder and got a job as a desk clerk in a hotel. He dyed his blond hair chestnut brown, took to wearing glasses, and put on twenty pounds. He gave up his education, his friends, and even his family: his mother and father and sister, still living in Ohio, who swore they never once heard from him after he left in 1971.

But there was something so deeply ingrained in the man, so inextricably a part of his very nature that he could never give it up. He had to write plays, and inevitably, inexorably, his plays attracted attention. And that, of course, was his downfall, for William Wilder was so enormously talented that within a few years he had become Canada's most celebrated and admired playwright.

But certainly not its best-known. Wilder was so terrified that some drama critic or curious reporter would find out who he was that he became a virtual recluse, shunning the camera, refusing to attend performances of his work, denying all requests for interviews. He and his wife (whom he married before his plays began to attract notice) built a secluded house in the wilds of rural Ontario and lived very simply, with only a very few close friends. Not even Wilder's agent or producers had ever met the man.

But seclusion and privacy weren't enough. Wilder was so afraid of the consequences of being found out that when his work attracted the public's attention, he began constructing an escape hatch. Back in Kent, Ohio, when he was ten, his best friend, Derek Cooper, had been killed when the two boys were riding their bikes on the highway. Using what he knew about where and when Derek had been born, Wilder obtained the boy's birth certificate, a social security card, and a Michigan driver's license — not hard to do, if you know the ropes. He'd also begun squirreling away some of his resources, putting the money where Derek Cooper could get it when he needed it.

So by the time a young crime reporter named Ellen Holt had made the connection between the fugitive James White and the reclusive Canadian playwright, Wilder was already prepared to make a second escape, leaving his wife, his career, and his Canadian identity behind. With a dramatic irony that must have appealed to his playwright's soul, he was reborn as Derek Cooper, whom he himself had seen die some forty years before. When he discovered that Ellen was onto him, he crossed the border, bought a pickup truck and a camper and headed for Colorado, where only a few days later, he met Allie. By the time she got back to Texas, he was waiting for her, ready to start a new life in a place where no one would be likely to connect a drifter with no past to the missing William Wilder — and certainly not to James White, the fugitive who had long ago dropped into the cold-case files.

"There's got to be something more behind all this," Allie said, clasping her hands around her knees and hugging them against her chest. "Ellen must have had another reason for chasing this story." She gave Elizabeth a resentful look, and her voice became sarcastic. "I suppose it was ambition. She probably wanted to be the one to find the great playwright. She thought it would give a big boost to her career."

"Of course it wasn't ambition," Elizabeth said wearily. Her hands were folded quietly in her lap and her gaze rested on Allie's face. There was no anger in it, only a deep, quiet sadness. "It was a compulsion. And it goes back further than you can imagine, to the very beginning. To the robbery."

"I understand compulsions," I said ruefully. "When I got involved with a case, I was obsessed. I ate it, slept it, dreamed it. It wouldn't leave me alone, and I couldn't leave it alone."

"But Ellen wasn't a lawyer," Allie objected. "She was a journalist, and this was just a story. I don't understand why she got so involved with this story that she would hound a man to —"

"But it wasn't 'just a story,' " Elizabeth interrupted sharply. She took a deep breath and her eyes became intent. "The clerk who was killed during the holdup was our father's younger brother. Dad raised Uncle Carl after the two of them were orphaned. The two were very close, and he never got over his death. It was all the more dreadful for him, since Uncle Carl was killed right in front of him."

"And your dad was the off-duty policeman who shot the gunman, wasn't he?" Ruby added, clarifying.

Elizabeth nodded. "Dad was in the store

that night, buying ice cream for Mom, who was pregnant with Joan, my older sister. After the shooting, he ran outside to try to apprehend the driver of the getaway car. He was too late, but he managed to get the license number and identify White, and it was his investigative work that eventually resulted in the indictment. It might have ended there, but Dad wouldn't let it go. Until he died five years ago, he spent all of his spare time searching for White. He followed hundreds of leads, from California to Mexico — once, he even went to France." She sat forward, and for the first time that day, I heard bitterness. "Mother and Joan and I *hated* it. Dad's obsession took him away from us. But we had no choice. It was part of him, and we just had to accept it."

"So Ellen grew up with the story, then," Ruby said.

Another nod, and a small smile. "It was different for her, you see. Ellen was — well, she was Dad's favorite. She shared all his interests, including the search. When she was twelve, she organized his files — the background Dad had dug up about James White, the diary he kept when he was following a lead, his interview notes, everything. The two of them would pore over the files by the hour, looking for something they'd missed. The rest of us — well, we just didn't exist for them. Joan and I tried to get involved, but it was a closed circle, just the two of them."

I looked at Elizabeth, hearing the wistfulness in her voice, understanding what she couldn't say: that she had envied Ellen her closeness with their father. Allie was watching her, too, and from the look on her face, I thought she was beginning to understand.

"When Dad died," Elizabeth went on, "Ellen just took up where he left off. She majored in journalism, and I sometimes thought that she went to work as a crime reporter just so she could keep looking for James White."

The rest of the story was there, in Ellen's article, the details filled in by Elizabeth. Following an old lead developed by her father, Ellen had managed to trace James White to Ontario. Eventually, after an inquiry that did credit to her growing skill as an investigative reporter, she uncovered White's metamorphosis into William Wilder. At that point, confident of her facts, she could have broken the story and let the police and the FBI take over. But Ellen had wanted more. She wanted to meet and talk to Wilder — the man who had helped kill her father's brother. When she telephoned him, told him what she knew, and asked him for an interview, however, the man vanished.

That was over two years ago. Ellen went back to her job as a crime reporter for the Cleveland *Plain Dealer*, and kept looking. She wrote the story of her father's search and her discovery and was ready to release it as an article entitled "The Real William Wilder," with photographs from White's Kent State days and one lucky snapshot of Wilder that another reporter had managed to take in Toronto. She was hoping that somebody would read the story, spot Wilder, and report his whereabouts.

But shortly before her newspaper was ready to break the story, Ellen received a phone call from Wilder's wife, who by now was sick and tired of living with the unhappy consequences of his disappearing act and was about to file for divorce. One of the couple's few friends had happened to see Wilder at a fiber show in San Antonio, where he was filling in at Allie's booth. The friend stayed out of sight but managed to get Allie's business card, and that night, he phoned Wilder's wife with the information.

A day or two later, Ellen was on her way to Texas. Before she left, she logged onto the Internet, found and booked Thyme Cottage, and by the time she arrived, had come up with a cover story: She was gathering material for a book about small towns. All she had to do was locate Indigo, find Indigo Farm, and arrange a first meeting with Derek Cooper, who by now must have realized that he was not going to escape this persistent young woman, who was compelled by her father's grim purpose. They had driven out to the old quarry, where Brenda had seen them together and jumped to the wrong conclusion — something that all of us had been guilty of, especially where Ellen Holt was concerned.

"I guess it just goes to prove that you can't judge someone by her looks," Ruby said soberly. With an apologetic look at Elizabeth, she added, "China and I had your sister pegged for a . . . well, for a bimbo. We certainly didn't figure her for an investigative reporter on the track of a story."

I colored. What Ruby was saying was true. I had completely misjudged Ellen, and I was ashamed of myself.

Elizabeth laughed a little. "Ellen was

pretty good at creating that impression. She said that she got more information from people when they didn't feel threatened."

"But the thing I can't understand is why she would agree to meet him in that abandoned school," Ruby went on. "Didn't she suspect that he had tried to kill her with that booby trap in the Bluebonnet? Didn't she realize he was dangerous? Why would she —"

"But I don't think she *did* think he might be dangerous," Allie interrupted. "Everybody in Indigo believed that Casey had set that trap and blundered into it. Or that somebody had killed him to keep the town alive." She bent her forehead to her knees. Her voice was muffled. "I knew Derek better than anyone, and I had no reason to believe that he was capable of such violence. So how could she?"

"I agree," I said. "Ellen was in the crowd on Friday night, and from the look on her face, I'd have to say she was utterly shocked when Casey was killed — and unspeakably grateful that she wasn't the one who was lying there in the street. But I don't think she could have guessed that Derek had planned her murder. When they talked afterward, he seemed just as

431

stunned as she was that the place where they had agreed to meet had turned out to be booby-trapped." We knew this from a note Ellen had made in the small notebook that had escaped Derek's hasty search of the cottage. "She couldn't have known that Derek was putting on an act. And she obviously didn't realize how determined he was to keep his identity hidden."

"I think that's true," Elizabeth said gravely. "I think she underestimated him. After this was over, she could go back to her job, but he would go on trial for Uncle Carl's killing."

We knew something else from that notebook, too — that it had been Derek who called while I was in the cottage with Ellen on Saturday morning. That's when she agreed to meet him in the basement of the abandoned school, where he had killed her. Where Allie had seen the two of them together, just as they went into the building. Allie had jumped to the wrong conclusion then, too, which was why Ruby had seen her in tears, running down the street.

Ruby sat back. "Putting on an act," she said thoughtfully. "I guess that's not too difficult for somebody who writes plays."

Allie raised her head, looking out across the garden. "I think his whole life must have been an act," she said in a low voice. "He was always so busy pretending to be somebody else that he was never sure who he was. If I had only known . . ." Her voice trailed off.

"If you had known, you couldn't have helped him, Allie," I said quietly. "Derek, or James White, or William Wilder — it didn't matter how many names he had or how many different lives he began, deception was always at the center."

"I can't believe that," Allie said, shaking her head. "We all grow. We all change. When Derek came here, all he wanted was a chance to make a fresh start. If I had known, things would have been different."

I lapsed into silence. Maybe someday Allie would be able to deal with the truth that Ellen's story revealed: that no matter how many times James White reinvented himself, changed his stripes, took on new colors — whatever metaphors you wanted to use for his "fresh starts" — it would always have been the same.

Epilogue

When lovely woman tilts her saucer,
And finds too late that tea will staine,
Whatever made a Lady crosser?
What art can wash all right again?
The only art the stain to cover,
To hide the spot from every eye,
And wear an unspoiled dress about her,
The proper colour is to DYE.
— John Swartz
in *The Family Dyer and Scourer*, 1841

"Perfect!" McQuaid exclaimed enthusiastically, as we stood in the living room, surveying the handwoven rug Allie had just brought. It was a soft, stunning blend of heather grays and chocolate browns and dark reds, exactly the right fit for the space between the sofa and the fireplace. I'd given Allie the dimensions and the colors I wanted, and she'd done the rest. The rug looked beautiful, especially next to the Halloween pumpkin grinning on the hearth.

"Art for the floor," I said. "Wonderful, Allie! Thank you very much."

"I'm glad you like it," Allie said, from

the sofa. "I enjoyed weaving it for you. After all, you two did a great deal for me." She managed a small smile. "Although I have to admit that I didn't think so at the time. I would have been glad if Casey's death was never solved, and I'd certainly rather not have known the whole truth about Derek."

McQuaid sat down in the recliner. "I understand what you're saying," he said ruefully. "Contrary to popular wisdom, the truth doesn't always set us free. But I've got to believe that even though we may be hurt in the short run, the pain would be much worse if we found out the truth too late and had to live with the consequences of a terrible mistake."

He fell silent, and I knew he was thinking of Sally. He and Brian had told her the tale of Brian's bruises, and the Whiz had followed up that revelation with a discreet, tactful phone call about her client's unfortunate marital experience: a "word to the wise," as she put it. Sally got the message and broke off her relationship with Henningson — not without pain, I'm sure. But it is better to love and lose than to love and live to regret it. McQuaid worked out an arrangement that gives her more time with Brian, about as much as the two of them can handle, I suspect.

"I suppose I agree with you," Allie said. "About knowing the truth, I mean." She shook her head, half-smiling. "You should see Shirley. She's a changed woman, now that she's taking responsibility for herself."

"How's she doing with her reading lessons?" McQuaid asked curiously. "Is she making progress?" Miss Mayjean had volunteered to help Shirley learn to read, and the two of them were making regular trips to the library for books.

"I don't know about that," Allie said. "They're working at it, but the dyslexia is a major problem. Miss Mayjean is thinking of finding a reading specialist. Money isn't an issue, of course. The accountant and the lawyer are getting everything sorted out, and it looks as if Shirley is pretty well fixed for life. She's remodeling the old house — refinishing the floors and putting in some modern appliances. And she bought a TV set."

"And Les?" I asked. "What's the story there?"

Another doubtful look, and a shrug. "They're still seeing one another, but Shirley is reconsidering her options. Les is — well, he's Les. Born to be bad, I guess you'd say. She's changing, but he's not. If I had to guess, I'd say that she'll break it off with him in a few months. And he'll probably be glad she did, ultimately." Her smile was sad. "Like me. In the long haul, I'll probably be glad that Derek no longer has to run from himself. It'll be a while before I can get my mind around that corner, though." She stood up. "Well, I guess I'd better get back to the farm and do my chores."

"Wait a minute," McQuaid said. "We haven't heard about Indigo yet. What's going on there?"

"Oh, the usual," Allie replied, and this time her smile was unqualified. "The next big event is a holiday fiesta — Christmas at Indigo, we're calling it." She hummed a few bars of "I'll Have a Blue Christmas Without You." "That's our theme song," she added. "It was Stella's idea, and everybody loves it. Even Maxine."

"Shirley isn't going to sell the mining rights, I gather," McQuaid said.

"Not a chance," Allie replied firmly. "As it turns out, she owns quite a bit of land around the town, so Indigo will be safe, more or less." She made a face. "All the problems with the mine still exist, of course. We're all very much afraid of what will happen with our wells and the water in

Indigo Creek, once they start pumping out more groundwater. But we're going forward with the remodeling of the Cotton Gin Theater, and we'll be having a Spring Arts and Crafts Festival next April — with another performance of *Indigo's Blue*. I'm sure it would please Derek to know that his last play is a big hit." She picked up her bag and slung it over her shoulder. "Oh, I almost forgot. Please tell Ruby that a friend of mine is interested in taking her class on intuition. When will she be teaching it again?"

I laughed. "She says she's giving it up, although I'm not sure I believe her."

"Giving it up?" Allie raised her eyebrows. "Why?"

"Because of what happened in Indigo. She says she doesn't want to have any more experiences like that, and if that's what it means to be psychic, forget it."

Allie laughed, too. "Give her another couple of months," she said, "and she'll be the same old Ruby again."

"I don't know," I replied, more seriously. "I guess we'll just have to wait and see." Allie and I walked together to the door, where she turned.

"Thanks again," she said, and gave me a hug. "And whenever you're ready to start doing the dye workshops again, just let me know."

"I will," I promised, "after the holidays." I grinned. "I even have a new name to suggest."

Her hand on the knob, Allie paused. "Well, are you going to tell me, or do I have to guess?"

" 'You Ain't Lived Until You've Dyed,' " I said.

The Mysteries of Indigo Dyeing

Blue from indigo is bluer than the indigo plant.

— Chinese saying

I'm just a soul who's bluer than blue can be . . .

— "Mood Indigo"

Most of us are so accustomed to the rainbow of hues produced by synthetic dyes that we don't give a great deal of thought to the herbs that were used to color textiles before the 1850s, when a young chemist accidentally solved the mystery of the color violet while he was trying to synthesize a vitally important herbal medicine, quinine. But when you know something about natural dyes, perhaps you'll understand and appreciate more about the mysterious world of plants and the ingenious and inventive ways humans have put them to use.

The story of natural dyeing begins with the most ancient of civilizations, around 30,000 BCE, when early Stone Age people buried their dead on mounds of red ochre.

For centuries, color was used primarily for magical and ritual purposes and associated with social status and economic power, with death and the afterworld, and with the occult. In many cultures, blue was the most important color, for it was the color of sky and water. Ordinary people couldn't use it: it was reserved for use by the gods, by the nobility ("blue bloods"), and by the dead. For example, the Hindus depicted Krishna as blue; the Mayans indicated their social status by wearing blue clothing; the daughters of the Egyptian pharaohs painted their breasts blue and gold; and blue grave cloths are among the earliest textile artifacts discovered around the Mediterranean.

A number of plants have been used to create the color blue, but among them, indigo (*Indigofera sp.*) is the most cherished and the most valuable, and the societies that cultivated or used the many varieties of the plant developed important traditions and rituals around it. Producing indigo dye from the leaves of the indigo plant was an unpredictable, complex, and carefully guarded process, beginning with harvest and continuing through several stages of fermenting (a smelly business!), whipping, adding ash or urine, heating, and finally, drying the indigo blue paste, which was pressed into lumps and cubes. Because of the skill that went into production, indigo dye was a relatively rare and precious commodity, and until the end of the nineteenth century, when the color was synthesized from coal tar, it was almost as valuable as gold. In fact, the British exploitation of Indian indigo ranks right up there with its exploitation of the mineral resources of South Africa, and the development of synthetic indigo was seen as a trade disaster of staggering proportions.

In some cultures of Africa and the South Pacific, where the color blue was said to have been given to a woman by the gods, indigo dyeing belonged exclusively to women and involved what one researcher has called a "cult of female secrets" hedged about by taboos and ritual practices. Among the Sumbanese islanders of Eastern Indonesia, post-menopausal Kodi women — known as the "blue-handed women" — were the only ones permitted to practice "the blue arts," linked to female reproduction, to healing, and to death. But every Kodi woman was intimately involved with indigo, from the day she learned to weave her first indigo-dyed shoulder cloth to the day she wove her own indigo burial shroud — the only textile that belonged, entirely and inalienably, to her.

Today, the art of natural dyeing has been nearly forgotten, except by the dedicated artists and craftspersons who seek out and preserve the old ways. But we can't forget the mysterious feelings associated with indigo, its connection with sadness, with dark moods, and with death. And every one of us knows exactly what we mean when we say that we're singing the blues, that we're in an indigo mood, or that we're "bluer than blue can be."

Resources

To unravel the mysteries of dyeing with indigo and learn more about the fascinating history and lore of the oldest and most important dye plant, you may visit Susan Albert's website, www.mysterypartners.com, or consult one of the following sources.

Adrosko, Rita J. *Natural Dyes and Home Dyeing.* Dover Reprint, 1971.

Bliss, Anne. *North American Dye Plants.* Interweave Press, 1993.

Buchanan, Rita. *A Dyer's Garden: From Plant to Pot.* Interweave Press, 1995.

———. *A Weaver's Garden: Growing Plants for Natural Dyes and Fibers.* Dover Reprint, 1999.

Dean, Jenny. *Wild Color: The Complete Guide to Making and Using Natural Dyes.* Watson-Guptill Publications, 1999.

Dendel, Esther Warner. *You Cannot Unsneeze a Sneeze and Other Tales from Liberia.* University Press of Colorado, 1995.

Hoskins, Janet. "Why Do Ladies Sing the

Blues? Indigo Dyeing, Cloth Production, and Gender Symbolism in Kodi," in *Cloth and Human Experience*, ed. Annette Be. Weiner and Jane Schneider, Smithsonian Institution Press, 1989.

Lesch, Alma. *Vegetable Dyeing.* Watson-Guptill Publications, 1970.

Liles, J. N. *The Art and Craft of Natural Dyeing.* University of Tennessee Press, 1990.

McRae, Bobbi. *Colors from Nature: Growing, Collecting, and Using Natural Dyes.* Storey Communications, 1993.

Miller, Dorothy. *Indigo from Seed to Dye.* Aptos, 1981.

Sandberg, Gösta. *Indigo Textiles: Technique and History.* A&C Black, 1989.

Utterbach, Christina. "Indigo: Mystic Blues," *Herb Quarterly*, No. 52, pp.38.

About the Author

Susan Wittig Albert grew up on a farm in Illinois and earned her Ph.D. at the University of California at Berkeley. A former professor of English and a university administrator and vice president, she now lives with her husband, Bill, in the country outside of Austin, Texas.

X